ONE MAN'S PAIN

DOMINIC BRANCA

ISBN 978-1-0980-0407-1 (paperback)
ISBN 978-1-0980-0653-2 (hardcover)
ISBN 978-1-0980-0479-8 (digital)

Copyright © 2019 by Dominic Branca

All rights reserved. No part of this publication may be reproduced, distributed, or transmitted in any form or by any means, including photocopying, recording, or other electronic or mechanical methods without the prior written permission of the publisher. For permission requests, solicit the publisher via the address below.

Christian Faith Publishing, Inc.
832 Park Avenue
Meadville, PA 16335
www.christianfaithpublishing.com

Printed in the United States of America

CHAPTER 1

Thunder, lightning, and endless rain—just another stormy night. It seemed like they had a thunderstorm every night in that stupid little town. But what did I care? Every night and day was another thunderstorm for me. I just lay there like I did every night, sad and lonely, wishing I could go back to the way things were before. Wishing I could have my old life back. Wondering why it had been taken from me.

I woke up to hear the sound of the birds chirping. A lot of people probably would thought that a sunny, bird-chirping morning was nice after a stormy night, but not me. I just lay there for a while not really feeling much like getting up, nothing new there. Somewhere in the back of my head, I remembered that it was Easter Monday, but that was not something I cared about anymore.

Eventually, I wandered downstairs, ate breakfast, and lay around my house. Today would be like every other day. I would just sit there and wallow in my own suffering. It was a nice day outside, one of the nicest the early April spring had to offer yet, but I still didn't care. Like I said, I was just sitting there unhappy and having nothing to do but wallow in my own suffering. A knock at the door woke me up a little.

When I opened the door, my self-pity turned to anger after I saw who was standing there. As soon as I saw the white collar, I slammed the door before he could even get a word in. Guess his reflexes weren't so bad either because he knocked again before I could turn around. This time, he started talking before the door was even fully open.

"Hi, I'm Father Blair. I'm from St. Jude Catholic church—" *slam*. Guess he got the message that time because he left. I went back to my wallowing, and eventually it got dark; another storm started, and like every other night, I lay there and listened to it until I fell asleep.

The next morning, I left the house to get some groceries. I always hated going out because I had to put up with all the smiling happy faces out there. All those people had no idea what suffering is? The ones who would complain if the price went up ten cents or if something wasn't on sale anymore and they had to pay full price. There were times when it was all I could do not to grab one of them and throw them headfirst out the door.

As I walked into the store dreading another one of these same experiences, who did I see but that same priest again. I walked past him with my head down, hoping he wouldn't recognize me. He just stared at me with a sad look on his face and kept going. I was glad he didn't try and stop to talk to me because I sure didn't want to talk to him. I just wanted to get what I had to get and leave.

As I approached the checkout counter, some there was a kid crying about something I did not know or care what. For a second, a memory started to push its way forward, but I shot it down. I was not going there. Instead, I just stood behind them for a few minutes while the parents tried to calm the kid down. Finally, I couldn't take it anymore, and I started to go off.

"Can't you control your kid!" I screamed.

That only encouraged him to scream louder and apparently didn't go over too well with the parents either. The father got right in my face and started screaming at me to mind my own business. Not to be outdone, I started screaming, and the next thing I knew, we were shoving each other. Some store associates got between us before, while another one went to call the police.

By the time the associates could get us apart, the sheriff arrived to see what was going on. The second he walked in, I could see by the look on his face this was not a nice man or a nice sheriff. It occurred to me that after nearly five years of living here, I should probably know who he was, but I didn't. I had never paid much attention to what was going on in town or bothered to get to know anybody. The store manager explained to him what had happened, but the sheriff didn't really seem to care. He just looked the other guy and me up and down, and the look on his face seemed to say that in his mind, it was entirely up to him whether or not he was going to arrest us.

After a few minutes, he walked over and addressed the father; clearly, they knew each other, and what up until now had been a look of toughness on the father's part suddenly turned to fear. That seemed to satisfy the sheriff who then turned his attention to me. I simply stared at him with the same what-are-you-looking-at look I gave everybody. That obviously did not satisfy him, and he demanded to know who I was. I simply told him that I lived in town and that I wanted to be left alone. He leaned in close to me and whispered, "You can be alone as you want, but I'm in charge around here, so don't cross me."

I just stared at him and asked if he was planning to arrest us. When he didn't say yes, I threw some money down and stormed out.

As I drove home, I saw that he was following, and so I turned a different way down an old dirt road that led to the back of my house. I guess he didn't see me or the car because he didn't follow. As I drove along, I passed what looked like an abandoned church. I saw the priest who had been at my door a few days earlier. I wondered why he was here at an old abandoned church. Whatever his reasons, I wanted nothing to do with him or his church. God had abandoned me a long time ago, so I had no time for him. I just drove home and went back to my daily routine of wallowing in sadness all day until another night of thunderstorm, and crying myself to sleep came along.

CHAPTER 2

The next morning, I woke up to the sound of a power saw and hammering. For a minute, I was back in my garage, at home, woodworking, kids playing…no I'm not going there. I looked out the window to see what was going on and could just make out the sight of the priest working on part of the old church along with a few other people. I could see the church from my bedroom window. For some reason I don't know, I decided to walk down there and see just what was going on.

As I approached, I noticed that the folks helping the priest looked like they were working in two separate groups. The priest saw me, and a look of surprise came over his face. He stopped what he was doing and walked out to meet me. "What are you doing here?" he asked.

I just stared at him, not sure what to say. I had no idea why I had come down there. "Why are you working on this abandoned old place?" I asked him.

He explained to me that it wasn't abandoned, just rundown because the local congregation was so small that the archdiocese hadn't been able to spare a priest to send there. Fortunately, he had been able to come there and take over. He explained that the parishioners had been going to other parishes in other towns, but now they were all trying to build the local parish back up.

He asked me why I had slammed my door in his face the other day. I told him that I had no interest left in faith and that I didn't want anyone trying to tell me otherwise. When he asked me why I just stared at him, I realized I had said too much already. The whole reason I came to this town in the middle of nowhere was because no one would know who I was. Here, I could hide from my past and never have to deal with it again. He looked at me puzzled, and I realized that a tear was streaking down my face. That made me incredibly angry; after all, who did this guy think he was digging into my past?

"Never ask me about my past again," I screamed at him and then stormed away and headed home.

By the time I got home, I was pretty angry, though I wasn't sure why. I wasn't sure what to do about it, so I pushed over a chair. Then I pushed over another one, and then I just sat there yelling. I went on that way for a while until eventually I was tired, and I just fell onto my couch, feeling sad and confused. I couldn't understand why I had gone to the church or why some part of me was almost glad about it. As I sat there, I couldn't help it—the memories started flooding into my head. Meeting my wife in college, my wedding, my years as a patrol officer, the kids being born and growing up, my promotion to detective, the first time I heard *his* name. The memories continued to flood in, and I lay there sad until eventually I fell asleep to the sound of another thunderstorm.

CHAPTER 3

Midway through the night the sound of something going on outside my house woke me up. I looked outside and saw some teenagers spray-painting something on the driveway. I became enraged, grabbed a shotgun I owned, and ran outside. I snuck up behind them and kicked one of them down to the ground. They all turned and looked up, and I pointed the gun straight at them and told them to get off of my lawn. They all ran away, and I was so angry, I fired a shot into the air just to make my point. After that, I went back inside but was too angry to sleep another wink.

As I lay on my couch later in the morning, I heard my door open and someone walk in. I grabbed the shotgun and probably would have fired on the spot if I hadn't realized it was the sheriff. Not that this made me any less angry that he had just walked into my house.

"What do you want, and why are you in my house?" I asked him.

"I wanted to talk to you," was the response I got.

"Last time I checked, this was private property off-limits to everyone but me, and that includes you."

"I'll go wherever I want, whenever I want," was his reply.

"What do you want to talk to me about?" I asked him.

"Last night did you threaten some boys with that shotgun," he said pointing to the gun still in my hand.

"What's it to you?"

"Yes or no."

"Why don't you get off my property before I threaten you with it?"

He just stared at me and gripped his gun still in its holster.

Our standoff lasted about a minute before I finally explained to him that those boys were trespassing and that I just wanted them off my property.

"Is that why you kicked one of them down on the ground?" he replied. "Because that boy is my nephew," he continued.

"I don't really care if he's your son. He and his idiot friends were still trespassing on my property."

He just got in my face and stared at me, and I got right back in his face and stared right back at him. He gripped his gun in his holster, and I held my shotgun down at my side. Finally, I broke the silence "We can argue about whether or not what I did was illegal, but I know for sure that you busting in here like this is definitely illegal."

"And just how is it you know?" A look of recognition and like he had just figured something out came over his face. "What did you say your name was?" he asked.

"I didn't," was my reply. "And I don't have to tell you," I answered him. "Either way, you have no right to be here, so get out of my house."

He just gave me this sly look and headed for the door. As he did, he turned and smiled and said, "You haven't seen the last of me."

For a minute, it occurred to me that he might be able to look up who I am. The vision of newspaper headlines and pictures in the paper and online went through my mind. Images so painful, I couldn't help it, I started to cry again. And for the first time in a long time, I talked to God: "Lord, why, why did you let this happen?"

For a minute, the Old Catholic me started to make its way to the surface, and I just didn't know how to feel or what to do. One thought that was going through my head was that I had to find out more about that sheriff. Clearly, he had some kind of hold on this town, and I was determined to find out what it was.

I lay on my couch for an hour or so trying to figure out what to do next when the sound of hammering interrupted my thoughts. And at that moment, it occurred to me that the priest, Father what's his name, might know something about the sheriff or this town. I headed down to where they were working on the old church. Even though it had only been a day since I had last seen it, I could see that they had made some progress.

A combined look and surprise and hope came over the priest's face as I walked up. We walked toward each other until we were a few feet apart, and then we just stared at each other. I wasn't really sure what to say. I wasn't proud of the way I had treated him in our past encounters, but that didn't mean I felt my actions weren't justified. I guess my face showed that a little bit because he walked up to me like we had never met and said, "Hi, I'm Fr. Blair," and held out his hand for me to shake. I stared at him and then accepted his handshake. I wasn't sure what had just happened or how to feel about it.

He asked me why I had come down to see him, and I stared at him for a second and then told him why and what had happened earlier. He looked at me with a kind of sad, almost pitiful look.

"You know things used to be a lot better around here," he said. "This used to be a beautiful church, but sadly everything changed."

I wasn't really sure what to make of his answer, but I knew it didn't tell me anything about the sheriff. Before I could ask another question, one of the parishioners working on the church came over to ask Fr. Blair if he could help them carry in a Mary statue that had apparently been delivered early. Fr. Blair looked at me with a curious look on his face as if he was wondering if I would volunteer to help. For some reason I didn't understand, something inside me made me offer to help. The statue wasn't too big, and a couple of us were enough to carry it.

We carried it across the outside and up the steps, but as we approached the door, something made me stop. Everyone else stopped too, and I just stood there and stared at the door for a minute. And I couldn't help it; another memory forced its way from its suppressed place to the surface. This time me sitting in front of a church, four caskets next to me, everyone is very sad and crying.

Outside reporters from TV stations and newspapers write and record what is happening. The funeral ends, and I stand at the back, looking at the cross with more anger and hate than I have ever felt before in my life. At that moment, I look up and vow to Christ on the cross and to God that I will never enter a church or worship him again. I flashed back to the present, and for a minute, I think about breaking the vow I made that day, but I just can't; it hurts too much. Instead of just angrily running off like before, I apologized to the priest and just calmly walked away and left.

CHAPTER 4

As I walked into my house, I thought I would be angry, but I wasn't. Instead, I felt sad and confused. I felt at a loss for what to do next. I thought about all the times I had entered a church for so many years of my life, and now I couldn't bring myself to do it. Once there was a time when I swore that would never be me, that I would never be one of those people who just gave up, no matter what happened. I just sat there on my couch thinking about everything I had and how I had lost it all.

Eventually, I was interrupted by a knock at the door. I opened the door and, for some reason, wasn't at all surprised to see Fr. Blair standing there. We stared at each other for a minute, and I was almost shocked to hear myself invite him in to talk. While that part of me was shocked, another part of me was almost glad. He walked in and looked around for a minute before he turned to look at me. He had this look of sad curiosity on his face that I didn't completely understand. It seemed like he wanted to ask me why I left, but he wasn't sure where to start or didn't want to open old wounds by mistake. Finally, I broke the silence: "What can I do for you, Father?"

"Honestly, I was wondering why you left," was his reply. "You seem like you're having some sort of…faith struggle," he continued.

"Well, I'm definitely having a struggle."

"Why?"

For a second, I was tempted to go off again and just throw him out of my house, but something made me stop. Something inside of me, instead, made me stay and talk to this man. "Why does God allow so much evil and so many bad things to happen?" I asked him with a tear coming into my eye.

He looked at me with a look of caring and pity and responded, "I don't know what to say. The only answer I can give you is that maybe it's because he can bring some good out of it."

"But how can that be?" I replied. I couldn't understand his answer or what could even bring him to say something like that. I guess my face showed just how confused and upset I was by his answer because he stared at me like he wanted to tell me something but didn't know how.

"The best answer I can give you," he continued, "is my own personal story."

"Personal story of what?" I asked.

"Personal story of how suffering led to something better."

I just stared at him almost stunned. The idea that anyone could suffer and still practice religion, let alone be a priest, was hard for me to believe.

"What is your story?" I asked him.

He just looked at me with a sad look on his face. But I also sensed something else, like somehow it almost inspired him, at least faith-wise.

"It's not an easy story for me to tell, but if you want to hear it, okay," he said.

After that, he basically recounted his entire life to me. He told me all about his parents and grandparents. His grandfather had fought in WWII and had been wounded and almost killed. He said he could remember as a kid wondering why, but that his grandmother had told him that they shouldn't ask why and should be thankful to God that his grandfather had survived the war.

But his father wasn't so lucky. Just after he was born, his father was drafted and shipped off to Vietnam. He was gone for almost a year and had only been able to write letters home. And then just a few weeks before he was supposed to come home, a sergeant showed up at their door and told his mother that his father had been killed. The news was devastating, and as for Fr. Blair, he was so young, he just couldn't understand. How could his father be one of those people he saw on TV bloody, wounded, dead? It just couldn't be possible. But he said what he remembered the most was his mother just sitting there on the couch crying for what seemed like forever.

After that, life was hard. His father had left behind some money, but not much, and his mother had to work to support them. His grandfather also went back to work to help contribute, so his grandmother took care of him. He said that life wasn't easy, but they loved each other, and they got through. But the stress of working and taking care of a family again was hard on his grandfather, and when Fr. Blair was fourteen, his grandfather passed away. He said at fourteen, he couldn't understand why he had to lose his grandfather and probably would have walked away from the church then if it wasn't for the faith of his grandmother. He said he could remember her at his grandfather's funeral praying and thanking God for the fifty years she had with her husband.

After that, life got better for a while. He managed to get graduate college and get his degree in psychology. He also met who he thought would be his future wife. Like him, she was Catholic, and her family structure had been altered by the loss of her father in Vietnam. She was planning to be a teacher. He had applied to graduate school to become a therapist; she had found a teaching job, and they were planning to get married that summer. But just a week before their wedding, his fiancé, along with his mother, were driving back from some last-minute shopping when they were in a car accident. Neither of them made it, and Fr. Blair was devastated and suddenly found himself alone in the world.

He said he could still remember the police coming to notify him that they were both gone and being in total shock. Before he could go on any further, I burst into tears. I just couldn't help it. Father stopped talking in midsentence and just stared at me with a look of sadness in his eyes. After about a minute, he apologized for making me upset and said he would leave if I wanted him to. I told him that I didn't want him to leave, that he wasn't the reason why I was crying. For a minute, I thought about telling him the real reason why I was crying, but before I could get a single word out, we were interrupted by someone banging on my front door.

I got up to open it and was surprised and angry to see the sheriff standing there, with a look of victory on his face. Any serenity or calm I had started to feel talking to Fr. Blair quickly subsided, and all I felt was anger.

"What do you want?" I demanded of him.

He just looked at me and before I could stop him stormed past me into the house. Before he could get a word out, his smile dropped a little when he saw Fr. Blair sitting there on the couch. Fr. Blair, for his part, just kind of sat there with a look of sadness and surprise on his face. The sheriff stared at Fr. Blair for a minute before turning his attention back to me.

"What do you want?" I asked again.

The look of victory came back over his face as he handed me a computer printout from a newspaper archive with a headline about me on it. It read "Self-described 'Most powerful criminal ever' kills detective's family!" A subline read "Police at a loss as to his whereabouts!" I just stared at the headline stunned and at a loss. I had come here to hide from this, and here it was right in front of me. Guess the priest was wondering what I was so stunned to see because he pulled the paper out of my hand. After looking at it for a second, he looked up at me with a look of pure sadness in his eyes.

I turned back to the sheriff who was still standing there with that look of victory on his face. And I couldn't help but become enraged; after all, who did he think he was?

"What do you think of this you—?" *crack*, I swung and hit him right in the jaw. He went down before he knew what hit him but just as fast he was back on his feet, and we were fighting. We wrestled around exchanging punches, and we each tried various police training measures to restrain each other. Fr. Blair for his part tried to get between us, but that just got him knocked to the ground. Eventually, after a few minutes, the sheriff managed to get me down and handcuffed.

"What are you doing?" I screamed at him.

"Arresting you for assaulting a police officer," was his response. I was enraged, but what could I do?—he was the sheriff, and I had hit him.

CHAPTER 5

Just when I thought I knew that this town had an overly powerful corrupt sheriff, I saw just how powerful he really was. After a night in a holding cell, he dragged me into court. It looked pretty kosher at first: a judge and a prosecutor, and a public defender who was supposed to be on my side. I stood at the table and waited while the prosecutor read the charges. That was the first time I found out I had punched the sheriff in an unprovoked attack. Apparently, I was in my house screaming, and he knocked on my door to see if I was okay, and I punched him.

After the prosecutor was done, I turned to my lawyer expecting him to deliver some defense of me, but all he did was stand there. After a minute, I spoke up and said that the sheriff's story wasn't true. The judge seemed interested at first, but then the sheriff stepped up and walked right into the gallery and said, "Judge, this guy is a flaming liar. Don't believe a word he says."

A cop addressing a judge as judge, not in any courtroom I had ever been in. Not to mention, the way he addressed the judge was more like an order than an argument. The prosecutor for his part didn't object or say a word about what the sheriff was doing.

The judge and the sheriff stared at each other for a minute before the judge agreed with what he had said and ordered me place on bail and sent back to jail until I paid it. As the sheriff led me away again, he looked back at the judge, and I got the sense that something wasn't right. Maybe they were involved in some kind of scam or corruption together. Either way, I had a new problem: how was

I going to get myself bailed out? While I was sitting there trying to figure that out, the sheriff came down and opened up my cell.

"Back for round 2?" I asked him.

He just stared at me and stepped aside to reveal Fr. Blair who was standing behind him.

"What are you doing here?" I asked him.

He just motioned for me to follow him, and we left the jailhouse. As we drove home, I thanked him and started to ask him why he had come to my assistance. But as the words came out of my mouth, I just sort of stopped for a second, feeling kind of shocked. At first, I wasn't sure why, but then I realized that it was the first time in a long time that I had thanked anyone for anything. We drove the rest of the way back to my house that way. When we got there, Fr. Blair turned and looked at me and asked me why I had gotten so quiet.

I just stared at him for a second, not really sure what to say. "I'm not really sure what to tell you," I said. "It's been a long time since anyone did anything for me to thank them for. Why did you do it?" I asked him again.

He just smiled and said that I seemed like I needed someone to reach out to me, and he thought maybe it was supposed to be him. I just kind of sat there for a second, not really sure what to say. For the first time in a long time, I felt something that wasn't hate or contempt or anger, and toward the last person I would have ever expected to feel it, a priest.

In the shock and sort of newness of this moment, I forgot for a second everything that was happening and why I was so upset with God. It dawned on me that Fr. Blair probably wanted to ask me about my past and all. I figured I owed him that much, considering how kind he had been to me after the way I treated him, but I just didn't think I could work up the strength to tell it. But there was one thing I was determined to do, and that was to find out more about the apparently crooked sheriff. I just wasn't really sure how to go about it. All the investigations I had done in my past, you would think I would have known where to start.

"So you said you're from around here, didn't you?" I asked him.

He just stared at me for a second and nodded his head in agreement.

"I'm not interested in what happened to you when you were younger. I just want to know more about the sheriff." I figured he didn't want to talk about his past any more than I did.

"Why?" he asked me.

"Because he's clearly up to no good, and I want to figure out what his true motives are."

"Power, that's his motive," was the response I got.

"But why?" I asked.

"I just told you, power."

"What do you mean by 'power'?" I asked him. It didn't make sense to me: what did the sheriff gain from being a bully?

"Look, Sheriff Blank isn't a nice man, and he never has been." He continued, "He's like a mini J. Edgar Hoover. He has dirt on everybody, and nobody wants to cross him."

"Does that include you?" I asked him. I wasn't really sure if I asked the question out of curiosity or if I meant it as an attack. In a weird way, that was a step forward because up until then, it definitely would have been an attack.

"No, it doesn't include me, which is part of the reason he hates me so much. He has the whole town eating out of the palm of his hand."

"More like he has a gun to their head," I replied.

"In a way, yes," he replied.

At that, I got out of the car and headed into the house. As I walked in, I sat down on the couch and thought about everything that had just happened. A few days ago, I hated everything having to do with religion, and pretty much the entire world in general. I didn't want anyone to have any idea who I was, and I just wanted to be completely left alone. Now I was beginning to form a friendship with a priest, and the sheriff knew exactly who I was and all the things about my past I wanted hidden. I got the sense that Fr. Blair knew more about him than he was telling, and I wanted to know what it was. At the same time, I was sympathetic and didn't want to drag up painful memories for him.

I wasn't really sure why I was so determined to take the sheriff on, but I was. It occurred to me that I was taking out all of my problems on him, but there was something else. Something that I didn't understand was driving me. Anyway, what did it matter and why? The important thing was that I was determined to do it. As I was sitting there, I heard a burst of thunder and saw some lightning. I figured it would start pouring any second, and then the same old feelings of anger and hatred began to overtake me again. But at the same time, I felt something else. I didn't really know what it was or how to interpret it. It was just there. I just lay back on the couch and reflected on it as I fell asleep.

CHAPTER 6

The next thing I knew, someone was knocking on my door.

I looked at the clock, saw it was after eight, and then remembered I had to be in court at nine. I went and opened the door, still half asleep and saw Fr. Blair standing there. He looked kind of rushed and told me he wanted to make sure that I wasn't late for court.

"You really think the sheriff will turn down a chance to arrest you again?" he asked with a smirk.

"No," I replied.

And then, I did something I hadn't done in I couldn't remember how long. I smiled. It was a quick smile, but it was still a smile. I sat there and reflected on that for a minute, and Fr. Blair and I just stared at each other. I think we both realized that this was a significant moment. After that, I ran off to quickly get myself ready for another appearance in court. Although whether I was really appearing before a court of law or a court of the sheriff seemed to me another question entirely.

I walked into the courtroom and saw the same group as before: prosecutor, judge, and public defender who clearly didn't care about my case. I had already been arraigned, so now the next step was for the state to prove to the judge that it could move forward with its case. Considering what I had seen during my last court appearance, I didn't think that was going to be any challenge for them. The judge asked the prosecutor if he was ready to call his first witness, and surprise, surprise, they called the sheriff. He got up and walked to the witness stand shooting me a sly smile as he passed by. *I wonder if he's polished his lies at all since the last time we met,* I thought to myself. Just as I was thinking this, the courtroom door opened, a man in a suit walked in and started talking. "Excuse me, your honor, sorry I'm late, I'm here to represent Mr. Brado," he said.

The second he walked in, the sheriff looked at him stunned and frankly not too happy. For my part, I turned and looked at him, having no idea what to say. Before the judge could get a word in, the sheriff stood up and screamed, "What are you doing here?" He yelled.

Clearly, this guy acted however he wanted even on the witness stand, I thought, but never mind that; the way he said it was like he knew who this new face in the courtroom was. The judge, who had initially started to ask the same question, stopped and gave way to the sheriff. *Okay, clearly the sheriff had something big on this judge because there's no way any judge would let someone act that way in their courtroom,* I thought to myself.

The new guy for his part walked over to my table and said, "I'm here to represent this defendant." He turned to the public defender and said, "I don't think we will be need you anymore."

The public defender just stared for a minute and then looked up at the judge and argued that this wasn't appropriate and that he was my attorney. I stared at the two for a second and then decided that despite what I didn't know about this new guy, it was pretty clear to me that the public defender wasn't on my side.

"Your honor, I think I'll take whoever this other lawyer is," I said.

The judge looked at me and then looked at the sheriff like he had no idea what to do. The sheriff looked back at him and shook his head indicating no, and then quickly stopped when he saw that the new guy and I were both watching him.

The judge sat there for a minute and then adjourned the court and told the sheriff to follow him out of the courtroom. I stared after them as they walked away. The new guy walked up to me and started talking, but I didn't catch a word of it because I was too busy pushing past him to follow the judge and sheriff out to the hall. I followed them down the hall to the judge's chambers and then listened at the door while they spoke.

"Where the hell did he come from?" I heard the sheriff screaming at the top of his lungs.

"How am I supposed to know?" the judge responded. "I never thought we would see or hear from him again," he continued.

"Well, now, he's here, and you better not let him start making noise," the sheriff yelled back at him.

"What do you want me to do? If I don't let him step in, it will look like we have something to hide."

"*You* do have something to hide," the sheriff said in what sounded to me like a threatening tone. "And if I go down, I promise you, you will go down with me," he continued.

At that, I heard him turn and start to head for the door, so I quickly ducked into the bathroom across the hall to hide from him. He turned and headed down the hall, and I waited until he was safely out of sight before I came out. I walked back down the hall toward the courtroom and saw Fr. Blair and this new guy standing there talking. Somehow, I got the sense that they had some sort of history together, but it went right over my head, which was still turning over the conversation I had just overheard.

As I walked up, the two of them stopped their conversation and turned to look at me. Fr. Blair looked sad and kind of disappointed, while the new guy turned and introduced himself to me, "Hi, I'm Bill Pricley,"

"Hi, Bill Pricley. Who are you and why are you here?" was my response.

He looked at Fr. Blair for a second and then turned back to me, "I'm an attorney. I heard about this case and thought maybe you could use some help."

I just kind of stared at him for a second, not really sure what to make of what he said or what was going on. "And how is it you think you can help me?" I asked him.

"Well, for starters, the sheriff hates me," he answered.

"Well, that definitely makes me trust you more," I replied somewhat sarcastically.

As we were having this conversation, Fr. Blair turned and just walked away, apparently upset. I followed after him and asked him what was wrong. He just looked at me with a very sad look on his face and walked away. I wasn't really sure what to do, but I decided it was best to just let him go for now. I didn't seem to be doing any good right now, so I figured maybe I could try to talk to him later. As he walked off, Bill caught up with me and just stared after Fr. Blair with a sort of frustrated look on his face.

"I wonder if that man will ever stand and fight for anything."

Believe it or not, I wasn't too thrilled to hear him talk about Fr. Blair like that.

"What's that supposed to mean?" I asked him.

He looked at me kind of surprised and said, "Oh, I guess you don't know."

"Know what?"

"Did Fr. Blair ever tell you anything about his past?"

"Just about his childhood and his fiancé dying,."

"Did he tell you how she died?"

"Just that she was killed in a car accident."

"Yes, she was killed in a car accident, with the sheriff, who was drunk as a fish at the time."

I looked at him stunned.

"Yes," he continued, "the sheriff was deputy at the time, and his brother was the sheriff. One day, he went out and got drunk, and then as he was driving home, he ran into Fr. Blair's mother and wife-to-be. Their car was totaled, and they were both killed."

"Why wasn't he prosecuted?"

"He ran away from the scene, and by the time anyone could catch up with him, he had managed to sober up some."

"So how the hell did he wind up being the sheriff?" I asked him very confused.

"His brother was a much better man than he is. He wouldn't have ever let the sheriff become another J. Edgar Hoover the way his brother has."

That seems to be a common perception of this sheriff, I thought. "So, anyway, what happened?" I asked him.

"The only reason he got caught is because another witness who was driving the opposite way saw him speeding away from the scene. He stopped and tried to help, but it was too late. When the current sheriff's brother heard what happened, he investigated and heard all about how many drinks his brother had consumed. It wasn't a far leap for him. He was going to fire his brother and arrest him for DUI. But only the witness, Fr. Blair, and the sheriff knew about it."

"So what happened?"

"One night, he was working late, and on his way home, he noticed the grocery story had been broken into. He went in to check, and the robber shot and killed him. He managed to get off a shot that missed but did at least some damage because when it was found, there was blood on it."

The whole thing didn't make any sense to me. "So how did the current sheriff get the job?" I asked.

"He assumed control as the deputy, and ever since then, he has run unopposed for reelection."

I just stood there for a minute trying to turn the whole thing over in my head and make sense of it. The one thing that I couldn't figure out was what happened to the person who killed the late sheriff.

"So who was responsible for the death of…?" I just stopped and stared at Bill for a minute. "It was the sheriff, I mean the current one, wasn't it?"

He just stared at me. "Yes, it was," he answered me. "But," he continued, "You and I seem to be the only ones who know it."

"What about Fr. Blair?" I asked him.

"Yes, he knows it. He just doesn't want to do anything about it."

"But why not?"

"I don't know. The way he sees it, it's better to just forgive and forget."

That didn't exactly ring with me, considering that all I wanted was revenge for what happened to me. Revenge against the scum that was responsible, revenge against God for letting it happen, revenge against everybody—that was a big part of my thinking.

"So where do you fit in to all this?" I asked Bill. We just started at each other, and my face told him I hadn't forgotten that I had no idea who he was or why he was here.

"Like him, I grew up here. But I never liked it, and as soon as I was done high school, I left for college and never looked back. By the time of the accident, I was already a practicing lawyer, but I came back for the funeral. I wanted to sue the sheriff, the current one, that is, for wrongful death. But Fr. Blair wasn't interested. He just wanted to forget it."

"How do you forget something like that?" I asked him.

"I don't know. I don't think I could," was his response.

I knew I definitely couldn't. "So why are you here now?"

"I heard about his case, and I thought maybe I could help you. In case you haven't figured it out, the judge and the prosecutor are both in the sheriff's pocket. The public defender isn't, but he may as well be for all he really cares. He knows better than to cross the sheriff."

"But you don't?" I asked him sarcastically.

He continued, "There's nothing here for me, and I don't have anything for the sheriff to try and expose me on, so frankly, there's not really anything he can do to me. And maybe, I can finally get him."

"How are you going to do that?" I asked.

"Well, rumor has it that you don't have any objection to taking on that corrupt jerk. Maybe, between the two of us, we can finally expose *him* and take him down."

That certainly sounded good to me. After that, Bill drove me back home. He told me that if I would let him, he would take on my case, and maybe together, we could take on the sheriff. I told him sure, what the heck, it didn't seem like anyone else in town was going to do it.

I got home and headed upstairs to change out of the suit I was wearing—never did like those things. As I looked out the window, I could see the old church Fr. Blair was trying to build up, and I could make out the sight of him working on something. I decided to finish changing and head down there. I wasn't really sure why, but I felt like someone should reach out to him. That and I wanted to know how he could possibly not want to take on the sheriff and see if he was willing to change his mind and try it.

CHAPTER 7

As I arrived at the church, Father looked up from what he was doing and just stared at me. "So what did you and Bill talk about?" he asked me.

"About the sheriff and about how to finally expose him for what he is, and about you."

He just stared at me for a second and then went back to what he was doing.

"Why are you so resistant to this?" I asked him, frustrated.

"Because maybe I don't want to go around holding grudges against people forever," he responded.

"Don't you want revenge for what happened to you, to your fiancé, and mother? Don't you think they deserve justice?"

"What do you know about justice?" he said, beginning to yell at me. "You think you're so tough because you just want to go out and kill somebody. Well, you're not, you're nothing but a winy baby."

By now, he had stood up and was screaming at the top of his voice. And I couldn't help it; I lost my temper and fired right back. "At least I'm not some coward who hides behind a collar, serving a God who doesn't care about him."

"What do you know about God? Just because something bad happened to you, suddenly you think he's just never cared about you? You think you're the only person who ever prayed. Well, you're not. Just because your family got killed doesn't mean that God doesn't care about you. He does care, and if you weren't so stupid, maybe you could see that."

"Care, *ha*, if he cared about me, he would have protected my family for me."

"Did it ever occur to you that that's what you were supposed to be doing? You thought you were going to be Mr. hotshot detective, and you were so busy looking after yourself you forgot—?"

"You don't know anything about anything, so why don't you just stay the hell out of it, you stupid fool," I interrupted him.

"You forgot to look after the family you *claim* to have cared about," he finished

"You listen to me, you stupid religious old fool. You don't know the first thing about me or my family or any of it, so why don't you just keep your big mouth shut? If you want to worship a God who doesn't care about you and couldn't even muster up the attention to prevent one negative event, then that's your problem. But don't ask me to be a part of your self-delusions."

"Get the hell off my church property," he yelled, pointing his finger back toward my house. "Take your hatred of the world and your self-pity and leave me alone. If you don't want my help, then fine, then go out and look for the revenge you think will be so satisfying, but leave me out of it."

"Fine, I'll do just that, and you can stay here and wallow in your self-delusions about your supposedly 'loving' and 'caring' God who doesn't love or care about you at all."

"Out of here now," he screamed, taking what he was working on and throwing it on the ground and shattering it to pieces. I just turned and left. I walked back to my house and stayed there.

CHAPTER 8

When I got back to my house, I went over in my head what had just happened. I was trying to figure out what had happened to me. I started out hating God, religion, and the like. Then I start developing a friendship with a priest, and somewhere inside of me started to reconsider those feelings. Then I'm getting arrested by a corrupt sheriff, and the next thing I know, what little connection I had developed with Fr. Blair is completely rocked by this huge argument. And over what, that stupid, corrupt, jerk of a sheriff. That settled it. I had to get him. Without Fr. Blair's help, I didn't know how to find out enough about the guy.

I spent the rest of the day working on that question until, eventually, it got dark, and what looked like storm clouds started to roll in. I stared out the window of my room as the thunder rumbled and the rain began to fall. But the storm wasn't too bad, and it occurred to me that maybe this storm was kind of like my relationship with Fr. Blair. We had hit a snag, but one we could get over and try and build a friendship. Suddenly, I caught myself in what I was thinking, and I almost couldn't believe it. After all of this, I was still interested in building a friendship with a priest. Was I actually considering returning to the church, to God? Did I really think that I should do that after everything that had happened to me?

I couldn't really come up with an answer to that question, so I turned my thoughts to other things, namely the sheriff. Whether or not Fr. Blair wanted to go after him, he had broken the law, and if he had killed someone, then there was no statute of limitations. If my years in law enforcement had taught me anything, it was that even the smartest criminals usually mess things up, so he must have made a mistake somewhere. But how could I find out about it? For some reason, I couldn't understand our first encounter. The day he stormed into my house kept running through my head. Then, suddenly, I remembered on that day he had mentioned a nephew as one of the kids who had been vandalizing my house that night.

If he had a nephew, that probably meant his brother had been married, and at some point had a kid. Maybe they could tell me a little more about the current sheriff. Since it was already late, I decided to wait until the morning and then try and look them up and see if maybe they could help me. It seemed like a long shot, but the worst that could happen was they told me to get lost. Maybe they could be of some help to me.

CHAPTER 9

Slam! That was the response when I told the sheriff's sister-in-law that I wanted to talk to her about her husband's death: the door slammed in my face. In fairness, I wouldn't have wanted to talk about my family either, but she didn't even know why I was there. So I guess, in a way, I couldn't blame her, but that didn't help me at all. How was I ever going to expose the sheriff if no one would help me?

I went back home and just sat and thought for a while. I stared out the window at the parishioners working on the church along with Fr. Blair. Part of me wanted to go down and talk to him. I felt as though I needed his help, that maybe he could guide me through some of the troubles I had been having for so long. I was never one for therapy. I always thought that whatever problems I had, I could just work them out on my own, or that they would just go away. But maybe, I was wrong. Then again, maybe I wasn't.

I felt at a loss, as though I didn't know what to do or where to go anymore. For a while, I thought that I was fine, that I could just come and hide here in the middle of nowhere. Hide from all of my problems, all of my sufferings, all of the feelings I didn't want to acknowledge were there. And now it seemed like it was all forcing its way to the surface. It occurred to me that seeking out help or talking to someone about my troubles would mean admitting to myself that it all happened. That it was all real and not some horrible dream.

I shook my head as if to shake off the idea. I just couldn't face that. If the old man wanted to be all sappy and forgive and all about his past, then fine, but that kind of stuff wasn't for me. I still wanted to get back at the person who was responsible for the deaths of my family, and I still wanted to get the sheriff. It occurred to me that my motives for wanting to expose him as corrupt weren't entirely pure, but what did that matter? If a corrupt sheriff who held an entire town hostage, at least symbolically, were taken out of power and prosecuted for his corruption, who cared what the motives behind it were?

I was also wondering how Fr. Blair was feeling about all this. It occurred to me that really he had suffered in life just like I had. That was the first time it ever occurred to me that anyone other than me had suffered in such a way. I thought about what Fr. Blair had said during our argument, about me not being the only one who ever prayed and what not. Maybe he was right. Maybe I hadn't ever really given God a chance. I stared out my window at Fr. Blair down there working on this old rundown church, and another symbol popped into my head.

Maybe that beaten-up rundown building was like a person like me. Someone who was struggling with scars and wounds, in my case psychologically, and just being run down from the stresses of life. Maybe, all I needed was someone like him to reach out, to be willing to help. I could remember the first time I ever looked at that building, and it looked like there was no way of ever building it back up. But now, it was really beginning to look like a church again. Maybe that was all I really needed, someone to reach out to me, to help me build myself back up and get over the struggles I always thought that I could hide from.

Maybe Fr. Blair was that man, and that was why God had arranged for us to cross paths the way we did. I was suddenly shocked by the weight of my own thoughts. Not in a long time had it occurred to me that God had ever done anything for me or helped me in any way. And for a long time up until that moment, I thought that I had been wrong all those years I followed that line of thinking. Now I didn't really know what to believe.

I decided to walk down to the church and try and talk to Fr. Blair. Maybe we could work things out, maybe he could help me. I was almost stunned to catch myself even thinking something like that. I started to head down there, but suddenly, I just couldn't do it. I didn't know what to say to him or how I even felt about him. Part of me was sorry for what had happened and what I had said. But part of me was also angry and just wanted to let whatever relationship we had fall away and go back to just being angry and wanting revenge.

I walked around town for the rest of the day and thinking about all of those things—how I felt, what I wanted, what was I going to do going forward. It seemed like I couldn't hide from my past anymore, so that only left one other option: to confront it. I didn't really want to do that, but it didn't seem like I had much choice.

I also thought a lot about my wife, who I used to take walks with all the time. I thought about all the time we had spent together and how I always thought we would be together forever. I walked around sad and lonely, thinking about her. But in a strange way, I was also happy, as that was the closest I had felt to her in a long time. I thought about the first time we met, at a party at the Neumann Center of our college. We spent the entire party talking and walked around half the night after that just talking. So after that, taking nightly walks became a tradition for us, at least when the weather was nice enough.

As I thought about my wife, I wondered what she would think of my new life. I wondered how she would feel about me abandoning the faith. She always took it so seriously. It was one of the reasons we had connected so well. It occurred to me that if things had been reversed, she probably would have carried on in her faith. She would have viewed it as a test. Honestly, there were times even when she was alive that she made the difference between me walking away and not walking away. She was always faithful like that. She probably wouldn't have been too happy to see me acting the way I was.

But then, it occurred to me that things weren't reversed and that she wasn't there. She was gone, my children were gone, my whole family was gone. The reminder of that fact tore at my heartstrings, it was as though I had never fully said it to myself like that before. It was as though consciously I had always known it but had never really accepted it. And boy, did it hurt. I caught myself starting to cry and break down worse than ever before, and I started running back toward my house, not wanting anyone to see me this way.

As I approached my house, I ran up my front steps and almost barreled right over Fr. Blair who was standing there about to give up and leave after apparently attempting to come by and talk to me. I didn't even stop to say anything, I just pushed right past him into my house and fell down onto my couch and just lay there and cried. He walked over to me and tried to comfort me, and I initially resisted him, but then I just let it go. I was feeling too upset to care. I just lay there and cried. I wanted more than anything in the world for what I was feeling to just go away. I had believed I could handle it by burying it, that if I ignored it, I wouldn't feel. Out of sight, out of mind, right, wrong.

It wouldn't go away; it was always there, always getting stronger. The hurt, the pain, the trauma of what I was going through. It wasn't in the past; it was in the present, right there in front of me, torturing me every minute of every day. And I was out of energy to deal with it. Out of energy to be angry, or to hate, or to want revenge. I was just sad and hurting, and I couldn't cover it up with anything anymore.

For his part, Fr. Blair just sat there next to me, not saying anything, just trying to comfort me. I sat up and looked at him, just staring, with tears in my eyes, wondering what to say in that moment. Because of that, I started to turn away from him, but he stopped me. And then, he quietly whispered to me, "Be still and know."

I turned and stared at him, absolutely stunned. I didn't know why I was stunned, but then I realized that those words gave me a sense of peace that I had not felt in I couldn't remember how long. Finally, I responded, "What did you say?" I had heard him clearly, but I wanted him to make sense of it for me.

"My son," he responded, "clearly you are suffering greatly. You believe that God has abandoned you, that he has forgotten about you. But he hasn't. God is right here walking and suffering this path with you. He has allowed you to walk this path so that he can bring you out of it and show you the greatness of his love. Just like he allowed his only Son to walk that path of the cross, he has allowed you to walk this path of suffering. But just like he raised up his Son, he can raise you up too. You have to have faith in God and in yourself. If you have faith that He can raise you up, just like He did His Son, then it will happen."

I sat there stunned, not because I didn't know what to say, but because what he had said hit me somewhere deep in the core of my psyche. He had tapped into something I hadn't even realized was there. That, maybe, my greatest hurt was the loss of faith I had experienced. The shock wave of that was like nothing I had ever felt before, but it also felt incredibly right. I felt as though I had really hit on something, and it was because of the guidance of this man who, despite how I had treated him so far, or maybe because of it, hadn't given up on trying to help me. This man who had continued to reach out to me despite my resistance and rejections.

In that moment, I knew that I needed his help, but I had no idea how to go about it or what it would look like. As if he had read my thoughts, he looked at me and said, "I can help counsel you through this if you want me to. We can work on these problems together. You don't have to go through this alone, you know. It says in the Bible, 'Who would give his son a snake when he asks for a fish?' Well, I think that all you really have to do is ask, and God will help you, and if you want me to, I will help you too."

For a minute, I thought about rejecting his offer, about just continuing on as I was. But some little place inside my heart told me to carry on. To let this experience that I had never foreseen in a million years take hold of me and carry me forward to what maybe could be a new me. A new me that was like the old me, the one who was happy and carrying on in faith and in life, not just going through the motions and suffering in silence, as I had been doing for so long.

"Okay," I answered him. "Let's do it."

He looked at me and smiled one of the biggest smiles I had ever seen in my life. And in that smile, and in the confidence of his voice, the way he had spoken, I knew he was sure in his ability to help me. Sure in his ability to take command of this situation and help work me through it. Part of me was still doubting, still believing there was no way out of this suffering. But part of me knew that there was, and it was that feeling that gave me the greatest hope. That feeling of knowing that I wasn't alone in this struggle that God was with me. That He had sent Fr. Blair to help me, and that together, we could work our way through this problem together.

Fr. Blair and I sat there for a minute smiling at each other. I think both of us knew that this would be a long and hard journey, but one that would ultimately lead to a better me and one that, maybe, could help both of us to gain a little more happiness and peace in life.

And so it began: a process of counseling, a process of trying to work through what it was that I was suffering. Father wanted to start meeting in the church, but I told him I just couldn't. I wasn't ready yet to go into a church. I made it clear to him that this wasn't a reversion. I had agreed to try and work through my problems with him, but that didn't mean I was ready to forgive God for what had happened to me or return to faith. He accepted that stipulation, but it seemed like he knew one other thing too, something I wasn't telling him: what he had said to me that night in my house had gotten to me. At least, part of me really did want to try and really did want to return to the faith.

But I didn't know how. How do you go back to something or someone, man or God, after all that time away, after all that hatred and anger, and constant rejection of them, and just act as though nothing had happened? It just didn't seem like something that I could do. Besides, I still wasn't entirely sure that I wanted to do that. I was still hurt and angry and sad and lonely, and I still couldn't understand why God would have let any of those things happen. I didn't understand how to deal with the emotional turmoil inside me.

But as we finished talking, I looked out the window and saw the sun shining. It was nearly May, and the most beautiful days of spring were upon us. It has always been my favorite time of year. As we were entering spring, it occurred to me again that this was a metaphor for my life. I had been in a winter for a long time, but now it was time to enter spring and a new birth. I wasn't sure if I could do it, but I finally decided I had to try.

CHAPTER 10

Sin! That was the topic I chose for my first counseling session with Fr. Blair, sin. I couldn't tell him why I chose that topic; that was just what had come to my mind. I guess maybe it was because I didn't understand why there was so much of it in the world and no one, least of all God, seemed to care. Why was it that I spent my whole life trying to avoid sin, and in return, I received endless bounds of pain and suffering? Why did I suffer while people like the criminal who had killed my family, or the sheriff for that matter, relish in their sins and benefit endlessly from them? Of all the things I couldn't stand in this world, that was at the top of the list.

I sat there talking about all this for a few minutes, and Fr. Blair just kind of stared at me and then began to chuckle. I couldn't understand his response, and I asked why he was laughing.

"Well, I was thinking about something my grandmother used to tell me," he said.

"And what was that?" I asked him.

"Well, whenever I would get upset about all of the bad things going on in the world, or why in the 1970s when I was growing up, there was a new generation called the baby boomers leaving the faith in waves, she always had the same answer for me."

"And what did she say?" I asked him somewhat sarcastically.

"She used to say the, 'The influence of the devil in the world!'"

I just started at him with a raised-eyebrow sort of look. "The influence of the devil?" I said in a questioning tone.

"Yep," he said almost proudly, but in a sort of sarcastic way of his own.

"And for a long time," he continued, "I didn't understand it. I used to think, oh come on there, has to be more to it than that. But nope, in time I came to see that yeah, she was right."

"So the excuse for everything is just 'the devil made me do it'?" I asked him. "Because," I continued, "I seem to recall something in church doctrine about the devil only tempts people to do things, but ultimately, we make our own choices."

"I said the *influence* of the devil, not the actions of the devil," was his response. He continued, "You're right. Ultimately, we make our own choices. And we have to learn to see clearly when the carrot of sin is being dangled in front of our faces, and we don't even realize it. We have to learn that when we think we have the devil all figured out, and we know exactly what our weaknesses are and how to avoid them, that's when we are the most vulnerable. The devil will know your weak points, and he will attack them. You have to learn how to fight back."

I just sat there, staring at him, a little stunned. I had thrown some of what I thought was the best material I had for denouncing God and the church at him, and he had completely debunked it and made a lesson out of it for me, all in a matter of minutes. Part of me was angry; what else was new? But part of me was also embarrassed. Embarrassed because some part of me had always sort of known what Fr. Blair had just said, but just didn't want to. The world is often so anti-God that no one ever stops and thinks that maybe the reason we never see God is because he's waiting for people to have faith in him.

I guessed he could tell that I was somewhat overwhelmed because he suggested that we stop for the day, even though we had only been talking for maybe a half hour. Whether I really was stunned or had just had enough religion for one day, I decided he was right to end our session. He got up and started walking toward the door, and just before he left, he smiled at me and said, "Try to think about what we talked about here tonight with your heart, not your head."

I didn't really understand what he meant by that, so I just looked at him for a minute and then watched him walk out and head back down toward the church where he was staying. After he left, I sat down on my couch and pondered the conversation we had just had. I thought about all the time I had spent angry at God for what had happened to me. I wondered if I was really angry because somewhere inside of me, I knew that I had let myself fall away. I realized that maybe I had been the person who made this bed I was in, not God or the devil, or the killer of my family, but me—the person who had ultimately done all the things I had done.

I was the person who had decided to run away from my home to this little mountain town no one had ever heard of. I was the person who had decided to blame God for my family's deaths. In the end, perhaps, I had done all of this to myself. Thinking about that, I began to have a strange feeling I could never remember having before, and I couldn't understand what it was. It was like somehow I had broken through to some inner part of me that I hadn't even known was there.

I sat there reflecting on this for a while, but I really just couldn't make sense of what it was. I decided to go for a walk and try to clear my head a little. I walked around town and thought about all of the things Fr. Blair had said. I thought about thinking with my heart instead of my head. It was the first time in a long time that I thought about what was in my heart. Naturally, the first thing to come to mind were my wife and my children, but then a new feeling began to appear.

I was thinking about my wife and how we used to take walks together, and it began to occur to me just how lonely I felt. I stopped in the middle of the sidewalk and just thought about that for a few minutes. I'm lonely—that thought just kept running through my head over and over and over again. I didn't know how to handle it, and suddenly, I found myself wanting to talk to Fr. Blair about it. I was a strange combination of stunned and confused! I couldn't believe that I actually wanted to talk to a priest about anything, let alone about how I felt about my wife and my family.

As I stood there, I felt someone push me forward and turned around to see the sheriff standing there behind me.

"What did you do that for?" I asked him.

"You were loitering in front of my house, that's why," was his response. "And I wanted you off my property," he continued.

For a second, I seriously thought about hitting him but decided against it. Letting a cooler head prevent my anger from getting the better of me, something else that hadn't happened in a long time. He stared at me with the same smirk he had shown me that day in court. It showed just how aware he was of his power and just how aware he was that no one was willing to stand up to him for the bully he was.

"Loitering or not, that doesn't give you the right to assault me," I replied.

"Maybe not as sheriff, not that anyone around here would take me to task for it, but as the property owner, I have every right to physically force you off my property. And if you don't believe me, ask your lawyer friend, who thinks he's so great."

It took me a second to realize he was talking about Bill Pricely, the only person who seemed to have ever wanted to make waves and stand up to this so-called sheriff.

"You bated me into a fight, so you could have something on me last time. I'm not going to let you do that to me again," I warned him, even as I began to feel my anger rise.

"Yeah, what are you going to do? Tell that stupid priest on me?"

I tried to keep my cool and just stared at him. "What are you talking about?" I asked him.

"I'm talking about all the time you two have been spending together lately," he replied.

"How do you know about that?" I asked him.

He leaned in close to me, like he had that day in the grocery store, and whispered, "I run this town, and I know everything that goes on in it all of the time." He continued, "And there's nothing you or anybody else can do to stop me."

I just stared at him, knowing that he was trying to bate me into attacking him. "So since you mentioned my 'lawyer friend,' as you call him, and since you know everything, what's happening with your case against me?" I asked him.

"That stupid cowardly judge is afraid to proceed because he's worried your lawyer has something on him," he answered.

"Does he?" I asked with a smirk.

"Whatever he's got, what I've got is worse," he replied.

I decided if I carried on any further with this conversation, I might wind up losing my temper and going off, so I turned around and headed back toward my house without saying a word. The sheriff, for his part, didn't say a word either. He just went back into his house.

By the time I got home, it was late, and I was tired. I crawled into bed and went to sleep with everything that had just happened in both my head and my heart. And that night, I slept the most peaceful I could remember in a long time, safe in the knowledge that, yes, all these things would still be there tomorrow, but that someone was there with me, and that I wasn't so alone in this fight anymore.

CHAPTER 11

The next morning, I woke up early to the sounds of construction. Looking out the window, I saw Fr. Blair was down at the church working on it with a group of volunteers. I got dressed and headed down there, wanting to see how I felt being so close to a church and being involved in its activities. Fr. Blair saw me approaching and walked out to meet me. As he did, I couldn't help but think of the parable about the prodigal son and how his father saw him off in the distance and came out to meet him.

He stopped a few feet away from me, and we stared at each other for a minute. He looked at me with a look of great hope on his face, like he could somehow feel today could be a big breakthrough for me.

"Need some help?" I asked him.

"Sure do," he responded.

He smiled at me like he had smiled that day at my house, and it felt good. It made me think about my wife and what a pretty smile she always had. I thought I would be sad, but instead, it made me happy to remember my wife's smile. It was always one of my favorite things about her. It occurred to me that, maybe, in a way, she was still with me smiling down on me from heaven, happy to see that I was perhaps making my way back into the church.

I looked up at the entrance to the church, the same one I had run away from before and felt a sadness in my heart when I knew I couldn't do it, I couldn't go in, not yet, at least. Suddenly, the weight of that thought hit me, and I didn't know what to say. I stared at Fr.

Blair for a second, wondering if I should tell him. I looked up toward the roof and saw that a few of the parishioners were working up there. I thought about my father, who was a roofer, and how when I was in my teens and college years, I used to help him some on weekends and during the summers.

I walked over to where there was a ladder and climbed up to the roof. Father followed behind me and introduced me to the parishioners working up there. I grabbed some tools and started working. The others just stared at me for a minute and seemed surprised that I knew so much. Not realizing this, I started asking for other tools that I needed, and when, after a minute, no one said anything, I looked up and realized that everyone, including Fr. Blair, was just staring at me. I stared back at them for a minute, and then someone started to giggle, and that quickly snowballed into the entire group, including me, busting out laughing.

"Maybe I should have mentioned I have some experience with doing this in the past," I said.

I told them about how I used to do this with my father and all that. We spent the rest of the day working on the roof of the church until late in the evening. As we finished for the day and came down from the roof, some of the people who had been working with me on the roof seemed to be having some sort of staring contest with some of the other parishioners. I watched this for a minute, and as I did, I couldn't help but remember the first day I had gone down there and noticed the workers working in two separate groups. Eventually, Father stepped in and sent both groups home for the day.

"What's with them?" I asked.

"They're busy competing over who sings better. They've formed two different choirs, and they're competing for who is going to sing at the opening mass for the new church."

I just looked at Father and chuckled sarcastically, and he did the exact same thing. I think both of us understood how trivial that kind of thing was after the things we had each been through in our lives. And once again, I was struck by the significance of the moment. Here I was forming this relationship, this sort of bond with a person who not long ago I wanted nothing to do with. I also began to feel as though I was having a lot of these moments.

I guess my eyes must have given away what I was thinking because Father stared at me with a sort of curious look.

"What are you thinking?" he asked.

"I was thinking that you and I are starting to have a lot of these moments," I replied.

"Moments?" he asked questioningly.

"Moments where I realize…" my voice trailed off. I wasn't sure how to explain to him what I was feeling. We just sort of stared at each other for a minute, and I think we understood each other perfectly. In a way, it reminded me of the quote "Pray always, use words when necessary." It was a moment sort of like that. And I think I began to feel the bonds of friendship truly begin to form.

"Would you like to stay for dinner?" Father asked me. "And maybe we could pick up our meetings where we left off last time?" he continued.

I sat there for a minute trying to work up the energy, but I just didn't feel like I had the strength to work on what was troubling me. Besides, I actually had a good day for the first time in I couldn't remember how long, and I didn't want to spoil it with a lot of bad memories. I explained this to Father, and he accepted it, but although he tried to hide it, I could tell it upset him. That bothered me some because I didn't think he was understanding what I was feeling, but I just ignored it and focused on what we were doing.

We ate dinner together in the rectory kitchen, which looked like it could use a few upgrades itself once the church was done being rebuilt. As I looked around at it, Fr. Blair asked me what I was thinking, and I told him, "Yep, this place definitely isn't a palace, but it does the job." I chuckled and thought about all those stories I had heard growing up and going to Catholic school. Stories about the prophets and the saints and how they were poor and lived humble lives. I had always thought those people were so far removed from me and my life here in the twenty-first century, but now it seemed like there was one sitting right in front of me. For the first time, it occurred to me just how much Fr. Blair had sacrificed and was still sacrificing to work for the church and be a priest.

He must have sensed what I was thinking because he looked at me and said, "The life of a faithful, God-fearing person isn't an easy one."

I could tell he meant it as a lesson for me, and in a way, I was humbled. I was really beginning to come around to this idea that maybe I wasn't unique in what I had suffered, and that other people, like Fr. Blair, had suffered too. As I thought about that, I also began to think about God and my relationship with him, which, you might say, had been distant for quite some time. I explained to Fr. Blair how I was feeling, and to my surprise, he looked at me with a look of hope on his face.

"I think maybe we did have one of our sessions after all," he said to me.

"What do you mean?" I replied.

"Well, it looks like you had a breakthrough and without any help from me," he said.

For a second, I was puzzled, but after thinking about it, I understood what he meant. And the weight of that shocked me. Maybe it was because of that that I didn't realize I was smiling. I was actually happy at the thought of making my way back up the mountain of faith. We finished eating, and I helped Fr. Blair clean up. After that, I started to leave, and as I did, Fr. Blair turned and said, "Good work tonight, let's keep it up."

I smiled at him, and he smiled back at me, and that was all. I turned and left and walked back to my house, smiling the entire way. For the first time in a long time, I began to feel some measure of peace in my life and in my heart. Much hurt and anger and sadness still weighed on me and on my heart, but still there was a measure of peace. I looked up at the sky, at heaven, at God, and smiled and simply said, "Thank you." That was the second time I had thanked someone; the first time being when Fr. Blair bailed me out of jail, and now the second time was to God. I still had a long way to go and still wasn't sure I wanted to return to a faith life, but I knew something was happening, and I thought I was starting to like it.

CHAPTER 12

The rest of the spring and summer flew by like that. I spent my days helping Fr. Blair and the parishioners build the church. Everything from drywall to electric and plumbing to the roof needed to be replaced. The work moved slowly but steady. Still, there were a lot of setbacks. Some days it felt like it was half step forward, two steps back. But each time we had a setback, Fr. Blair would just say that we had to keep moving forward and pray to God for patience.

He was better at that than I was, but I still tried. I tried when a pipe I was helping to fix broke because of my mistake, and I got covered in water. I tried when some tiles fell off the roof and landed on my foot. I tried when I nearly set the church on fire trying to install some electrical lines, even though the electrician in the parish had told me exactly how to do it. After that, he had a great time teasing me that it was too bad the pipe hadn't broken on me the same day because at least then there would have been something to put out the fire. I knew he was only teasing me, and so I just smiled. And it actually felt good to just sit and laugh with someone.

But, most importantly, I tried to make progress in the counseling Fr. Blair and I were doing together. I tried to share with him how I felt. I tried to go to places I had never gone, emotionally speaking, and confront my demons. I tried to learn to see the past in a new way. I tried to learn to see meaning and purpose in my suffering. Each time I learned about myself and about my suffering was kind of like learning my mistakes in helping to build the church. It seemed like a good analogy. Sometimes our difficulties are the results of our own mistakes; however well-intentioned, sometimes things just fall on our heads, like roof tiles.

As time went on, I began to learn more about myself and began to heal just a little from my suffering. Not that it was a nine-to-five operation. I kept Fr. Blair busy, often calling him at all hours because I needed to talk to him more about what had happened or how I was feeling. And he was always so gracious. I truly came to be grateful for the help he was giving me, even if I didn't always show it.

On Labor Day weekend, we even put on a barbecue with some of the other parishioners. It was the first time in a long time I had started to feel a part of anything. Even though I still was very hurt and still hadn't come back to church yet, it felt good to be a part of a community. Fr. Blair smiled the entire time, and I thought that he could see how I felt and was happy to see me becoming a part of something.

Near the end of the summer, Fr. Blair and I sat out behind the church just talking for a while. We talked some about me, about him, about all that had happened that summer. We talked for a while as the sun went down and a breeze began to blow up. We sat there for a while as it got darker and listened as the wind whistled through the trees. It was a moment of stillness. A moment when I could start to see some beauty in the world again. My heart was still very heavy, but that didn't mean I couldn't see some beauty in the world.

CHAPTER 13

The next morning, I woke early, around 6:00 a.m. and was struck by something, but I couldn't figure out what it was. I got up and walked over to the window and opened it a little. I saw the sun coming up and heard the birds and realized that I was again enjoying the beauty of this moment. I looked at the calendar and saw that it was the first day of fall. I started thinking about my wife again; fall was her favorite time of year. She always loved seeing the different colors on the trees, and when we first got engaged, she could only think of one time of year she wanted to get married: the fall. At that, I remembered that our anniversary would be coming up in a few weeks.

At that thought, I felt very sad but at the same time happy. And surprisingly, I wasn't angry. For the first time since our last anniversary that she was alive, it felt like I wasn't dreading the day, or at least dreading it less. I decided to head out for an early-morning walk and then started to chuckle thinking about my wife. She was always more of an evening than a morning person.

I got dressed and headed out just as the sun was starting to come up. I thought about stopping in and checking on Father to see if he wanted to come with me. Maybe this would be a good time for another one of our sessions, but I wasn't sure if he would be awake yet. I decided to head the other way toward the town, which I figured would just be starting to stir this early in the morning. Not like the big city, which was always bustling 24-7. I walked around for about an hour and a half, just enjoying the peace of the early morning.

It was amazing to me how far I had come in such a brief time. I didn't feel like I was carrying around as big of a weight as I had been before, or like I was carrying around so much anger. And I knew that I had Father to thank for a lot of that. Somehow, his presence, his not giving up on me, had made a big difference. Even though I had only known him for a matter of months, those months had been some of the most significant of my life in a long time. Yes, I was still lost and confused, not to mention far from healed of my wounds, but I had more peace and calm in my heart than I had in a long time.

As I made my way into town, I headed for a small corner diner that was open early. I couldn't remember the last time I had been out to eat, let alone out to breakfast. Unless you counted the endless eating on the run and fast-food eating I used to do as a cop. Endless eating that drove my wife crazy. She always wanted me home for dinner more. She thought it was important for us to eat as a family—me, her, and the kids. For a minute, I felt very sad, thinking about how that was one of my biggest regrets, not spending more time with my family. It occurred to me what Fr. Blair had said that day when we had our argument about me wanting to be a hotshot cop, or whatever, was actually true. And ultimately, that distracted me from what I loved the most in the world, until one day they weren't there anymore.

Suddenly, I just stopped right where I was. It hurt me to think what I had just thought about, but the thing was that wasn't something I had been consciously feeling until that moment. More than anything, I was surprised. It was something I wanted to explore more, and I decided after breakfast I would stop in and see if Fr. Blair had time to talk with me. I walked into the diner and sat down in a corner booth. As soon as I sat down, I looked across the diner and saw two familiar faces, the sheriff and the judge. It looked like they were having an important private conversation. My guess was they were discussing whatever secrets, they were afraid of Bill Pricley, using my case to drag up. I couldn't hear what they were saying, so I ducked down out of my booth and ducked behind the counter, making my way over to where they were.

"What do you want me to do?" the judge asked.

"I want you to let me prosecute that jerk before he starts causing serious trouble," came the sheriff's response.

"I'm not the only one with the things to hide." The judge continued, "If he ever finds a way to prove what you did, he'll go running straight to that lawyer, and before you know it, we'll both be locked up."

"The key word there is *prove*," the sheriff countered. "No one has anything on me except accusations that are completely unfounded and untrue." *Yeah, right,* I thought, and I think the judge was thinking the same thing. "But the same can't be said for you."

I could hear the anger in the judge's voice as he fired back, "There's plenty of proof. You and I both know if that doctor who stitched you up that night lived here instead of just passing through, she would have figured it out, and there would be enough evidence to convict you."

"Maybe you think I'm stupid enough to say something incriminating in response to that, but I have news for you: you're going to have to do a lot better than that."

At that, the sheriff got up and walked out without paying any money. I wondered if he had something on the diner owner too, or if he was just that obviously corrupt. I stayed in my hiding spot for a minute, not sure what my next move should be. I thought about just approaching the judge, and in a moment of what was either shear boldness or sheer stupidity, I walked around the counter and approached his booth just as he was about to get up and leave.

We just looked at each other for a second.

"So what does he have on you?" I asked him.

"What are you talking about?"

"The sheriff, what does he have on you? Clearly, based on the way he treats you and acts in your courtroom, it's something pretty big."

"If I tell you, you'll just try and use it against me too, then I'll be stuck between him and you."

"So he does having something on you," I said with a smile.

The judge just looked at me and, realizing he had been tricked, pushed past me and headed for the door.

"Does that lawyer Bill Pricley know?" I yelled after him. "I know you haven't proceeded the criminal case against me because of him," I continued.

He turned back and just stood there for a minute with a look on his face like a deer in headlights. I almost told him what I had overheard him and the sheriff talking about in his chambers that day, but then thought better of it. The judge opened his mouth for a second to say something but then just turned back around and walked out of the diner and away down the street.

I thought about what I had just learned and was so interested in it that I forgot I was hungry. The judge had confirmed for me what I already pretty much knew—that he wasn't proceeding the case against me because apparently, Bill had the same thing on him that the sheriff had. But the other thing, the thing about a doctor who had treated the sheriff for his wound. I remembered Bill telling me that there was a bullet with blood found on it in the store where the previous sheriff had been killed.

In that moment, I forgot about everything I had been thinking about faith and my family and whatever else. Once again, my mind turned to getting the sheriff for exposing me and my past. I decided to give him a call; he had left town to go back to his office but had told me to call him if they set a court date for me or anything like that. I was wondering if he knew anything more about this doctor or where the only piece of physical evidence that might convict the sheriff could be.

CHAPTER 14

I almost tripped over Bill's suitcase, walking into the lobby of the motel as he was walking out.

"Where are you going?" I asked him.

"I'm leaving. When I didn't hear from you all day, I figured you weren't coming. I have a practice to get back to. Clearly, nothing is ever going to change around here."

It was Saturday, and he had agreed to come to town for the weekend. But it had taken me all day to get over to the motel to see him.

"Maybe it can change, maybe we can change it together."

He just looked at me for a second. "And how exactly is it that we are going to do that?" he asked. "Are you going to get some kind of proof that the sheriff killed his brother and then prosecute him?" he continued sarcastically.

"That's exactly what I intend to do," I said with a smile. "But only if you help me."

"How can I possibly help you?" he asked skeptically.

"You can start by telling me if there were any doctors visiting this town during the time that the sheriff's brother was killed."

Bill stared at me like I had just asked him to get me a private audience with the pope himself. Frankly, I may have had a better shot at that than finding out what I wanted based on his reaction.

"You want to know if fifteen years ago a doctor came and stayed in this town, which, by the way, is after I had already left?" was his eventual response.

I just smiled and stared at him with a sort of you-know-you-want-to look.

"It's impossible. How could that possibly help us?" he asked negatively. "There's no way we could ever find her, and even if we did, what difference would it make, like she would remember anything? She was just visiting on vacation and what help could she…" He trailed off as I just continued to smirk at him. Finally, he just sighed. "How do you propose we do this?" he asked.

"Well, during my years as a cop, I did pick up a thing or two about finding people," I replied sarcastically.

"Okay, Mr. know-it-all," he replied with a smirk. "Where do we start?"

"How about right here?" I said.

"What are you talking about?" was his reply.

"Well, unless there is anywhere else in town to stay, he probably stayed here, right?"

"Sure he, or she, or they, if it was a couple or a family, or a medical convention, or God knows who else. Do you have any details on when this doctor was supposedly here?"

"Only that it was during the time that the sheriff's brother was killed. You must know when that was."

"Yes, I know when that was."

"Well, then all we have to do is search through the records right here of who stayed here around that time."

"And assuming they still exist, how do you propose we get access to them?"

I stared at him for a second, not willing to admit he had stumped me. When I was a cop, I would have just gotten a warrant or subpoena or something, but those days were gone. Besides, even if I could apply for one, there was no way that corrupt judge would give it to me and no way the sheriff was going to enforce it for me. Finally, I decided to try a somewhat more underhanded way. Pulling a fifty out of my emergency cash stash I always kept on me, I motioned Bill to follow me inside.

We walked up to the desk where some clerk, who looked like he couldn't possibly care less, was sitting behind the counter reading some book. I asked him if we could see the records of who had stayed there and where they kept archival ones. He just looked at me, and his face told that apparently he could have cared less before and that now he did. I waved the fifty in front of him, and he reached for it. I pulled it away and told him what I wanted to know and offered him the rest of the day off on my dime if he told me what I wanted to know.

Bill for his part just stood there, somewhere between disbelief, surprise, and to some extent, amusement. The situation was a little more comical than it was dramatic. After a minute, the clerk agreed, told us what we wanted to know, and headed out the door, fifty dollars in hand.

As he left, Bill stared after him and then looked back at me, apparently not sure what to say. "Well, that was productive. If nothing comes of this, at least we can say we didn't violate our principles," he said sarcastically.

"Maybe you didn't violate yours," I shot back at him sarcastically.

We just looked at each other and then headed into the back storage room where the clerk had told us the records were. We spent the rest of the afternoon and evening looking for the records but couldn't find anything. It was after midnight, and we were both getting tired and about to give up when I noticed a book at the bottom of the box I was looking through. It had the right date on it. We started going through it, and there it was on the last page: Dr. Emily Sharpton.

She had left the town almost exactly to the day. I yelled to a sleepy-looking Bill that I had found it, and then we cleaned everything up after writing down her name and the dates she had stayed. I glanced at Bill's watch and knew it was too late for him to drive back to the city. He went back to the desk and got a different clerk to re-rent him his room. One nice thing about this little town, there was always a room at the inn. Running that through my head made me think about the nativity story—no room for baby Jesus—and then I remembered Fr. Blair. I hadn't thought about him since early that morning.

Thinking about him made me remember everything that I had been thinking about my family and my faith, and how maybe I was actually beginning to heal. I wondered if it was too late to drop in on him. I didn't think so, but then again, I wasn't sure if he would understand this anyway. Considering what Bill had told me that day at the courthouse, I really didn't think so. I wasn't sure how to feel about that. I walked back home thinking about that and everything that had happened that day. Something about going after the sheriff felt so right, but at the same time, something also felt wrong. It was almost like I was doing the right thing but for the wrong reasons.

As I approached my house, I thought seriously about heading down to the church rectory to talk to Fr. Blair but ultimately decided to reconsider what to do after a night's sleep. I changed and climbed into bed but couldn't fall asleep thinking about all that was going on. I rolled over and looked out the window just as some storm clouds started rolling in and some thunder and lightning started to roar. I finally fell asleep, but didn't sleep much as I tossed and turned trying to figure out what to do and how to go forward. The only thing I could figure out was that I felt conflicted. The previous day was a perfect example of what was going on inside of me. Part of me wanted to go after the sheriff and expose him for what he was, although I still didn't fully understand why.

Another part of me wanted to proceed down the path Fr. Blair and I had started. I couldn't deny there was a part of me that liked the idea of healing, of letting go of all of my anger and hate and maybe making a new life for myself. But the questions still lingered: what would a new life look like? I certainly couldn't stay around town Rocky Hills, not after all the trouble I had stirred up. But what about Fr. Blair? Believe it or not, I didn't want to leave him. I felt like if I was really going to continue down this path I was on that I definitely needed his help. As I lay there, I remembered the first time Fr. Blair and I had spoken. How he had quoted the Bible verse "Be still and know" for me. And that made me remember the passage in the gospels where Jesus tells us about not worrying and letting tomorrow take care of itself. On that note, I rolled over and fell asleep, resolving that a few hours rest could not make my problems worse and could only make me a little stronger in my ability to face them.

CHAPTER 15

First thing in the morning, I went to the inn and met Bill, and we started trying to find out more about this Dr. Emily Sharpton.

"So, Mr. know-it-all, where do we start?" Bill asked with a smirk.

"Well, here in the early eighteenth century, we have this magic thing called Internet. There's all kinds of amazing pieces of information on it," I shot back sarcastically.

"Okay, enough of this sarcastic back-and-forth. Where do we start?" he replied.

"Well, where can we get access to the Internet around here? Even a small town like this must have it."

I knew that I didn't have it at home, and I didn't think Fr. Blair would have it at the rectory, plus I wasn't sure I wanted to involve him in this anyway.

"I think they have some Internet access computers right here," Bill replied.

After paying a fee at the front desk for access to a computer that looked like it had been built somewhere around the time of the *Titanic*, we got online and googled her name. We pulled up the website for her practice, and I saw that it was in the center city of Philadelphia. At that, I just stared at the screen, not sure of what to do next. I wanted to find her, see what she knew, what she remembered. Find out if she could help me in my quest to expose the sheriff for what he was. But at the same time, I knew what going and finding her would mean.

It would mean going back to everything I had left behind. Back to the place where it all started. I just didn't think I could face that. I was so conflicted, and that feeling made me angry. I was finally starting to make some headway in this quest, and now my impossible-to-face past was in the way. It just seemed so unfair, I was caught between two forces. Something that I wanted to do, and my inability to face my past getting in the way. It was at that moment that I realized for the first time just how much I had lost control of my life. And boy, was I angry about it.

I got up, pushed past Bill, and stormed out the door. He got up and followed me out, yelling after me to stop, but I didn't. I just got in my car and left. I drove straight home, went in my house, and just sat there stunned, angry, and sad. I thought I was making some progress. Talking to Father was helping me a lot, and I really thought that maybe I had started to heal, just a little. But now, when faced with the possibility that I would have to go back to the place where it all started, I just couldn't.

I wasn't really sure where to go from there, but one thing struck me. I wanted to move forward. I wanted to change my ways, to heal from my hurt, maybe even give God a second chance. But apparently, that process wasn't going to look like what I thought of it. It was as if I actually had some idea. My thoughts were interrupted by Bill knocking on the door. I let him in, and he just looked at me.

"What happened to you back there? One minute you're all excited, the next minute you're running away?"

I just looked at him, not sure what to say. "I just had to get out of there," I finally replied.

"Why?" he asked.

"I just did," I insisted.

"Okay," he continued, "what do we do now? I guess you're going to say we should find this doctor and see if by some off chance she actually remembers anything."

I only half heard what he was saying as I was lost in my own thoughts trying to understand what I was feeling.

"I need to talk to Fr. Blair," I finally said, a little surprised to hear myself say it.

"You need to what?" he replied, confused, and I think a little shocked. "Why do you want to talk to him about this? You and I both know he wants no part in any of this whatever 'this' is," he answered me.

"Maybe not, but I need his help. I don't think you'll understand," I replied.

I got up and walked out of the house and down toward the church. Bill followed behind me like he was just curious as to what was happening. And he wasn't the only one. I was pretty curious myself. Wanting to talk out my problems with anyone, let alone a priest, was still new to me. We walked onto the church lot, and I went over to where Fr. Blair looked like he was working on, rebuilding what he had destroyed the day we had our argument. I guess my face must have shown that I was upset because as soon as he looked at me, a look of concern came over his face.

"Everything okay?" he asked.

"Can we talk?" I replied, not sure what else to say to him.

"Sure, should we get some privacy?" he asked.

I just nodded in agreement, and we walked away and into the church rectory, which I learned for the first time wasn't air-conditioned, and since it was still warm even though it was fall, it was uncomfortable. Apparently, that was one more sacrifice Father was making to rebuild this church. Once again, it occurred to me he really had sacrificed a lot.

"So what's going on?" he asked me, sitting down at the table inside the kitchen. "It looks like something has really upset you."

I sat down on the other side of the table and just stared at him for a minute. I wasn't really sure where to begin. "Was it hard for you to come back here, to this church, after everything that happened to you here?" I finally asked him.

"Initially, yes, but in the end, I think it was actually helpful to me," he answered.

"How could it be helpful?" I asked skeptically.

"In the end, I think it helped me to make some peace with my past."

"But how?"

"I'm not sure how to explain it to you," he answered me. "But maybe," he continued, "it was so that God could help me to be in the right place and time to help you."

I couldn't really argue that point with him, seeing as I had already thought the same thing myself.

"Why do you ask?" he asked me.

"Recently, the possibility of returning to my hometown, and so facing some of my past, came up," I said, avoiding saying how it was that that opportunity presented itself.

"How did that come about?" he asked. "And does it have anything to do with Bill Pricley being here with you?"

The way he said that almost sounded confrontational and annoyed me some. I could tell there was some sort of issue between the two of them based on what Bill had told me that day at the courthouse.

"Can we just leave him out of it for now?" I asked Fr. Blair.

"Okay, back to you then," he replied. "What is it about your past you don't want to face?"

I didn't know how to respond to that. There was so much. Memories so painful I couldn't even bare to play them out in my head, let alone tell them out loud to anyone. "Where do I begin?"

"Well," he replied, "the beginning is always a good place."

I guess he meant that as advice, and also to try and lighten the mood with a little humor, but in my already-confused and angry state, that was not how I took it. I knew where I wanted to start but was sure that I could not face that memory at all.

"I don't think the beginning is a good place for me right now," I said.

"What if we talk about your family?" Fr. Blair asked me.

That question caught my attention, and I just stared at him, not sure how to feel about it. I remembered the first time he made me remember my past, and even though our relationship had progressed since then, I still wasn't sure that it was fair of him to ask me about it. And I just couldn't make myself face the memories; it was just too painful.

"I don't want to talk about this," I said firmly, beginning to raise my voice. The confusion and anger I was feeling was beginning to show.

Fr. Blair for his part just looked at me. I could tell he wanted to yell back at me but was trying to resist it. "Okay," he finally replied, "what do you want to talk about?"

I couldn't help it. I let my anger start to get the better of me and just started firing at him. "Why don't we talk about why you want to focus on my past so much and avoid talking about your own?"

He just stared at me with a look of confusion/anger on his face, but before he could say anything, we were interrupted by one of the parishioners coming in to announce that the sheriff had just pulled up.

"What does he want?" Fr. Blair asked.

"I don't know," the parishioner replied. "But he says he has something you need to see immediately."

The two of us got up and walked outside. As soon as he saw us, the sheriff came walking toward us with that same victory look on his face the day he showed me the newspaper printout. He handed it to Fr. Blair who looked it over and then just handed it to me, looking at the sheriff, not saying a word to either of us.

"What is it?" I asked him.

"See for yourself," he replied.

I looked at what he had just handed me and realized it was a court order issued to Fr. Blair by the judge to stop working on the church. I just stared at it for a second, completely unsure of what to do next. While officially the sheriff was here to enforce a court order, I knew what had really happened. The judge had run straight to the sheriff and told him about our conversation, and this was the sheriff's answer. Obviously, he had this judge completely in his pocket. There were apparently no limits on his power.

Fr. Blair, for his part, just stood there with a blank look on his face, like he had no idea how he was supposed to react to this. I yelled for Bill to come over and showed it to him, hoping maybe there was some sort of legal error or loophole he could find. But he couldn't find anything wrong with it. He did demand to know from the sheriff what the legal basis for the order was.

"Whatever I say it is," was the reply we got. He never failed to let you know he was in charge.

"Why are you doing this?" I asked him. "Because of me?"

"Because of you, and just because I can," he shot back at me arrogantly. "As long as you keep talking to that judge, or anyone else around here about me, not so much as another nail is going to get hammered into this place," he continued.

"You can't do that," was the only response I could come up with.

"I can do whatever I want, and there isn't anything you can do to stop me," he answered me.

"Oh," he continued, "and your little Internet searches aren't going to help either."

It took me a second to realize what he was talking about. "How do you know about that?" I asked him. I couldn't believe even he was that all-knowing.

"I know everything that goes on around here. I told you that," he answered me.

"And," he continued, "if you and your little buddy here make any more noise, I'm going to come back with an order to demolish this place to the ground and put your little priest friend here in jail. And trust me, I'll make sure to charge him with so many offenses, no one will ever be able to get him freed."

I just stood there incredulous. I couldn't believe just what an arrogant megalomaniac he was. He just smiled that same sly smile I had gotten to know rather well and turned away to leave. But at the last second, he turned back toward me and said, "If you wanted to know about that doctor you went looking for, all you had to do was ask your priest friend there. He can tell you all you need to know about her."

At that, the sheriff got in his car and left. The parishioners, all of whom had stopped working to watch what had just happened, just stood there, not sure what to do next. After a minute, Fr. Blair looked around at them and then sadly and quietly told everyone to just go home until he could figure out what to do next. One by one, they just all turned and left, not saying a single word. After they left, Fr. Blair turned and just stared at me.

"I hope you're happy now," he said sarcastically and then turned and started to walk away.

"What the hell is that supposed to mean?" I shouted after him.

"It means exactly what I said," he replied without even turning around or even stopping.

I walked toward him, got in front of him, and got in his face and repeated my question. "And just what hell is that?" I asked him.

"It means that now you can have what you want," he started yelling at me. He continued, "You can go back to being angry and walling in your self-pity all the time. You can go out and find whatever you think is out there about the sheriff. You can just stay angry at the world all the time, and now you don't have to worry about me getting in your way. Thanks to this, I can't do what I came here to do, so now I can just leave, and you will never have to hear from me again. Congratulations, you're free of the only thing that was standing in your way. If you want to leave here and give up on this church, feel free, but don't ever, even for a second, blame it on me."

I fired right back at him, "The fact that you're a weak leader who can't even get a little church rebuilt, or even unite a small group of people you have here is not my problem."

"Don't make the mistake of confusing your anger with strength because, believe me, there's a difference," he shot back at me.

"What would you know about strength? You've spent your whole life being a weak person waiting for your God to do all your fighting for you."

"Why are you still here yelling at me?" he asked in an angry, sarcastic tone. "Don't you have a doctor to go and track down?"

"Well, apparently, you can tell me everything I need to know about her," I fired back. I hadn't forgotten what the sheriff just told me. "So what exactly is it that you know?"

He just paused for a minute and then finally spoke, "She was a friend of my mother's," he said, tears beginning to form in his still-angry-looking eyes. "She came here for my mother's funeral. After the funeral, she stayed here for a while. Her last night here was the night that the current sheriff's brother was killed. That same night the current sheriff went to see her very late, with a wound in his side, like a bullet had gone through it. She didn't know what had happened yet, no one did. So she treated him, stitched him up, and left the next day, having no idea what she had just helped to cover up. The only reason I know is because a year later, she sent me a letter to see how I was, and in it, she told me what had happened. I hadn't put it all together yet, but I did then, and ever since, I have carried the weight of knowing the same awful truth that you do. That a great tragedy struck not only me and altered the course of my entire life, but struck the people in this parish and this town and altered their entire life. The difference is that, unlike you, I have actually tried to bring some sort of good out of it, not just go out and look for revenge."

I just stared at him, half stunned and half enraged. And in that moment, every bit of hurt, anger, and any other emotion I had left in me, exploded at this man who I thought was becoming my friend. I grabbed him by the shirt, knocking his white collar off, and lifted him up the ground and started screaming at him. I can't even remember what I said. I had just lost all control of myself. Apparently, the old man was a better fighter than he had showed that day at my house because his immediate response was to kick me, doubling me over and then grab my head with his hands. I responded with a defense maneuver of my own, and our fight escalated.

We wound up on the ground wrestling and trading punches. Eventually, I managed to grab him and throw him up against the wall of the church. He reached out and grabbed what he had been working on and, destroying it for a second time, swung it at me. I retreated backward and ducked to avoid it. It slammed against the wall of the church and fell to the ground in pieces. That gave Bill, who had been trying previously, to no avail, the opportunity to get between us and break up our fight.

I walked backward and just stared at Fr. Blair, and he stared back at me, both of us angry and sad. "I can't believe you knew all this time and you never told me or did anything about it," I said, continuing to stare at him almost in a state of shock.

"Get out of here, and this time don't come back," he said angrily but plainly, as if the words didn't bother him at all. "You're a failure," he continued, "you can't be helped. Live with your wallow and self-pity and leave me the hell alone."

I guess I had run out of things to say because I just turned and walked away. I was so lost in my thoughts that I didn't see the car pull away to from the end of the road where the church sat. I didn't see the sheriff sitting inside of it. I didn't see him smile an evil smile that the devil himself would have envied. A smile that showed just how proud of himself he was. Because he knew that he had just neutralized the only two people who might ever be a threat to his power. Each in a different way, but the same threat. Instead, I just went back to my house, having no idea what to do or how to fix this situation. I didn't think about God, or the church or faith, or the sheriff, Fr. Blair, Bill, Dr. Sharpton, anybody or anything. I just cried.

CHAPTER 16

At some point during my crying fit, I must have fallen asleep because the next thing I knew it was morning, and actually a nice one, for whatever that was worth. I started to get up and was startled to find Bill asleep in the chair across the room, still dressed in his suit. As I started to wake up more, I began to recall everything that had happened the day before. I tried to clear my head and figure out what to do next. For the second time, I thought about leaving Rocky Hills and finding somewhere new to start out. Somewhere new where I could just go back to hiding from everything that had happened to me.

I headed into the kitchen and started ruffling around for something to eat. The noise I was making woke up Bill, who came stumbling in half asleep. He walked in and just stared at me. I didn't say a word to him, just continued to do what I was doing.

"You want something to eat?" I asked him.

"I guess," he finally mumbled out after stumbling over to a chair and sitting down, apparently not fully awake yet.

We stayed like that for a few minutes, me trying to make some food, and him just sitting there watching me. Finally, he asked me the question we were both thinking, "So what do we do now?"

I ignored him and just continued to make breakfast. And he continued to stare at me, looking very confused. What I didn't want to admit to him was that I was just as confused.

"Are you going to answer my question?" he asked me.

"No," I responded quietly.

"Why not?" he asked me.

"Because I don't have an answer," I told him.

"Well, that's just great," he started shouting at me. He continued, "Well then, what the hell am I supposed to do? I have a life of my own. I can't hang around here and wait around for you to think of something."

"Then just leave," I said without even turning to look at him.

"Leave?" he asked.

"Yes, leave. If you hate it here so much, then just leave. No one forced you to come here, you know. You quite literally just burst through the door one day and involved yourself in all of this. So maybe what you should do next is ask yourself why you are here."

He sat there, looking stunned at the question. I don't think he had ever asked himself that before. "I came here to try and help you avoid becoming another victim of the sheriff's reign of terror around here," he finally replied. But I wasn't sure it was very sincere answer. I got the sense there was something else happening.

"Is that really why you came here?" I asked him sarcastically.

"Why else would I come here?" he replied to me in a half-sarcastic, half-questioning tone.

"Maybe because you felt guilty," I challenged him.

"Guilty for what?"

"For leaving," I answered him. I continued, "You can't really tell me that everything was just wonderful around here until the sheriff's brother died and the sheriff took over, and then all of a sudden, it was Jonestown where everyone is hostage. Things were probably going downhill for a long time before that, and you just left. You left at least one friend and probably others behind. And now that other people are standing up and trying to make it better, you want to try and play a part in it to feel better about yourself."

The way I said it wasn't in a yelling or accusing tone, or like we were having some sort of argument. Instead, I said it quietly, in a straightforward, conversational tone. Almost as if I was giving him a piece of wisdom I felt he should have. He just sat there staring at me, stunned. I don't think he ever for a second imagined having a conversation like this.

"You don't know anything," he answered me, sounding upset and confused and looking at me with a sad look on his face.

For some reason, I didn't understand our first meeting went through my head. What he had told me about a witness who had seen the sheriff driving away from the accident. I looked at him with a look of curious suspicion.

"You never told me who the witness was who saw the sheriff driving away from the accident scene all those years ago," I said to him.

"What are you talking about?" he asked.

"Who was the witness, I mean, it certainly would help us, wouldn't it?" I asked him almost accusingly because I thought I already knew the answer.

"Why does it matter?" he answered.

"It was you, wasn't it?" I asked him. "You were the witness. That's why you came back here, that's what's really the issue between you and Fr. Blair, and that's why the sheriff is afraid of you. Because you have that on him."

He looked at me half-angry, half-sad. "Yes, it was me," he finally admitted. "I was out late driving, still trying to get over the death of my father and considering Fr. Blair's offer to be his best man at his wedding. I saw the sheriff's car swerve into Mrs. Blair's car and knock it off the road into a rock formation. They don't call this town Rocky Hills for nothing, you know. I tried to help them, but it was too late. They had been killed on impact. I called the sheriff at the time, and based on what I told him, he quickly made the case against his brother. He was waiting until the funerals were over before he was going to make the arrest. But then, he was killed. I wanted to make noise about it, but Fr. Blair said no, he wanted to move on. So I just left. I never saw Fr. Blair again until the day I showed up at the courthouse."

I didn't say anything, just looked at him. He looked like a person who had finally gotten a weight off his shoulders. Just like Fr. Blair, it was clear to me that Bill had suffered, just like I had. I guessed it was a powerful moment for both of us. For a minute, neither one of us said a word, and then Bill broke the silence, sounding confused.

"So what then?" he finally asked. "The old man tries to shrink you, so you try to shrink me. Is that what's going on? Well, I don't want any part of it."

"Then what do you want?" I asked him, not sure how to feel about this role of therapist I was apparently playing.

"I want to know what it is that we are supposed to do next. Apparently, if we keep going after the sheriff, he will just keep coming back with more court orders. And next, he's going to start putting people in jail."

"Well then, I guess it's a good thing you're here," I replied to him. "Because last time I checked a lawyer is just what you need when someone wants to put you in jail."

Bill smirked a little bit at that, and it helped to lighten what had become a very tense mood.

"And what about this court order?" I continued. "Is there some way to fight it?"

"There are only two ways to get it reversed," he answered me. "One: get the court that issued it to repeal it, which is definitely not going to happen. Two: appeal it to a higher court and hope that they repeal it."

"Well, maybe if we say *please* and ask real nicely, we can get the judge to repeal it," I said with a smirk.

"The only way that's going to happen is if we sink to the sheriff's level and blackmail the judge with whatever the sheriff is blackmailing him with, or something worse," he replied.

"Don't tempt me," I replied. I continued, "What do you think it is that the sheriff has on him?"

"Who knows? One thing you have to give the sheriff credit for is that he keeps his methods a secret."

"So then our only hope is that he hasn't found a way to blackmail an appeals court?" I asked Bill.

"Pretty much, yes," was his response.

"I was afraid you were going to say that," I replied.

"Why?" he asked me.

I didn't answer him, although I think in a way he already knew. And whether he knew what the answer was or not, I did. I was afraid to leave this little world I had created for myself. I had vowed never to go back, to never venture out into the world again. I would stay here and hide from what had happened to me. And even though I was realizing more and more every day that I couldn't hide from my past, and that at some point I would have to face it, and not have a tantrum when someone asked about it, I didn't know how. It occurred to me to go and talk to Fr. Blair, but then I remembered I had pretty much burned that bridge already.

"Do you know anything about the sheriff's family? Or really his brother's family?" I asked Bill.

"Not really, why?" he replied.

"The first time I met him, he mentioned having a nephew. Did his brother leave behind a family?"

"Yes, he had a wife, Sarah, I think her name is, and a son, but he was just an infant when his father was killed. I doubt if he even has any memory of him."

The mention of a son with no memory of his father reminded me of the story of his past that Fr. Blair had told me. "Do you think they could be of any help to us?" I asked, recounting my last, very brief encounter with the sheriff's sister-in-law.

"Well, I would have said probably not, but after hearing that, I would say definitely not," he replied.

"So that leaves us with the court order or Dr. Sharpton then," I answered him.

"Pretty much, yes," was his reply.

"Is it possible for you to prepare an appeal to the court order from here, or would you have to go back to your office?" I asked him.

"I could try and do it from here, but here or there, it doesn't matter, unless you can get Fr. Blair on board," he answered me.

"Why?"

"Because the court order was issued to him, so he has to be the one to appeal it. Unless I'm representing him, or his archdiocese, I have no legal standing to do anything."

"So basically, our options are find Dr. Sharpton and see if we can get the archdiocese to care about fighting a court order to stop a little church that's irrelevant anyway. Because with all the other legal battles the church is currently involved in, I'm sure they'll push that to the top of the docket," I said sarcastically.

"Like I said before, 'pretty much yeah' that's it," was his reply.

"Then we have to back to the city," I declared, shocked and scared to hear myself say it. I was still torn between wanting to do it and not feeling able to.

"Okay, when do we leave?" he asked me.

"I don't know, I guess as soon as possible," I replied.

"What about Fr. Blair?" he asked me.

I just let out a sigh and didn't say anything. I was at a loss for what to do about that, so I just stared at him. After the way we had it out the night before, I guessed any relationship or friendship between us was pretty much finished.

"Did you know the sheriff's sister-in-law before, I mean before her husband was killed?" I asked Bill.

"No, the first time I met her was at his funeral, but what does that matter, as you just pointed out, she's not going to help us?" he answered me.

"Maybe she will," I replied.

"And just how are you going to get her to do that?" he asked me.

"I don't know," I answered him. "But it's worth a try."

"What the heck," he replied to me. "There isn't much logic to any of this anyway, so why not? The worse she can do is slam the door again."

What I really wanted to say was that the worse she could do was go running to her brother-in-law, and that he would follow through on his threat and lock us all up. But I didn't say that. Instead, I followed Bill out the door and headed for the sheriff's sister-in-law's house hoping that maybe she could help us. And that this whole thing wouldn't blow up in our faces.

CHAPTER 17

As Bill and I approached the house, I began to feel a sense of nervousness I hadn't felt in a long time. It was the same sense I would get anytime I had a nervous witness on a case, and I had to try and get them to tell me what they saw or knew. Remembering that connected me to my past in a way I hadn't connected to it in a long time: thinking about some part of it other than the tragedy it became. I stayed lost in that thought until Bill brought me back to reality, yelling my name, telling me we had arrived.

I sat in the car for a second staring at the boy standing in the yard, cleaning up some leaves that had started falling in the early fall. I looked around and realized that this yard was the only one with any leaves on it yet. It reminded me of our next-door neighbors in the first house my wife and I ever lived in. They always had a pile of leaves on their yard by Labor Day. Apparently, this tree was cut from the same cloth. And for the second time in as many minutes, I encountered the feeling of remembering something from my past that wasn't about my family or the tragedy that had come to define my life.

As we got out and approached, I recognized the boy as the one I had kicked down the night I caught him and his friends spray-painting on my driveway. He looked up and just stared at me, looking half-surprised and half-nervous. I walked over to him and stared at him not sure what to say.

"So you're the guy that punched my uncle in the face?" he finally asked me with a sort of half smile.

"Maybe," I replied to him. "Why does that make you want to smile?"

"What do you want?" he asked us.

"Maybe I want to know why you and your friends were vandalizing my driveway one night a few months ago," I answered him.

"Why did you kick me down and shoot at us?" he fired right back at me. The kid had guts; I had to give him that.

"Because you were trespassing on and vandalizing my property. So back to my question, why were you doing that?" I answered him.

"It was my friends' stupid idea. We thought the house was still empty. It was for a long time," he replied. "But I guess I owe you an apology."

"Well then, I guess I owe you one for kicking you," I replied.

"What about shooting at me?" he asked.

"Don't push it, kid," I replied in a sort of firm but sarcastic nature.

"Okay, how about we just call it even?" he asked me.

"Deal!" I answered him.

"What's your name?" I asked him.

"Jimmy," he answered. He continued. "So back to my original question, what do you want?" he asked me.

"I was going to ask the same thing," came an unhappy voice from behind us.

I turned around to see the same woman who had slammed her front door in my face a few weeks earlier standing there. Bill and I looked at each other, apparently trying to decide which one of us was going to speak first. The situation probably would have been comical if it weren't so serious and if the events of the preceding days hadn't occurred the way they did. Bill's face seemed to say "well this was your idea," so I figured I would be the first one speaking.

I looked back at her not really sure what to say. I stared at her for a second, and she stared back at me, and as we stared at each other, I suddenly, to my surprise, felt something that I hadn't felt in a long time. Even though I didn't fully understand it at the time, it was an attraction. The sister-in-law of the person who I hated most, save for the criminal the killed my family, and I just had a moment of being attracted to each other. I pushed the feeling aside and tried to focus on the present, but instead, another memory welled its way up.

It was the memory of the first time I ever saw my wife at the party where we met. I sat there lost in that for a minute, once again totally oblivious to the world around me until Bill finally shook me out of it.

"What do you want?" she asked me angrily. She was obviously not happy to see me.

"The same thing I wanted the last time I came here," I answered her.

"Well then, my answer is the same as last time," she replied to me.

"Why won't you just talk with me?" I asked her, my voice showing some of the frustration I was feeling.

"Because there's no point to talking to you, and because I don't want to," she replied, sounding equally upset.

"Well, I don't know about there being no point, but I definitely believe that you don't want to, or at least that you wish you didn't," I answered her.

"What is that supposed to mean?" she fired back at me.

"I think maybe you *do* want to help me, but you're afraid," I answered her, not sure what I meant by that.

"Even if I did, it wouldn't do any good, it wouldn't change anything," she replied. She continued, "My husband would still be dead, and his brother would still rule this place. No one around here will take him on, or haven't you noticed that? Everyone would just look the other way out of fear he would come after them. No one is brave enough to stand up to him."

"Your husband was brave enough," I answered her, not confrontationally but in a soft way. I was trying to set an example for her of values to live out, sort of in honor of his memory. I didn't really know if it would work, but I thought maybe it would touch her somehow. Truth was I didn't really have anywhere else to turn if she refused to help me.

"And look what happened to him because of it," she answered me. She continued, "You don't really think I never figured out what happened to him, do you? How any of these naïve people can't see it is beyond me. I guess they just never knew and have never known my brother-in-law, as well as me. The only people who ever knew him were myself, the priest, and your lawyer friend here, and apparently you. And he left"—she said, motioning to Bill—"the priest went off to find religion. I never heard of you before a short time ago, and I was here all alone with an infant to raise by myself. Do you really think I was going to go making noise and leave my child to be raised by the likes of that so-called sheriff? No, sir, you can reference my husband all you want, but that fact is he isn't here to help me, so it doesn't matter what he did."

"Why not?" The question came from behind me, and I turned and realized it was the boy who had asked it. "Why doesn't it matter what he would have done?" he asked again. He continued, "I never knew my father. I only know what everyone says about him. They use words like 'brave' and 'honorable' to describe him. And if what this guy is claiming is really true, if he really was killed by his brother because he was going to hold him to a higher standard, than he was just as brave and honorable as everyone says. And if that really is true, then I think that we have a duty to honor his memory and to stand up to someone who betrays everything he stood for and, apparently, killed him for it."

The three of us, Sarah, Bill, and myself, all stood there and marveled at these very wise words of such a young man. In a strange way, it reminded me of the story of when Jesus was twelve and his mother and father found him in the temple, amazing the elders with his questions and knowledge. Finally, his mother spoke up, "My husband is dead, that *can't* be changed. That's why it doesn't matter what he would have done. And shame on you for trying to use his memory to guilt me into helping you. You know, so far in all of this, you haven't told me anything about you. Who you are, what you want, why you're even here. For all I know, you're another person he's blackmailing, and you want me to give you something to help weasel out of it. Well, sorry, go somewhere else. There's no way you can ever understand the pain that I feel. There is no way you can ever know what it's like to lose your family and be left behind. And you can't force me to go back and reflect on my husband, reflect on the pain of losing him. I don't know who you think you are to try and involve me with this, but I want no part of it. Now get out of here and keep away from me and my son." She walked past me, grabbed the boy, and started to head into her house.

"You're wrong," I yelled after her. It seemed like a short answer for what she had said to me, but it said all that I needed to say.

She turned back around and walked back toward me with a look on her face that I have never been able to fully describe. All I know was that I could see the pain in her eyes, and I knew that I understood it fully, even if she didn't know that I did.

"How could you possible know anything about it?" she asked me. She continued, "How could you possibly know what I've been through or the pain I've experienced? The answer is you can't. So you also can't stand there and tell me I'm wrong."

"Actually I can because I know exactly how you feel," I answered her. "I know the pain that you have felt, I know the loses you have suffered. I know more than you can possibly imagine I do."

"How can you possibly know anything?" she asked me angrily.

"Because I've suffered the same losses you have, and for the same reasons, a sense of duty and courage and service to others," I answered her.

"What are you talking about?" she asked me half-angry, half-confused.

"My name is Detective Thomas Brado," I answered her, tears coming into my eyes.

She took a step backward and stood there, looking shocked. Obviously, she had heard my name before. Even in a small town like this, where no one may have known my face, most people had come across the story at some point.

"You're that police detective?" she asked me. "The one whose family was killed by the criminal he was chasing. The one who got lured away one night, the one who—"

I cut her off. I didn't need her to retell a story I had already lived out and heard over and over again a thousand times since. One I could not seem to get away from no matter what I did. One that finally drove me away from the place where I grew up to here, the middle of nowhere were I could hide from it. I had had that thought so many times, about coming here to hide from it. And now I was using it to try and make a connection with someone who had had a very similar experience. Someone who had suffered just like I had.

Once again, I thought about what Fr. Blair had said to me during our first argument. About how I wasn't the only person who had ever prayed or suffered. About how I wasn't the only one who felt abandoned by God. As if he, or Bill, weren't examples enough here was another one right in front of me. And now I was presented with the full memory of what had happened on that horrible night that my family died. The story I had read and heard a thousand times but could never tell with my own lips. The worst and most painful memory of them all, the one I never wanted to face, even though all along, part of me knew I would always have to. The memory, the event that had come to define my life. The one that I measured every other memory against, both before and after. And now I was using my own suffering to try and connect with someone else.

And for the first time, I began to understand just what it was that drove me to chase after the sheriff the way I did. I began to see that maybe, just maybe, God was using my suffering to help me connect to others. That he was taking some of the most horrible evil that could ever be and using it to unite a group of people together for good. That maybe, like Fr. Blair had used his suffering to help him connect with me, now I could use mine to connect with this woman and hopefully bring some good out of it.

In that moment, I was struck with awe by the power of what I was thinking. I had been toying with the idea of returning to faith and God for a long time, but I had never been able to because I just couldn't see any reason to. But now I was starting to see through it all. To see that there was a purpose for what I had suffered. But it was hard. The weight of what I was thinking, the idea that somehow it fit into my life and wasn't this cosmic disaster, that I always thought it was, wasn't easy to bear. If that really was true, it was a reality I knew I couldn't face alone. Once again, I thought of Fr. Blair and wondered if maybe we could repair our relationship, and he could help me.

But for right now, I had this situation to deal with. The sister-in-law was sitting there, apparently waiting for me to say something. But once again, it was the boy who shook the conversation with his words: "What about the bloody clothes?" he asked, directing the question at his mother.

His mother turned around and looked at him and then looked back at me, tears in her eyes. "I think we should go somewhere we can't be seen and talk," she said.

I suggested we go inside her house, but she said she didn't want anyone to see me there or know that she was talking with me. She agreed to come with Bill and I to my house and talk with me. We rode there together in silence, her look, very sad most of the way. As for me, I was still trying to make sense of how my earlier thoughts weighed on me and the pain I felt. It was a short trip, and we arrived and all four of us walked into the house and stood there in silence.

I could see from the look on the sister-in-law's face that there was something she wanted to say, but it was like she couldn't make herself do it. Once again, it was the strength of her son that encouraged her: "What about the bloody clothes you talked about once?" he asked her.

She stood there looking sad, the rest of us staring at her waiting for her to give an answer. Finally, she spoke, "Do you have any idea how hard it is for me to stand here and tell you that not only was my family forever traumatized but that it was because my husband was betrayed by his own brother?" She paused for a few seconds and then through tears finally told us what she knew, "The day after my husband was killed, I went to the sheriff's office. You can imagine there was quite a lot going on. My brother-in-law was running around trying to investigate his brother's murder, or at least that's what I thought he was doing. Everyone from the town council was there, along with some local reporters. There were all sorts of commotion, and I finally had to just step out for a while. I walked around to the back of the office and saw the car sitting back there in a small garage where no one could see it. Inside on the driver's seat, and on the door handle inside and out, there was blood all over. That was when I started to put it together.

"I went back inside the station and started looking around for I didn't know what. I was just trying to make sense of everything that was happening. I went into my brother-in-law's office, and in a box under his desk were his bloody clothes. I recognized them because I had seen him wearing them before. I just got out of there and ran home. I couldn't make sense of what was happening. My husband was dead, and his own brother had killed him. And it's not like it was any mystery why. But the only person who would have ever known his motive is dead, and I'm sure all of that evidence is long gone by now."

She turned and looked at her son, who clearly had no memory of any of this. Neither of them said a word; they just embraced each other and shared the power and emotion of this moment. Clearly, she had just lifted quite a weight off her shoulders. As for the boy, I thought he was handling the whole situation very maturely for his young age. He was trying very hard to be strong and to be there for his mother.

I watched as the two of them embraced, and I couldn't help but remember all of the times I had hugged my own children like that. Never under circumstances like that, but the level of embrace and emotion was the same. A tear began to streak down my face, and Bill, noticing this, walked up and put his hand on my shoulder to comfort me. Clearly he and I were starting to form a bond of friendship, something else I never would have thought to do again. And the four of us just stayed there like that for a few minutes.

Finally, I looked around at this group of people assembled in my house, and it occurred to me that God had brought us all together for the purpose of helping us all to heal and maybe to help this town recover from two great tragedies that had been dragging it down for so long. I really was starting to think that a lot. That God had not simply allowed a series of bad things to happen to me because he had forgotten me or didn't care, but because he knew that he could truly bring good out of them. As that thought went through my head, I looked around and couldn't help but feel that someone was missing from this group. And I realized that person was Fr. Blair.

As I was thinking this and trying to figure out how we could possible repair our relationship after our last encounter, the boy looked around and said, "So what do we do now?" As he asked that, he turned and looked at me, and so did his mother and Pricley. Apparently, God had not only put this group together but had made me their leader. And that was probably one of the most powerful moments I had had since all of this started because I accepted that. I accepted as a purpose from God that He had put me here to be the leader of this group and to help the people of this town recover their lives from the tragedies that had come to define it. I let out a breath and just tried to understand what I was feeling in that moment. It was as though something in me had broken. Like a weight had started to be lifted off me. Like I had made a huge step on a long journey I hadn't even realized I was taking. And at that moment, I felt a faith come alive in my heart again, and I felt the courage to face my past like I hadn't before.

"We aren't going to achieve anything just staying here," I replied to the question. I continued, "I think we should go back to the city and try and find Dr. Sharpton."

"Who?" Sarah asked.

I explained who she was and what we had talked about doing.

"Do you really think she will remember after all this time?" she asked me.

"I hope so," was my response.

"If I go anywhere with you, my brother-in-law will get very suspicious," she said.

"Fine, then, you stay here and just keep going along as if nothing has happened or is happening. I won't tell you anymore than I already have so that he can't accuse you of anything. Besides, based on what he said last night at the church, he already knows that we're looking for her anyway."

"So what should we do?" Jimmy asked. He continued, "I don't want to just sit around and wait for you to do something. I want to help. I want to play a role in helping bring my father's killer to justice."

"I think you have already played a very big role," I replied to him with a smile. "You helped give your mother courage to come forward with some very important information."

A look of pride came over his face and, despite her sadness, the same look came over his mother's face as well. It was clear to me that she was proud of her son for the way he had acted that day, even if it was hard for her to accept what was happening. I looked at her, not sure what to say, just trying to comfort her somehow. She looked back at me, and again for the second time that day, I felt an attraction to her. And that time, I was sure that she felt it too. We stared at each other for a few seconds, and then she quickly looked away.

"I guess we will just go for now then," she said, motioning toward the door.

Something inside of me told me to stop her, but I didn't think that would be a good idea just then, so I simply said goodbye and told her I would be in touch at some point. At that, she and the boy left. After she left, Bill looked at me with a smirk on his face.

"You like her," he said like we were seventh graders, and he was teasing me for having a crush.

I just kind of smirked back at him, and our teasing once again helped to lighten a very tense mood. It also showed me for the second time that we were beginning to become friends.

"We have to form a plan," I said, returning to a serious tone.

"I thought our plan was to go back to the city and find Dr. Sharpton?" he asked me.

"Yes, but what do we do once we find her?" I replied to him. "I'm not really sure about that," I answered him. "I guess we find out if she remembers anything, and if she will tell us."

"And then what? Do we go to the police? We would have to go to the state police or to the Feds and hope one of them is interested in taking the case," he argued.

"A cop killer, I think they will be interested," I answered him.

"Maybe, if we can bring them enough evidence," he replied.

"Well, then, we will have to," I answered.

"And what about Fr. Blair?" he asked me.

Once again, I just sighed. I still didn't know what to do about that situation. After all that had happened between us, I wasn't sure how to go back to him. In the past, I had felt that my actions were justified during our arguments, at least somewhat. But I was ashamed of how I had acted the previous day. Never before in my life had I let any type of dispute or argument lead to physical violence, with the exception of my fight with the sheriff.

At the same time, I still felt betrayed by what I had learned about Fr Blair. That he had always known what had happened with the sheriff and his brother. And that he had known that evidence was out there but never did anything about it. I just didn't know how to rectify those feelings.

"Maybe we can go talk to him together," Bill finally offered. "Maybe we can talk him into appealing the judge's order to stop working on the church."

"I don't know what that man will or won't do," I replied, letting out a breath of frustration as I said it. "He just doesn't seem to want to do anything. He just thinks he should forget everything that ever happened to him," I continued, sounding confused and frustrated.

"He takes his mission of forgiveness seriously, I guess," Bill replied, sounding equally baffled.

"I just don't understand him. How can he not want any justice for what's happened to him?" I asked out loud, again sounding confused and frustrated.

"Well, I don't think we're going to achieve anything sitting here debating it," Bill said.

"Your right, we're not," I replied, agreeing with him. I continued, "If we're going to leave here and go through with all this, then we may as well try and get him to go along with us. But I think maybe we should wait a little longer. Give him a few days to collect himself and recover from what happened. After all, he did tell me to leave and not come back."

"Yes, but he didn't really mean that. He was just angry," Bill replied.

"Maybe," I answered him, not really sure if I believed that or if I wanted to believe it.

"So how should we proceed with all this?" Bill asked me.

"Why don't we take a few days to get ourselves together and plan out exactly what we're going to do and all that, and then when we have everything in place and we're ready to leave, we'll go and talk to him together and see if we can get him to come with us?" I suggested.

"Okay," Bill said, agreeing.

And that was it. We called it a day, and Bill left and went back to the motel. I spent the rest of the day thinking about Fr. Blair and what relationship we might have going forward. I tried to look at it with the peace I had felt in my heart before. That feeling I had had that God was there and that he would take care of things. I just reflected on all of that and on everything that had happened, asking God to help me make sense of it all and to guide me in what to do going forward. And I knew I had Fr. Blair to thank for helping me be able to take that step.

CHAPTER 18

Bill and I spent the next few days planning out the details of our trip. He suggested mapping out a driving course, but I already knew how to get where we were going. Getting there wasn't going to be my struggle; going there was. We made arrangements to stay for a few nights, since neither of us was sure how long we would be there. Once all of our preparations were in place, I knew that there was only one thing left to do. I knew that I had to talk to Fr. Blair. He was a part of all this.

Late in the afternoon on the day before we planned to leave, Bill and I headed down to the church looking for him. We tried the rectory first, but he wasn't there. I looked in the window, and I could see a lot of his clothes and possessions sitting out along with some suitcases. It looked like he was planning to leave. While I did that, Bill tried looking in the church and came back saying he had found him there. I walked up to the door and was able to make out the sight of him sitting in the front pew, not praying or anything but just sitting there.

Bill was just standing at the door. Apparently, he had stopped and was waiting for me to go in first. The scene reminded me a little of the gospel story about the first Easter: how the other disciple had waited for St. Peter to go into the tomb first. That seemed to fit with what had happened to me a few nights earlier. How I had made the decision I was accepting a mission from God to lead our small group in whatever was happening here. Kind of like how St. Peter had accepted the role of being the first pope and leading the early Christian church. He didn't really know what was happening, or what he was doing for that matter, but he accepted it and let God guide him.

I did have one big problem though: I couldn't go in. I remembered back to that day a few months earlier when I was helping the parishioners carry in the statue. I hadn't been able to go into the church that day, and I wasn't sure that I would be able to do it on this day either. From my position outside the door, I looked up at the altar and realized that there was no cross. Despite that, I just stared at the spot where there should have been one, and the memory ran through my head again of the day I had vowed never to reenter a church.

As I stared at the spot where the cross would hang, I felt something in my heart. It was the same feeling I had before, like my faith had come alive again. I felt a strength I could only describe as divine. At the same time, I remembered all the hurt and anger I had felt, and I thought about just walking away. But I couldn't resist the strength that I felt, the urge to go inside. So I took a breath and dived in headfirst. I just walked inside and stopped. So many times in my life, I had done this without thinking about it, but today it was a big event. It was an important event.

I walked forward toward where Fr. Blair was sitting and called out to him. He turned around and looked at me, and his face showed a whole plethora of emotions, from joy to surprise to anger and sadness. I thought that maybe he was happy that I had come into the church, but at the same time unhappy to see me. In part because he truly did believe the words he had spoken to me a few nights before: that I couldn't be saved.

We stared at each other, neither of us sure what to say. For a minute, he turned and looked at the spot above the altar where a cross would hang, and then turned back and looked at me again. I think he felt the same thing I did. I walked all the way up to where he was sitting, neither of us saying a word. I was very confused about what I was doing, but at the same time, a part of me was happy. It was like I was really making the choice to have God be a part of my life again. Even if I was still very hurt, and lost, and angry. I was on a journey, but it wasn't one I was taking alone.

"Mind if I sit?" I asked him.

He didn't say anything, just moved over a little in the pew so I could sit. I turned around, looking for Bill, and saw him standing at the back of the church, just watching all of this go on. It occurred to me that maybe he had the most interesting role in all of this. Just sort of watching it unfold, playing an important role, yes, but at the same time doing what he was doing now, watching it all happen. Whatever it was. At the same time, I thought about Fr. Blair sitting next to me. I thought, as I had a number of times now, about how much he had sacrificed to be here with me. Even if God had brought him to this spot just so he could help others, he had lost and sacrificed quit a lot.

One thing that had always struck me about priests, and those in the religious life or even people who spent their lives working as missionaries or in charity work, was what they gave up. And I often wondered what compelled them to do that. Was it something in their brain that made them different from the rest of us, or just a deep religious devotion? Or was it something greater? A greater sense of purpose, of duty to help, and serve, and above all love their fellow man? And was that something that maybe, just maybe, was present in all of us, even the worst kinds of people, if we just searched for it. I didn't know the answer that day, but I knew that, despite the upset I still felt toward him, there was an example of that devotion sitting next to me.

Despite all those thoughts going through my head, I didn't really know what to say to him. I guess he didn't either, and so we just sat there in the church staring up at an altar without a cross. Once again, I was reminded of the quote about praying always but only using words when necessary. And once again, a memory of my previous life wove its way into the moment. Sitting there praying with Fr. Blair made me think about the last time I had prayed with someone else. And that was the last time I every prayed with my family before I lost them. The night before what was their last day in this world, I prayed with my wife and children, and then we all went to sleep.

I started to cry some as I thought about that. But then I collected myself and tried to return to how it was that I was going to handle this moment.

"So are you planning on leaving?" I asked him. The question just popped out of my mouth. Guess it was as good a place to start the conversation as any.

"Maybe, there isn't really anything here for me anymore, is there?" he answered me.

"Maybe there is," I replied.

He just let out a sigh. "How can there be anything here for now if it's illegal for me to do this?"

"The only law that makes it 'illegal' is the law according to the sheriff," I answered him. I continued, "And last time I checked, that wasn't the law any of us lived by."

"So what do you propose I do?" he asked me.

"Bill and I are going to the city, and I want you to come with us," I answered him, presenting him with the whole reason for my visit.

"Why?" he asked me.

"Well, according to F. Lee Baily back there, we can mount a legal challenge to the sheriff's court order, but only if you get on board," I answered him.

He didn't say anything, just sat there staring off into space. I had hoped the "F Lee Bailey" remark would lighten the mood a little bit, but it didn't seem to have any effect.

"I don't really see a point to anything anymore," he answered me. He continued, "It seems like my whole life, everything I have ever tried to do has just blown up in my face, including this little project of mine here."

"I can't believe I'm going to be the one saying this to you," I answered him, "but maybe you just have to have faith in God that still has a few tricks up his sleeve."

He turned and looked at me and just started to laugh. For some reason, that moment seemed to strike him as funny.

"You know, they say God works in mysterious ways," he said to me as he laughed, "but if now you're encouraging me to have faith, maybe he really does want me to do this."

Once again, I was reminded of the early Christians. How they had an entire empire arrayed against them, but they still fought on, and in the end they won. If they could withstand that, then we could withstand this. That was an interesting thought—*we* could survive this. I really was starting to think of things in terms of someone other than me, that there were other people, including Fr. Blair, involved in this too, and that I was a part of something bigger. Something being put together by a God much bigger than all of us.

And that was the best argument I could come up with to convince Fr. Blair to join us in this fight, so I just threw it out there: "We're in this together, you know," I told him.

He turned and looked at me with a combined looked of confusion and surprise. "We?" he asked me.

"Yes, we," I replied to him. I continued, "You have helped me so much, you've been a friend to me and been there for me when no one else was. You didn't give up on me, even when all I did was push you away. I know we hit a major snag in our relationship, but we can push past it. Nothing is perfect, at least nothing human, and so that includes all human relationships, including our relationship with God. But I still feel a bond of friendship with you. I still feel as though God brought us together for a reason. And I think that reason was to help both of us find some peace and to find justice. But we have to do it together.

"You know sitting here with you and thinking about our little group and about what we're up against reminds me of the story of the early Christians. How despite having a whole empire, really the only world they knew, up against them, not to mention their own hometowns and communities, they banded together and fought back. And eventually, they conquered the world. And I think if we band together, we can each conquer, and we can conquer our shared enemy."

"What shared enemy?" he asked me.

"Our shared enemy of the losses we suffered and the demons we have had to live with as a result of those losses. We can conquer them together," I answered him.

"And you really think that taking the sheriff to court will help us somehow?" he asked me.

"I think that, like the early Christians, we can't surrender just because we're up against a powerful political force. I think that the greatest victory for the sheriff is if we just give up and let him go on ruling the way he does. It is what has kept him so powerful so far and what has allowed him to bully this entire town and to quite literally get away with murder," I answered him. I continued, "You helped me face my demons, now let me help you face yours."

He just sighed and didn't say a word. But his face said it all. I could see how sad he was and how much his suffering weighed on him. I couldn't really blame him for not wanting to face it. I put my arm around him, and we sat there in the pew like that. After a while, I stared up at the spot where the cross should be, looking for that same strength I had felt earlier. And this time, I prayed with what I thought were some necessary words: "Oh, Lord, give my friend here strength to face his demons, as you have given me the strength to face mine. Let me help him, as he has helped me."

And that was the first time I prayed anything in a long time. Part of me felt like I had betrayed what I had come to believe: that God was never there for me, so why should I ever follow him? If all he would do was let me suffer, then I had no time for him. But another part of me felt like I had welcomed an old friend back into my life. I was very conflicted, but at the same time, I experienced a measure of peace that I had not felt in a long time.

Fr. Blair for his part just continued to sit there. He was obviously very confused about what he should do. "I just don't think I can do what it is you're asking of me," he finally said.

Hearing him say that was very saddening to me, and I wanted to try and talk him out of it. But, instead, I just let it go. I figured he had to find his own path and maybe his was different from mine.

"So does that mean you're leaving town?" I asked him.

"I don't know," he replied.

I didn't know what to feel. Truth was I wanted him to stay. I felt like I was really benefiting from knowing him, and I wanted that to continue. And I was also feeling afraid. For all the time I had known him, Fr. Blair had always taken the lead in our relationship. He was there for me as a guide, a confidant, and a spiritual advisor. He was the strong one who was there for me when I needed it. And he was wise enough to see that I needed his help, even if I couldn't see it myself. But now it seemed as though I was going to have to take on that role myself. I was going to have to be there for him. That was hard enough, but knowing that I could be losing his support that I had come to rely on made me very afraid.

I decided to just leave and go back home and hope he changed his mind. I told him I was leaving and that if he changed his mind and wanted to come with us that we were leaving in the morning. At that, I got up to leave, but before I did, I had one more thing left to tell him: "I want you to know that despite how I may have acted in the past, I really am grateful for the help and guidance you have given me. And even if you decide to leave, I won't ever forget you or the help you have been to me. And you will always have a place in my life. But I hope that you don't leave, that you stay and come with us and fight this fight. A fight one wise apostle once called 'the good fight.'"

He didn't say anything, just looked at me. I walked toward the exit of the church, and Bill and I left. We went back to my house, neither of us saying a word. Bill left and went back to his hotel for the night. After he left, I went into the kitchen and started looking around for something to make for dinner, but I wasn't really hungry. I had way too much on my mind. The thought that tomorrow I was going to not only leave this place where I had come to hide from my past, but go back to the place where it all started. I tried to keep in mind that I had a reason for doing this. That it was important to do this because it was the only way to bring a bully and murderer to justice.

It was a nice night, so I decided to sit outside in my backyard and try and enjoy the beauty of the nightfall. I hoped that would bring me some peace. I looked up at the stars and felt the gentle breeze, and just being there in that moment, enjoying the natural beauty of the world helped to calm my feelings. As I sat out there, I heard my front door open and someone calling my name. I recognized Sarah's voice and yelled to her that I was out back. I got up and met her just as she was coming outside.

"Is everything all right?" I asked her, concerned that the sheriff may have found out what she told us or something like that.

"Yes, everything is fine," she reassured me. "I just wanted to come and see you before you go."

"Why?" I asked her.

"I don't know, I just did," she answered me.

Truth was it didn't really matter to me why she had come over; I was happy to see her. What Bill had said a few nights earlier was true—I did have feelings for her. And I suspected that it was mutual, even if neither of us was sure how to feel about it. We sat out there and talked for a while. We talked about what had happened already, about the sheriff, and about what we thought might happen going forward. We talked some about our respective spouses, but it wasn't a topic either of us was able to discuss much.

As the conversation went on, we both just kind of stared at each other. I looked at her sitting across from me, and she seemed to fit so well with the beauty of the night and the moment. Looking at her once again reminded me of the first time I met my wife. I was struck by what I was feeling. Up until then, I had thought I would never feel that way toward anyone again, but in that moment, I felt like maybe could I not only love God again, but I could love another person. She looked back at me, and I couldn't shake the feeling that she was thinking the same thing.

The kiss came as a surprise to both of us. It just happened. We were drawn together in the beauty of the moment we were experiencing together. Under a different set of circumstances, it probably would have been different, but in that situation, it was romantic and at the same time painful. Our kiss lasted only a few seconds, and then we pulled away from each other and just stared at each other. I knew what I was feeling: a mixture of sadness and at the same time happiness. Happiness in a sort of I-just-met-somebody, puppy-love kind of way. And also happiness in the sense that I felt the emotion of love start to come alive in me again.

At the same time, I felt sadness from the fact of what was happening. It was hard to imagine having a moment like this with anyone other than the wife I had loved so much. Or to imagine moving on and loving someone other than her. It occurred to me that Sarah was probably experiencing something similar. After a few seconds, she looked away from me and then got up to leave.

"I think I should go," she said.

"I'm sorry if I've upset you," I replied to her.

"I'm not upset. I'm just very confused," she answered me.

"I think I understand," I replied to her.

At that, we headed for the door, and she left. As she walked out, she said, "Good luck, I hope you find what you're looking for."

"Thanks," I answered her and then watched her get in her car and leave.

I closed the door behind her and then went upstairs and went to sleep, trying again to remember the Bible verses about not worrying but praying. As I fell asleep, I asked God to guide my heart and help me to understand what was happening. I also asked him to bless our trip tomorrow and to help us to find what we were looking for. Above all, I asked him to watch over Fr. Blair and help him with his struggles. All this I kept in my heart as I fell asleep that night, wondering what tomorrow and the next few days would bring.

CHAPTER 19

"I don't think he's coming," Bill said.

We had met at my house early in the morning and packed the car, ready to head out on the three-hour drive to Philadelphia. I had spent all that time looking for Fr. Blair, hoping that he had changed his mind and would show up. But he hadn't, and now it was time for us to leave.

"What if we just wait a few more minutes?" I replied to Bill.

"You've been saying that for almost a half hour now, it's time for us to get going," he answered me, beginning to sound very impatient.

"I guess you're right," I replied to him, feeling disappointed. "He isn't coming."

"He isn't necessary for what we're trying to achieve," Bill said, trying to sound comforting and at the same time talk me into leaving already.

"Yeah, I guess so," I replied with a sigh, not really convinced.

"What are we going to do when we find her?" I asked Bill, beginning to have doubts. I continued, "How do we convince her of who we are, or to help us? What do we have to offer her to prove that we really are trying to achieve something good and that she should help us?"

"I think maybe I can help with that," came a voice suddenly from behind me.

I turned around and was pleasantly surprised to see Fr. Blair standing there, holding a packed bag. He had this strange look of sad determination on his face. As though he knew he had to do this, but he did not want to face it. That was apparently a struggle we were both having. I wasn't really sure how Bill felt about Fr. Blair showing up at the last minute. He just kind of stood there, I think more frustrated that we weren't leaving than anything else.

I walked over to Fr. Blair and just smiled. "I'm glad you decided to come with us," I said to him.

"I'm glad one of us knows how to feel about it," he replied to me half-sarcastically, half-confusedly.

"What made you change your mind?" I asked him.

"Last night, after you left, I continued to sit in the church for a while. Eventually, I fell asleep and had a dream."

"What did you dream?" I asked him.

"I dreamt about my family. I saw my mother, and my grandparents, and my fiancé. They were all standing around watching a man in his midtwenties play with a little boy no older than about two or three. I didn't know who either the man or the little boy were. As they played, the man began to fade backward, as if he were fading away. The boy started to run after the man but couldn't catch up to him before he faded away completely. He looked all around but can't find him anywhere. Suddenly, he turned completely around to look behind him, and when he did, he was a fully-grown man.

"He looked at my family and asked them how he can go on alone. They encouraged him to carry on and not give up, but he was still not entirely convinced. Suddenly, he heard the voice of the man who disappeared, and that man told him to be strong, that he was proud of him, and encouraged him to stand and fight against evil. The last thing the man said was 'I love you, son, run this good race, fight this good fight.' Suddenly, a vision of the altar in our church appeared, with a cross hanging on top of it. The same man was standing there looking at it, beaming with pride. He turned and looked at the spot in the pew where I was sitting and smiled. Then I woke up!"

He looked at me, clearly waiting for my response, but I didn't have one. Of all the powerful moments I had over the past few months, and that Fr. Blair and I had together, this was probably the most powerful. I remembered all the stories I had heard over my life of Bible characters being encouraged or pushed along by inspiring dreams. The biggest example that popped into my mind was the story of St. Joseph marrying Mary after a dream told him to do so. Once again, here was an example, right in front of me, of what I thought were ancient practices and experiences removed from our modern-day lives.

"What do you think all of that means?" I asked him.

"I think it means that I'm supposed to go with you, that God has made me a part of this mission even if I don't fully understand it," he answered me.

"What about the man in the dream? Who was he?" I asked, confused by that part of it, and why a mysterious figure like that seemed to have so much influence over Fr. Blair.

"I think he was my father," Fr. Blair answered me.

"Your father," I replied questioningly.

"Yes," he replied to me. He continued, "A few nights ago when we had that big fight, the object I swung at you was a project I've been working on. It was the second time I destroyed it, the first being after the first argument we had."

"Yes, I know," I answered him. "I saw you working on it, and I saw you destroy it from my house the first time. What does it have to do with anything?"

"The project I was working on was a cross for the church. You see, before he was in the military, my father was a carpenter. He had a regular job, and on the side, he did his own woodworking. The last job he was commissioned to do was to build a cross for a new parish church that was being built not far from where we lived. Unfortunately, he was drafted and ultimately killed before he could ever complete the project. I've been working on building a cross for our church as a tribute to his memory," he answered me.

"And you think that your dream was him encouraging you to come with us and to stand up to the sheriff?" I asked him.

"Yes, I do. How can I build a cross for a church if there is no church?" he answered me. He continued, "Even if I'm not sure about doing this, I believe that I am supposed to."

I didn't say anything to him, just smiled at him, happy that he was coming with us. I walked up to him and offered him a handshake. "Speaking of our fight the other night, I think I owe you an apology. I'm sorry for the way I behaved and for allowing it to become physical. All of this can't be any easier on you than it is on me, but sometimes, in my arrogance, I forget that."

He accepted my handshake and answered me, "I accept your apology, and I forgive you for what happened. And I hope you can forgive me for keeping the secrets I have kept. You're right when you say this hasn't been easy on me. But I need to take some of my own advice and confront my demons, like you have tried to do."

"We can face them together," I replied to him.

We smiled at each other, and I felt as though we had undone at least some of the damage done to our relationship from our fight that night.

"Can you face them in the car on the way to the city?" Bill asked sarcastically. "Because we really need to get a move on if we want to get there sometime this century," he continued.

Fr. Blair and I both laughed, and then the three of us got into Bill's car and headed for the city. As we pulled away, I felt a knot in my stomach and a wave of anxiety come over me. I was headed back to the place in my life that I thought I had left behind. But I knew that it was important. I knew that I had to do this. I looked out at the road ahead and both literally and metaphorically wondered what it had in store for me, and for all of us.

CHAPTER 20

Traffic! That's what the road ahead held for Bill, Fr. Blair, and myself as we drove toward Philadelphia. What should have been a three-hour drive turned into almost six by the time we got there. In a way, it reminded me of the journey of my life. It hadn't gone as I planned it to. Of course, the same couldn't be said for Bill, who was visibly frustrated. Not that that stopped Fr. Blair and I from teasing him about it.

"You know, maybe God's giving you an opportunity to learn some patience, Bill," Fr. Blair said to him, smiling.

"Yeah, or maybe he's just giving us an opportunity to entertain ourselves at your expense," I replied.

"Or maybe he's just giving me a chance to rethink why I ever started hanging around with you two in the first place," he answered us sarcastically, with an eye roll.

"You can ditch us if you want. Just make sure to leave the car," I shot back at him with a smile.

"Okay, you can have the car, but the keys are coming with me," he answered me with a laugh, finally starting to cheer up.

"Guess you're out of luck, Tom," Fr. Blair said with a laugh.

"Hey, whose side are you on?" I replied to him.

"Whoever's driving, so I don't have to walk," he answered me.

We all laughed at that, and the laughter helped to alleviate some of the anxiety and stress I was feeling.

The rest of the trip was like that, lighthearted on the surface but underneath filled with anxiety and a sense of uncertainty. I think Bill and Fr. Blair felt it as much as I did.

"Hey, look, you can see the city skyline," I heard Fr. Blair say.

I looked up, and as it came into view, I felt a rush of emotions. On some level, it actually felt a little bit like I had come back home to visit after a long time away. But that was overshadowed by the pain I felt. All of those memories I had tried to resist before came back again. I just stared out at the city line as the memories rolled through my mind. I was totally tuned out until Fr. Blair tapped me on the shoulder and brought me back to reality. "You okay?" he asked me, putting his hand more firmly on my shoulder, attempting to comfort me.

"Yeah, I'm fine," I answered him.

I tried to turn my thoughts back to what the three of us had come here to do and how we were going to do it. I figured, with Fr. Blair on our side, we could probably get Dr. Sharpton to tell us what she knew, but that was assuming she remembered. After all, it had been many years since the death of Fr. Blair's mother and everything surrounding that. And even if she did remember, I wasn't sure it would be enough to convict the sheriff. For a minute, I thought about just forgetting the whole thing, turning around and just going back to town, collecting my things and just moving on to some other town where I would just go back to hiding from my past.

But I didn't. Instead, I turned my thoughts to the feelings of faith I had in the previous days and how I had resolved myself that God had given me this mission, even if I didn't want it, and that I had accepted it. And I thought about Sarah. After what had happened between us the night before, I didn't want to just leave her behind. I felt something for her, and even though it scared me, I couldn't shake the urge to pursue my feelings. I mauled all of that over in my mind as we drove into the city and to the motel where we were staying.

It was late in the afternoon by the time we got there, and we decided to check in and then find a place to have dinner. We ate dinner at a small diner, not far from our motel. It occurred to me that I might run into someone, anyone, from my past, and I hadn't been able to figure out how to handle it, but I didn't. During dinner, we talked about what we would do in the coming days. We agreed that Bill and Fr. Blair would spend the next day or two working on the appeal of the sheriff's court order forbidding Fr. Blair from building the church. After that, we would go on looking for Dr. Sharpton.

After dinner, we headed back to the motel and settled in for the night. Fr. Blair and I were in a double room, and Bill was in the room next door. I felt like I needed a shower after the trip and the long day and all, so I went into the bathroom to take one. I was in the shower about fifteen minutes, and when I turned off the water, I heard the sound of someone talking. I got dressed and walked out into the room expecting to see Bill or someone else talking with Fr. Blair but, instead, saw him kneeling on the side of his bed, praying before going to sleep.

I stood there quietly, not wanting to interrupt him. He looked up and, noticing me standing there, invited me to join him. I just kind of stared at him for a second, not really sure what to do. Once again, I thought about praying with my family the night before the day they died. That was the last night I had ever prayed before going to sleep until this night.

I accepted Fr. Blair's invitation, and together he and I said a short prayer. I prayed for the success of the goals that had brought us here. I prayed for Fr. Blair and for Bill, and for me. After a few minutes, I got up and went to bed without saying anything. I had just done something I hadn't done in a long time, and once again, I was a little closer to the faithful person I was before. But once again, it was very hard, and so I didn't really say anything about it. I just went to sleep, continuing to keep all these things in my heart and try and feel peaceful and not worry about tomorrow.

But peace didn't come to me that night. Instead, a very sad and confusing dream did. In the dream, I saw my family. All of us, including me, were sitting together on the edge of a cliff, watching the sunset. Then suddenly, the scene changed, and instead, I was in my old house that I shared with my family, standing just inside the front door. I was alone, but I could hear my wife and my children calling out for me. I started to head into the house looking for them, but only made it down the entrance hallway before I woke up.

I sat up in bed feeling very confused. I looked at the clock and saw that it was about 4:00 a.m. I sat there for a minute, trying to mull over my dream and what it might mean. I tried to lie back down, but I couldn't sleep; there were just too many thoughts going through my head. I got up and decided to sit outside for a few minutes. I looked over at Fr. Blair asleep on the other side of the room. For a second, I thought about waking him up and talking to him but decided not to. I walked outside and stood on the balcony outside our room. I wasn't sure what the dream meant, although I had a suspicion.

I sat outside for a while and just stared up at the night sky. I looked at the stars and imagined the vastness of the universe. It reminded me of the Bible story of Abraham and how God promised to make his descendants greater than the stars in the sky. I thought about how beautiful the world really was, and how so many people never even took the time to look up at the stars in the night sky. I had hoped this setting would give me some peace, but it didn't bring me much. Instead, it began to occur to me that I was one of those people who had never bothered to look up at the stars.

Instead, I had become one of those people who lived to be angry, and anger was the only thing that kept them living. I hadn't looked around at the world and seen just how much other people, like Fr. Blair or Sarah, suffered. Their suffering didn't diminish mine, but it showed me that what Fr. Blair had said to me in our first argument was true: I wasn't the only one who ever prayed. And God hadn't forgotten about me. He helped me to come through all of this, to get to the point where I was at. To get to the point where I was able to let Fr. Blair into my life. And He had, perhaps somewhat indirectly, led me down the path to trying to stop the sheriff from what he was doing and from getting away with his crimes.

But now, I had this whole new mystery on my hands in the form of the dream I just had. I had so many questions: What did it mean? Why did I have it? Was the timing really a coincidence? As I was mulling all of this over, I heard the door to our room open behind me, and Fr. Blair stepped out. "Trouble sleeping?" he asked me.

"Something like that," I answered him.

"What's troubling you?" he asked.

"Well, did you know there's no room service at this motel? Seriously, I'm hungry and no room service," I answered him with a smile.

He smiled back at me with a sort of "that's funny, but now is the time to be serious" look. "Well, I'll see what I can do about that," he answered me. "But in the meantime, anything else you would like to talk about?"

"Yes, there is," I answered him. I told him about my dream, and I asked him if he had any idea what it meant.

"Did you know what my dream meant when I first told you about it yesterday?" he asked me.

"No," I answered him. It seemed like a strange question for him to ask me.

"Right, it was my dream, and I had to be the one to interpret it and understand it. So I think that you have to do the same thing."

"So I'm on my own in this?" I asked him.

"No, I will certainly help you, and I'll bet I'm not the only one," he answered, looking up at the sky with a smile.

I didn't really have a response for that, so I just looked back at him and hoped that he was right. "Will you say some of those prayers you say for me?" I asked him

"I've been doing that every night since I first met you," he answered me.

His answer both surprised me and at the same time didn't surprise me. But what did surprise me was how it made me feel. I felt grateful. Grateful that he had cared enough about me to pray for me and grateful just for the fact that someone was asking God to help me. Not long ago, I would never have felt that way, and never would have wanted to.

"Thank you," I said to him.

Two little words, but for so long, I never said them to anyone because I didn't think that anyone deserved to hear them. And now I had once again thanked a priest and, of all things, for praying for me. It really did make me feel loved and cared about to know that he was praying for me. That was the first time in my life that I had ever felt truly loved since I lost my family. And it occurred to me that maybe part of what hurt me so much was that lost love. I had already realized that I was lonely, and that the loss of my faith had hurt me, so in a way, feeling as though I missed the love I had lost seemed to fit well with this journey I was on.

At the same time, thinking about my family again reminded me of how sad I was and what had brought me to this point in the first place. And yet, I was already beginning to feel new bonds forming in my heart. A bond of friendship with Fr. Blair and with Bill too. And, on a deeper level, a bond of intimacy with Fr. Blair in that he and I had formed a special sort of relationship. He had become my confidant, someone who was helping me deal with the great pains that I felt. But it was more than that. There was a connection in the way we had shared our stories and experiences with each other, and in a way, that sharing is what brought us close together. And I was beginning to feel romance again with my feelings for Sarah. Yes, I was feeling all kinds of new bonds of love in my heart.

Thinking about that helped to bring me some of the peace I was seeking. But thoughts of my dream and what it meant still lingered. I started to hear the sounds of birds chirping and saw that the darkness of the night had given way to some light. I realized that the sun would be rising soon and decided to try and get a little more sleep. I went back into our room, and Fr. Blair followed behind me. As I lay down, I thought about the scene I had just witnessed outside. Like the heavy traffic the day before, that scene reminded me of life. Only this time, I was thinking that maybe the darkness in my life was starting to turn into light, and the birds were starting to chirp again. But much hurt still lingered, as did the great uncertainty I felt about my dream.

CHAPTER 21

The big city! It was there like a prize surrounded by thorns, waiting for me to come and conquer it. All I had to do was fight through the thorns. They, of course, were my inability to face my past. I had managed to sleep peaceably until about eight that morning and then gotten up and tried to figure out what to do next. Fr. Blair, Bill, and I ate breakfast at the same place we had eaten dinner the night before. Bill wanted to go into the city to a law library to look up some past cases he thought might help ours.

"How long do you think it will take?" I asked him.

"It will probably take me a couple of days to prepare the appeal, and then we send it off to the state superior court. After that, it's up to them what happens."

"How can we help you?" I asked him.

"Well, I can always use some help doing research," he answered me. He continued, "Why don't you come to library with me and see what you can help me find out?"

I didn't say anything, just sat there. I knew I wanted to go, but I didn't know if I could. The motel and diner were one thing, but venturing out into the world I had left behind was still something I couldn't quite fathom. I had shut it out. I had just accepted that was life now. There were just some things I couldn't do, and that was the way it would always be. That was the way I had viewed things. But now I could see the flaw in that view, and I wanted to change it. I wanted to move to a point where I wasn't held back by my past any longer. Because as long as it held me back, it wasn't really the past.

"All right, let's do it," I answered him after thinking about all that for a minute.

"Okay then," he replied.

We finished our breakfast and headed out the door toward the car. We drove off farther into the city toward where Bill wanted to go. As we drove along, I just sat there with a knot in my stomach and a feeling of pain in my heart. Here I was back in my hometown, the place where all of this started. In that moment, the strongest feeling I was having was like it was happening all over again. Being back in town made me feel like I was reliving the hurt, the pain, the trauma of what happened to me and how my life was never the same again.

But, at the same time, there was something else. A feeling that maybe this was part of making a new start for me. Part of making a new me. A new me who wasn't angry, or hateful, or sad. A new me that wasn't just going through the motions of day-to-day life, not caring about anything, really just waiting to die. A new me who had friends again, who had love in his heart again, and above all, had God again.

I stared out the window thinking about all of this, oblivious to the world around me. I stared up at the clouds in the sky. Like the night before I thought about the beauty of the world and of its creator. As I looked at the clouds, I tried to see shapes in them, but they looked plain to me. I tried to picture them as different shapes or as different things. As I did, a metaphor popped into my head. That this new me I was working on was like the clouds. I could mold the new me into anything I wanted if I just worked at it. And if the same God who created those clouds would help create the new me.

The three of us got to the library and spent the rest of the day researching case law that could help with the appeal. By the end of the day, Bill felt like he had some solid precedents to cite and believed that he would finish the appeal in the next day or two. We left the library and headed back to the motel. On the way back, we stopped for dinner. I was still anxious that I would run into someone I used to know, but we didn't see anyone. We just ate a quiet dinner and then went back to our motel and settled in for the night.

Before going to sleep, Fr. Blair and I said a short prayer together again. This time, I prayed for me, and for God's help in forming a new me. I also prayed for a peaceful night and for God's help in interpreting my dreams. I went to sleep once again trying to feel peaceful. But peace did not come to me that night either. I had the same dream I had the previous night, only this time I got further into my house, and I could hear the sounds of my family calling for me even louder than before. But, once again, before I could get to them, I woke up.

I lay there in bed, not even sitting up, so confused. Apparently, there was something going on inside of me that I wasn't aware of and didn't understand. But I was so tired from having been up part of the previous night that I rolled over and fell back asleep. I managed to sleep better for the rest of the night, but really I felt like that was only because I was so tired.

I woke up in the morning hoping to talk to Fr. Blair about my dreams and everything that was happening. He wasn't there, so I went to take a shower and waited for him to come back. I turned on the water and stood there under it, hoping it would cleanse me of whatever was causing my confusing dream. I tried to understand what it could mean and why I was having it. I went over in my head again the biblical figures who had been moved or encouraged, or even troubled, by dreams. I remembered the story of Daniel in the Old Testament, and how he interpreted the king's dreams for him. *Maybe Fr. Blair could channel him for me,* I thought, chuckling a little.

I finished showering and got dressed. I thought about heading out for some breakfast, but I didn't really have much of an appetite. So I decided to take a little walk while I waited for Fr. Blair to come back. I walked outside and looked around wondering where to go. There were some woods right behind where our hotel was, so I decided to walk through them for a while and see where I wound up. I walked through the woods for an hour or two, careful not to get lost. As I walked, I looked at the trees that were changing colors in the midfall.

Again, I remembered how much my wife loved the fall. Her favorite thing about it was always the changing of colors on the trees.

She had always thought it was one of the most beautiful things ever. I looked at the leaves, and once again, an analogy between nature and myself popped into my mind. Maybe I could be like the changing leaves. Maybe I could change my colors and become something new. Wow, I thought, the universe seemed to be sending me a lot of signals that change was possible in my life. And maybe, really for the first time, I believed that I could become someone new. That I could remold and reshape myself into a new person. The person I had already imagined. The person who had love and faith in his heart again, and, above all, had God.

As I stood there, I saw a butterfly fly by. It seemed strange to me that a butterfly would be around this late in the year, but there it was just floating there around the trees. It was a bright colorful butterfly, with big wings made up of too many colors for me to count. And I couldn't help but think that it was a sign from heaven, from my wife, a sign that it was finally time to start putting my life back together again. Seeing that butterfly and not just believing, but knowing, in my heart that it was my wife, that she had come to visit me, made me truly want to commit to forming a new me.

Suddenly, the butterfly turned and flew away, high up into the trees, higher than I had ever seen any butterfly fly before. It was as though it had come from heaven and now it was headed back. As I watched it fly away, I hoped maybe it could come back and help me figure out the meaning of my dream. Despite wanting to create a new me that was something that was still holding me back. I had the feeling that if I could get past this obstacle, if I could understand this dream and push past the causes of it, I would finally, truly, be on a path to changing. I walked back toward our hotel hoping Fr. Blair was there, and hoping that he could help me with all of this.

When I walked into our room, Fr. Blair was sitting in a chair, reading the Bible.

"What are you reading?" I asked him.

"Just something from the book of Daniel," he answered me. Guess, he and I were thinking the same thing, I thought. "With all this talk of dreams lately, I was looking for some help, and maybe some inspiration in dealing with all of it."

"You must have read my mind because that's exactly what I wanted to talk to you about," I replied to him.

"Okay, talk," he answered me, closing his Bible and turning his attention to me.

"Well, I guess I want to understand what my dream means, or why I'm having it," I answered him, sitting down on my bed.

"What do you think it means?" he asked me, reminding me what he had said before about me being the one to interpret the dream.

"I don't know what it means. I don't even know why I'm having it," I answered him.

"Well, you said that you dream about being in your house and hearing your family calling for you, right?" he asked me.

"Yes, why?" I replied to him.

"Well, maybe they're the key to understanding what your dream means," he answered me.

When he said that, we looked at each other. I was sure Fr. Blair had learned by now that my family was not a subject I wanted to discuss. But I figured it was a new day, and I was working on a new me, so why not try changing that rule?

"Okay, let's talk about them then," I replied to him.

A look of surprise came over his face. I guessed he was expecting me to resist him or get angry at him again.

"Tell me about them," he said

"Well, there was Greg, and Peter, and Bobby, and Marsha, and Jan, and Cindy, and of course our maid Alice, she was the best," I answered him with a smirk.

A resisted smile forced its way across his face, and the humor helped me to relax. "Anyone else?" he asked me, parlaying my joke into a serious question about my family.

"Yes there was," I answered him, feeling sad and hesitant, but knowing I had to talk about it. "There was my wife, Carly, and my three children, Jill, Emma, and Tommy. They were my whole world." I started to cry a little when I said that, but I collected myself and continued to talk. "We were married for fifteen years. Our kids were twelve, nine, and the youngest was only four. He was kind of a surprise," I said, chuckling a little as I remembered our surprise when my wife first found out she was pregnant with him. We had thought we were done having kids at two, but apparently, God had other plans.

"What were they like?" Fr. Blair asked me.

"Where do I begin?" I said.

"Maybe you could start with your wife. How did you two meet?" he asked me.

"At a party in college," I answered him. "I was playing Ping-pong with some of my friends, and I was beating everybody. She came over and challenged me to a game. I responded by asking her out. So we made a bet on the game: if I won, she would go out with me."

"And what happened?" Fr. Blair asked me with a smile.

"She won," I answered him. "I couldn't believe it. No one had ever beaten me. Of course, my friends thought it was hilarious and began teasing me mercilessly. But I barely noticed because I was following Carly out the door. I caught up with her outside and proposed that date again. She turned and smiled at me and then turned and walked away again, like she was playing hard-to-get or testing me or something. I followed behind her and started talking about, of all things, Ping-pong. It was the only thing I knew we had in common. I guess it worked because she started talking back to me, and the next thing I knew, we had spent the entire evening walking around campus that way. I told her about wanting to be a cop, and she told me about wanting to be a teacher. After that, we started dating and then got married after we graduated from college."

I looked at Fr. Blair, and he was smiling, and seeing him smile at that story made me want to smile about it too. That was probably the first time I thought about that story since the death of my family and smiled at the thought of it. And in that moment, I felt my heart heal a little, and just a little bit of the hurt and anger I felt started to leave me. I guess my face showed that because Fr. Blair looked at me puzzled.

"What?" I asked him.

"Well, I was just thinking that this is about the happiest I have ever seen you," he answered me.

"It's about the happiest I've seen me in a long time," I answered him.

"So what happened next?" he asked me.

"We got engaged right before we graduated college, and we got married that fall. I was accepted to the police academy, and she started working for the school district. We rented a house close to both our jobs. Three years later, our first daughter, Jill, came. Three more years passed and Emma came along. After that, we bought our first house, and then I was promoted to detective. We settled in to a simple life. And then five years later, our 'surprise child' as we called him came along, our son, Tommy."

Fr. Blair smiled at me, and I started to smile back at him. Fr. Blair noticed it and started to ask me about it, but we were interrupted by Bill knocking on the door. Fr. Blair got up and opened it, and Bill walked in at first looking excited but then a little confused. "Am I interrupting?" he asked.

Fr. Blair and I both just kind of looked at him. I think both of us wanted to say yes but were resisting it because we thought that would be rude or something.

"What is it?" I asked him.

"I'm finished with the appeal. All that's left to do is mail it in and wait for a response. But first, I had an idea. I think maybe we should include a letter from you," he said, addressing Fr. Blair. "It could help. If you can show them you're not just there to make noise and cause trouble but that you actually have a legitimate purpose for the work you're doing, it could help convince them to rule in our favor."

Father thought for a minute and then agreed to do it.

"Okay then, what do we do now?" Bill asked.

"I guess we go and see Dr. Sharpton," I answered him. I continued, "That was the plan, wasn't it?"

The three of us looked around at each other, like we didn't know what to do next. It was like we had set out a course of action, but now that we had come to point of actually carrying it out, we were suddenly having second thoughts. But we had set out to do this, and I, for one, was not going to give up on it. Not after all I had been through to get to this point. So, acting in the role of leader of this group that I had taken on, I spoke up in an attempt to move us forward. "Well then, let's go find her and see what she knows," I said.

"And assuming she knows anything, what do we do with that information?" Bill asked me.

"We use it to try and expose the sheriff for what he is doing," I answered him.

"But how do we expose him?" Bill replied to me.

"I think our best shot is to do what we talked about before: to try and get the state police or the feds to investigate him. I mean, if we can really prove that he is responsible for the death of a cop, that has to be something of interest to them," I replied to him.

"If that's the case, then it would definitely help if we could bring them some evidence or a witness," he answered me.

"Who does the sheriff work for?" I asked, wondering if either of them knew.

"What do you mean?" Bill replied to me.

"I mean who does he work for. He must answer to somebody," I answered him.

"He's independently elected. The only people he's answerable to are the ones who elect him," he answered me.

I remembered Bill telling me the first time we met, at the courthouse back in Rocky Hills, that Sheriff Blank had assumed the office after this brother was killed and had run unopposed since.

"What about the town council?" I asked Bill. "They must have some authority over his office. I mean, there has to be some kind of check on his power if a case of corruption or misconduct ever happens, doesn't there?"

"There is a provision in the town constitution that the council can, by a two-thirds majority, issue a vote of no confidence in the sheriff. After that, a special election is held, and anyone who wants to can enter their name and run against the sheriff. But only if they are nominated by a member of the council or a citizen in the town," he answered me.

"So what if we try and get the town council to vote no confidence in him?" I replied to him.

Fr. Blair and Bill just sort of looked at each other and didn't say anything. "That's not going to happen," Fr. Blair finally answered me.

"Why not?" I asked him, even though I thought I knew the answer already.

"I think you know why," Fr. Blair answered me. "For the same reasons that we have talked about before. The sheriff is corrupt, and he has everybody under his control. He has dirt on a lot of people, and the ones he doesn't have it on he makes things up and threatens them with that. Either way, he's got everybody afraid to take him on. And we all know what happened to the only person who was ever brave enough to stand up to him."

That statement by Fr. Blair caused us all to fall silent. We all just sat there for a minute, as if we felt as though the stakes of what we were doing had just been raised and by a lot. Suddenly, it had been put before us that our very lives could be in danger here. Finally, I decided that if I was going to be the leader of this group, it was my job to come up with a course of action. Again, I tried to draw some inspiration from St. Peter and the first apostles. If he could lead a group of poor fishermen against an entire empire, I could certainly lead a lawyer, a priest, and ex-cop against one small town sheriff.

"Well then, we simply can't let that happen," I finally said. "Besides, the sheriff has only been able to get away with his crime because he keeps it hidden. But there is no way he could hide killing all three of us," I said that to try and bring some comfort to the two of them and to me.

"Maybe not, but he could make life very difficult for us," Bill answered me.

I was surprised that he suddenly seemed hesitant since he had been so trigger-happy to take on the sheriff when I first met him.

"Why are you suddenly so hesitant about this?" I asked him. "Weren't you the one who wanted to help me do this in the first place?"

"Yes, but wanting to do something and actually doing it are two different things," he answered me, as a look of hurt suddenly came over his face.

"Look, we're already here, and you have already completely prepared this appeal, and we have already set out a course of action for doing this. I say we stick to it and complete it. If we band together and fight back sooner or later, we will be able to overcome the sheriff, no matter who he has control over. That night that he caused Fr. Blair and I to fight the way we did, that wasn't an accident. He wanted that. He wanted it so he could divide us and, by extension, neutralize any threat we could be to him. We have to stick together and fight back against him."

I said that, hoping to inspire them past these doubts they were apparently having. Also, I was surprised that this was happening. But I knew that I couldn't let things fall apart. We had started something, and we needed to stick with it and see it through.

"Look, why don't we just file this appeal and see what happens?" I proposed.

"Okay, but I'm not sure trying to simply get the town to kick the sheriff out of power will work," Bill replied.

"Okay then, we will just try something else," I answered him.

After that, things settled down a little. Fr. Blair spent the rest of the day working on the letter to the appeals court, and Bill and I spent some time exploring some of the town around where the law library was. I was still very nervous and resistant to doing it, but I had come to a point where I knew it was important to do things that would help me move forward. And exposing myself to my past, and eventually being able to face and accept it, were important. So we explored the neighborhood and talked. As we spent the rest of the day exploring, I felt our bond of friendship deepen a little. After that, we returned to our motel and settled in for the night. There was a lot to come in the days ahead.

CHAPTER 22

Emily Sharpton, MD! The three of us stood there staring at the sign outside her office. I guess waiting to see which one of us would go in first. Earlier that morning, we had mailed the appeal of the judge's court order, along with Fr. Blair's letter, and then had made our way down to Dr. Sharpton's office. And now we were just standing there staring at the entrance to her office. We hadn't quite yet figured out what we were going to say. We had debated it for a while, and not being able to come up with anything good, we had just decided to wing it.

As we stood looking at the entrance to Dr. Sharpton's office, I once again was reminded of the story of St. Peter and the other disciples at the tomb on Easter morning.

"Well, we aren't going to get anything done just standing here," I said, pushing the door open and walking inside. I walked into her waiting room and looked around. There were a few patients sitting around reading magazines or looking at their cell phones, and a receptionist sitting behind a desk, looking bored. I approached the desk and asked if Dr. Sharpton was in.

"Do you have an appointment?" she asked me.

"No, but I would like to see her if she's available," I answered her.

"Is this a medical visit?"

"Well, no, but it is important."

"As you can see, Dr. Sharpton has patients to see, maybe if you come back later."

"Can you tell her Fr. George Blair is here?" Fr. Blair asked, speaking up from behind me.

"Look, I'm sorry, but unless this is a medical emergency, Dr. Sharpton is with a patient."

"Can you please just tell her that I'm here?" Fr. Blair answered her. "Please," he pleaded.

"All right, wait here," the receptionist answered him and then got up and walked away toward where the examination rooms were.

She came back a minute later and said that Dr. Sharpton had asked for us to wait for her in her office. She led us back there, and the three of us sat down and waited. I looked around her office, desk with pictures sitting on the edge of it, bookshelf with different medical publications and textbooks, diplomas hanging framed on the wall. Suddenly, another memory from my past popped into my head. I started remembering all the different times I had taken my children to a doctor's office just like this one.

I started to get lost in those memories when I was suddenly interrupted by Dr. Sharpton walking in. Despite the fact that she was an older woman, probably close to eighty, her wrinkles and gray hairs still seemed to say that she was a woman who had seen too many negative things in her life. As she walked in, she looked at Fr. Blair clearly surprised to see him. She walked over and gave him a hug.

"It's been too long, George," she said, addressing Fr. Blair.

"Yes, it has," he replied to her with a smile. Despite the circumstances, it was clear Father was happy to see her. Even if it did bring back painful memories for him.

"How's your husband?" Fr. Blair asked her.

"He passed away seven years ago," she said with a sigh.

"I'm sorry, I didn't know," Fr. Blair answered her.

"It's okay," she replied. "It happened pretty quick. I tried to get in touch with you, but I heard you were out of the country."

Bill and I both looked at Fr. Blair surprised to hear that he had ever been out of the country. But I figured I would just ask him about it later.

"What happened to him?" Fr. Blair asked Dr. Sharpton about her husband.

"He started to experience fatigue, and he often wasn't feeling well. He thought it was just a bug, but I could tell something was wrong. He went for some tests, and it turned out he had cancer, and it was serious. They tried to treat him, but the cancer spread quickly. He was gone within a few months. I was all set to sell the practice and retire, but after that, I decided to keep working. I wasn't going to become some old shut-in widow."

You could hear some determination in her voice as she said that, and it occurred to me that she had handled the death of her husband quite well.

"So what brings you here, George, and who are your friends?" she asked Fr. Blair.

Fr. Blair introduced Bill and me and then started to tell her why we had come, "The reason we're here is, well…" his voice trailed off. For whatever reason, he was hesitant to say what he wanted to say.

"Dr. Sharpton," I said, speaking up, "do you remember the last night that you were in Rocky Hills after Fr. Blair's mother's funeral?"

"Of course, I do, how could I forget it?" she answered me.

"Do you remember someone coming to see you unexpectedly that night?" I asked her.

"Yes, I do," she answered me hesitantly. "Why?"

"Can you tell us what happened that night?" I asked her.

"What do you mean?" she asked me.

"I mean, can you tell us who came to see you that night and what they wanted?"

"Why do you want to know?" she asked me.

"Because I think it's important to what we're trying to do here," I answered her.

"No offense, but I don't know you or what you want," she replied to me.

"Look, I'm not here to scam you or to trick you somehow, and I promise if you can just tell me what happened that night, I can explain everything to you," I replied, trying to reassure her.

"It's not that I think you're up to no good, it's just that you want me to tell you about a private encounter between a patient and myself. And I just met you a few minutes ago. That gives me serious pause."

"Emily, please, this is important," Fr. Blair pleaded with her.

I was glad he spoke up because I was running out of things to say to convince her, and I didn't want to wind up in an argument with her.

She just looked at Fr. Blair for a minute after he spoke and then sighed.

"All right. That night, it was late, after midnight. I was asleep when someone woke me up, knocking on my door. I opened it, and he was standing there, doubled over and bleeding. He said he needed my help. Of course, I couldn't turn him away. I wanted to go to the hospital, but he said no, he didn't think he could wait. I had my medical bag, so I treated him as best I could. I patched up his wound. It looked like a bullet had gone through him. I stopped his bleeding and, like I said, patched up the wound. But the biggest challenge was removing the other bullet that was lodged inside his hip—"

"Wait, there was a second bullet still inside him," I said shocked, cutting her off.

"Yes, it was lodged just inside of his hip," she answered me. She continued her story: "Anyway, like I said, that was the biggest challenge. I didn't think I would be able to get it out without getting him to a surgeon, but he insisted that I try, so I did. Eventually, I was able to get it out. After that, I gave him some antibiotics I had and then told him to go home and get some rest and follow up with another doctor the next day."

I was shocked. I had known from what Bill told me that day at the courthouse that there was a through-and-through wound, as it's known. But I had no idea that there was a second bullet that Dr. Sharpton had removed. Much more important she could testify to that wound.

"Did you know who that person was who came to see you? I asked her.

"Yes, it was the deputy sheriff," she answered me, confirming what I already knew. "After that, he left and told me he would be in touch if he needed me, but I never heard about it again. Not until you came into my office today," she said, finishing her story.

"What happened to the bullet you removed from the deputy sheriff?" I asked her.

"I put it in a glass jar I had and then gave it to the deputy. He said that he could take care of it," she answered me.

"I'll bet he did," I said, sarcastically, under my breath. But it also made me wonder what did happen to it. I figured the sheriff had probably gotten rid of most of the evidence, but I thought there was a chance that maybe he had hidden it somewhere where we could still find it.

"So now you know everything that happened that night, now will you tell me why it is that you're asking about something that happened over fifteen years ago?"

I looked at her and didn't say anything. I didn't think that telling her was avoidable, but I still didn't want to tell her. It hadn't occurred to me before, but now she would have to know what she had inadvertently helped to cover up. She looked at me and then down to Fr. Blair and Bill, all three of us sitting in front of her desk. We stared back at her; I think both of them feeling the same way I did. I looked at them and then back at Dr. Sharpton, who was still staring at me waiting for me to answer her questions. For a second, I thought about just getting up and leaving, but didn't. Instead, I just sighed and then told her the truth about why we were there. "Dr. Sharpton, fifteen years ago, on the night that you treated the deputy sheriff for his wounds, his brother, the sheriff, was killed. To this day, the identity of the assassin is not known."

"So was the deputy sheriff involved in whatever happened as well?" she asked me.

"Yes," I answered her, "but not in the way you think."

She stared at the three of us looking confused, and then very upset as she started to put it together. "Wait, what are you saying?" she asked me.

I looked at Fr. Blair and Bill and then back at her. "Dr. Sharpton, I'm saying that we believe that the sheriff was killed that night by his brother, the deputy sheriff, and that the deputy sheriff was wounded and came to you to treat him because he thought that was the best way to cover it up."

She just stared at me, incredulous. "What makes you think that?" she asked me. "I mean you don't really have any motive for making that accusation."

Again, I just sighed. "Doctor, when the sheriff died, he was about to arrest his brother, the deputy sheriff you treated that night, for a drunk-driving auto accident. One where two people were killed."

"What accident?" she started to ask me but then just stopped. "Wait, you mean that the accident where George's mother died, that accident was caused by the deputy sheriff? And that he killed his brother to prevent from being arrested for it? And that he was wounded and came to me to treat him and help cover it up? And now you have come here to tell me that I helped to prevent getting justice for my friend, that by doing what I took an oath to do, I allowed someone to get away with three murders?" As she said, tears started to form in her eyes.

"I wish I could say no, but, yes, that's what happened," I answered her.

The truth was I really did want to tell her no. It hadn't occurred to me until that moment just how emotional and difficult this moment might be for her. Up until she said what she said about doing what she took an oath to do and allowing someone to get away with three murders, I hadn't thought about how knowing the truth would affect her. There was a part of me that felt selfish for not having thought about that before. But I also felt like that was unfair. It was the sheriff who had caused all of this; he was the reason that she was feeling hurt, not me.

"Why are you telling me this?" she asked us.

"Because we want you to come forward with what you just told us," I answered her.

"Come forward?" she replied questioningly.

"Yes, we're hoping that with the information you just gave us, it will be enough to start an investigation into the sheriff and maybe finally get him prosecuted for his crimes. But we can't do it without your help."

"I'm not sure that I want to be involved in this at all," she replied to me.

"I know that's how you feel, but without your help, I don't know that we will ever be able to expose the sheriff. But if you help us and come forward with what you know, then maybe we will be able to get justice for your friend."

She didn't say anything, just sat there looking sad and a little stunned. She had just learned that she had inadvertently helped someone who had killed one of her friends get away with it. I started to think about how she must feel, knowing that someone had used her life's work against her, and I realized I could relate to her. No, I wasn't going there—that was a memory I couldn't face. And now was not the time to be trying to work that out. Right now, I had to deal with Dr. Sharpton.

"What do you think I should do, George?" she asked Fr. Blair.

"I know it's hard, but I think it's the right thing to do. I know that you just want to forgive and forget, but that doesn't mean that justice should be ignored. This man is a murderer, including the killing of his own brother, and he should be brought to justice for it. But he's had fifteen years to get away with all of it, and now we can only do it with your help. I was hesitant at first too, but I believe God is showing me that this is a path I have to walk down, and I think that you do too."

"I'm just a little to stunned to say or do anything right now," she answered him.

"I can understand that," I answered her. "Look, you don't have to say anything right now. Just think about it. Sleep on it and maybe call us tomorrow or the next day."

"I think that's a good idea. How can I contact you?" she asked me.

Bill gave her his cell phone number, and Fr. Blair gave him the number for the church rectory where he was staying. We told her that was the best way to reach us.

"Okay, then."

At that, the three of us got up and left her office. As we drove away back to our motel, I thought about what our next move should be. We had done the two primary things we had come here to do:

appeal the court order and make contact with Dr. Sharpton. Even though she wasn't totally on board with us yet, at least we had gotten her involved, and I had a feeling she would come around. Apparently, Bill was thinking the same thing I was because he asked, "So what should we do now?"

"Pray," Fr. Blair answered him, saying it like it was the most important thing we could do.

"Why? If God helps us, won't the sheriff just try to blackmail him too?" Bill answered him with a smirk.

Fr. Blair looked at him, in the rearview mirror, with a half-smirk, half-disapproving look on his face. I didn't say anything, just kept driving. As if I wasn't confused by everything I was feeling already, what Fr. Blair said made me a little more confused. Part of me knew he was right, that it was important for us to pray and ask for God's help. At the same time, I was still struggling to return to faith. I still couldn't understand why God would allow what had happened to me to happen.

"Well, then, let's pray," I said, surprised to hear myself say it. I hadn't really meant to say it; it just sort of slipped out.

"What should we pray?" Bill asked sort of sarcastically.

"How about a rosary?" Fr. Blair suggested.

"Why not?" I answered him.

Fr. Blair removed a rosary from his inside pocket, held it in his hand, made the sign of the cross, and started praying the Apostles Creed. I didn't join in at first, and he got about halfway through and then stopped and looked at me and at Bill to see if we would say the second half. For a second, I thought about resisting, but instead, I picked up where Fr. Blair left off and said the second half of the prayer. We went on that way for the rest of the car ride, Fr. Blair leading us in saying the rosary. Bill was kind of half-in half-out, but I tried to stick with it.

I stuck with it because praying the rosary made me remember my wife. It had been her favorite prayer, and she made an effort to say it at least once a week. Normally, that was something that would have made me sad and not want to pray anymore, but this time, something else happened. I thought about the butterfly I had seen in the woods the day before, and I thought about how seeing it made me feel that my wife was still close to me. Knowing that she was still close to me gave me strength and a desire to pray once again. And once again, something in me came alive, as though a part of me that had been dormant had come to life again. I channeled the love I felt for my wife, and the closeness I had felt to her that day, into faith.

I prayed for Dr. Sharpton, for God to help her through this difficult time, to help her come to terms with the awful truth we had just told her. I also prayed for guidance about what to do next. We had seen Dr. Sharpton, and we had appealed the sheriff's court order about the church. It seemed like we had done a lot, but somehow, I felt like we hadn't done anything. The sheriff's crimes were great, and we would need more help to take him down.

I think that was about the quickest answer I ever received to a prayer because just as we were about to turn down a road toward our hotel, I saw a sign for a state police barracks in the other direction. And I swore I saw a butterfly lift off it and fly away. I turned the car and headed down the road in that direction.

"Where are we going?" Bill asked.

"You remember when we talked about trying to get other authorities to investigate the sheriff?" I asked him.

"Yes," he answered me.

"Well, I think we should do it," I replied to him.

"And what makes you think that will make any difference, or that they will even listen? What we are claiming is pretty out there," he answered me.

"Yes, but we all know it's true, right?" I asked him.

"Yes, so?" he answered me.

"Well, if we all believe it, then maybe someone else will too. Besides, I was a cop for a long time. I think that I know how to talk to them," I replied to him.

"Still, it seems like a long shot," he replied.

"What do you think?" I asked, turning to Fr. Blair, who until now had been quite about our sudden change of direction.

"I think that God works in mysterious ways, so if you really think this is an answer to our prayers, then I guess it's worth a try," he answered me.

I was struck by the fact that he said *our* prayers. I guessed he had been praying for the same things that I was.

"Well, then, why not?" Bill said.

Honestly, I think he was still a little shocked by what he had gotten himself sucked into. He had come here to represent me, and now here he was about to go see the state police about getting the sheriff arrested. Then, again, I wasn't really sure what to believe about him. It had always been in the back of my mind that I didn't know much about who he was, or why he had come here and involved himself in all of this, but it was never something I had paid much attention to. But now, I was seriously beginning to wonder who he was and what he wanted. But that had to wait until later because at that, we were headed into uncharted waters, so to speak.

I pulled the car into the parking lot of the police station, put it in park, and turned it off. And the three of us just sat there, nobody doing anything. Personally, I had no idea what to do next.

"So what do we do, walk in and say, 'Hi, we're here to ask you to investigate a fifteen-year-old case in which the only evidence is an eighty-year-old witness, an angry widow, and a fifteen-year-old bullet that we say came from someone but have no way to prove it'?" Bill asked sarcastically. He didn't mean to put down what we were doing. I think he was just trying to point out how spontaneous and totally unplanned it was.

"Well, we should probably work out a better-sounding statement, but, yep, that's pretty much what we're about to do," I answered him.

Once again, I took the lead and got out of the car first and started to walk inside. Fr. Blair and Bill got out and followed behind me, and the three of us walked into the police station.

CHAPTER 23

The detective just stared at the three of us.

"That's quit a story," she finally said after what seemed like forever.

The three of us had gone into the police station and asked to see a detective to report a homicide. We had been directed to one and had told her everything: the sheriff, his brother, Dr. Sharpton, all of it.

"I know it sounds crazy, but it's true," I said to her, trying to get her to believe us.

"Crazy doesn't begin to describe it," was her response.

"Look, we're talking about the murder of a cop here. I thought that was something you would care about," I answered her.

"Of course, I care about that, but to believe that he was killed by his own deputy, who also just happened to be his brother, that's pretty far-fetched," she replied.

"Look, do you really think we would be here if we didn't believe it?" I asked her. "Why would we want to make something like that up?"

"All I know is in the twenty years I've been a cop, I have heard some crazy stories, but that one has to take the cake," she answered me.

"Maybe coming here was a mistake," I answered her and then got up to leave, motioning for Fr. Blair and Bill to follow me.

Her sarcasm and disbelief made me angry, and I felt like I needed to get out of there before I really started to blow up. Guess she wasn't that interested in what we had said because she didn't follow us out or try to stop us. I started to head for the door when I was interrupted by someone calling out my name. "Tom."

I turned around expecting it to be Fr. Blair or Bill but was stunned to see the very thing I had been dreading, someone from my past. Immediately, I was in another world as the memories of our time together, and ultimately of the bitter end our relationship had come to, began to fill my head. Memories of patrols, midnight shifts, and later investigating the city's biggest criminals. We both looked at each other, and, clearly, he was stunned to see me.

"What are you doing here? Where have you been all this time...?" his voice trailed off as he just continued to look at me, stunned.

Fr. Blair and Bill walked up behind me, both looking confused. "Who is this?" Bill asked, but I barely heard him, as I was still lost in my flashback to my past.

"Tom, are you all right?" Fr. Blair asked, shaking my arm a little.

"Fr. Blair, Bill Pricley, this is Bob Simmons, my old police partner," I answered them, still stunned to see him.

The two of them looked at each other, neither one of them having apparently any idea what to say.

"What are you doing here?" Bob asked me for a second time.

I wasn't sure what to do or what to tell him. I hadn't expected to run into him, but I started to wonder if maybe he could help me. At the same time, I wasn't sure I wanted to involve him in this because it would mean letting a part of my past back into my life in a way I wasn't sure I wanted to. But something in my heart told me this was what the sign I had seen earlier had truly meant, and I decided it was worth a shot.

"I'm here because I need help," I finally answered him.

"What kind of help?" he asked me.

"Is there somewhere private that we could talk?" I asked him.

"Let's talk in my office," he answered me.

He led us back into the station and down a hallway toward his office. On the way, we passed the detective I had just stormed away from. She looked at us, but didn't say anything. We walked into Bob's office and sat down, but before we could talk about anything, she knocked on the door and asked to see him. He walked out of the room, and while I couldn't make out most of their conversation, I could pretty much guess what she was telling him. After a minute, he walked back into his office and looked at me with the same look the detective had given me earlier.

"I take it she told you why we're here?" I asked him.

"Just that your story is crazy and that she thinks maybe we should investigate you," he answered me.

"For what?" Bill asked before I could get a word out.

"Relax, she's just very zealous about her job, and she doesn't like it if she thinks someone is trying to take her for a ride, that's all," Bob answered Bill.

"So where have you been all this time, Tom, and what are you doing here?"

I didn't really know what to tell him. I hadn't told anyone what I was doing. After my family died, and their killer had disappeared, I simply gave up. Packed my bags, put in my papers for early retirement, sold my house, and left town. I hadn't told anyone that I was doing it or where I was going because I didn't want anyone to come looking for me. I just wanted to go away and hide from my past. But once again, here was my past right in front of me.

"Well, like your detective out there told you, I don't know if you're going to believe the reason why we're here," I answered him.

"Frankly, I can't believe that you're here, period, never mind why," he answered me.

"Look, I know you probably want an explanation for why I disappeared and why I have suddenly reappeared, but there really isn't time for that right now," I replied to him.

"Okay, then, will you at least tell me why you're here now?" he asked me.

So for the second time that day, I told the whole story: the sheriff, his brother, Dr. Sharpton, Fr. Blair's mother, all of it. And for the second time that day, someone looked at me like I had just announced I knew where to find JFK's killer or something like that. Like I was a crazy man they needed to institutionalize or something.

"Well, Detective Manley wasn't lying when she said your story was crazy?" he finally replied to me.

"No, she wasn't lying, but there is one big difference between you and her," I replied to him.

"And what's that?" he asked me.

"You know me. You know I wouldn't just show up and make up a crazy story like this," I answered him.

"I think the proper answer there is I *knew* you," he answered me. "But now I'm not so sure. I haven't seen you in five years, and you never even told me you were leaving. No goodbye, notice, not even a note. I just came into work one day and found out you had left. So now I'm not really sure who is sitting in front of me."

For a second, I thought about just getting up and leaving, and giving up on this. But I remembered that sign I had seen on the way here, and I felt like it just wasn't a coincidence that I had run into the Bob like that.

"Look, I don't know what to tell you. All I can say is that things have been hard, and that I just felt like I needed to escape everything and get away. And through that and this weird series of events, I still don't really understand I wound up here, and I ran into you. And I'm hoping that even if I haven't been the most loyal person in the world, maybe you can understand why I did what I did, and that maybe you will help me anyway."

He just paused and stared at me for a second. "What is it I can do to help you?" he asked.

"Investigate this case," I answered him.

"Why are you so interested in this?" he asked me.

"Because this man left behind a family, a wife and a son, who need him but don't have him. Because he left behind a man who lost the love of his life and can't do anything about it, and above all because he left behind a brother who has and continues to this day to benefit from all of that. And because if you don't help us, he could very well get away with it." It occurred to me that the answer sounded overly dramatic, but I also felt like it drove the point home well.

Bob sighed and stared at the three of us for a minute. "All right, Tom, I'll look into this for you. Now where is this evidence you say that you have?"

"Well, I don't know," I answered him.

"You don't know?" he asked me, sounding even more skeptical than before.

"Dr. Sharpton said that the night she treated the sheriff, he took it and told her he would take care of it," I answered him, hoping that would explain it.

"So you claim this evidence exists, but you have no idea where it is?" he asked us.

"In a way, this actually helps our claim," I answered him.

"How?" he asked sarcastically.

"Well, it just shows that the sheriff has something to hide," I answered him.

"Maybe, but unless you know where he hid, it doesn't prove anything," he replied to me.

"Then we have to find it," I said, trying to think of just how to do that.

"Where can I find this Dr. Sharpton?" he asked.

I told him where her office was and gave him one of her cards so he could get in touch with her.

"Whatever happened to you, Tom? Did you leave because we couldn't find Fearhand?" he asked me.

"I left because I was devastated over what happened, and because I knew why it had happened, that it was my own fault."

"What happened wasn't your fault. You were doing your job, and the best way you thought possible," he replied to me.

"I was doing what I thought was the right thing, but I think the results of my actions speak for themselves," I answered him.

"But there was no way you could have known what happened would happen," he replied to me.

"Only because I was too distracted doing all the things I thought I had to do, whether or not I thought they would make a difference."

"So are you here now trying to redeem yourself? Is that what this is about?" he asked me.

"Maybe," I answered him. "Maybe, that's exactly what it's about."

That answer was followed by a moment of silence. I don't think anyone had any idea what to say.

"So what about you, Bob?" I asked him. "How did you wind up here?"

"About two years after you left, a friend of my father's contacted me about an opening for a detective spot here. I applied and was hired on. Two years later, the lieutenant position opened up, and they promoted me to it. And here I am."

The situation started to feel like two old friends catching up after a long separation, and for a second, I forgot why I was there.

"So, Lieutenant Simmons, will you investigate this case as a favor to an old friend?" I asked him.

"I'll look into it," he answered me. "But I can't promise anything."

"All we want you to do is try," I answered him.

"I will try. How can I get in touch with you?" he asked me.

Like before, we gave him Bill's cell number and the number to the landline in the rectory.

"You don't have a phone?" Bob asked me.

"Nope," I answered him, the tone of my voice indicating I really didn't want to talk about it anymore. I hadn't ever bothered to turn on the phone service to my house after I moved in. And I had gotten rid of my cell phone. I didn't have anybody to call, and I didn't want anyone trying to call me."

After that, Bob walked us out of the police station and promised that he would look into the case. The three of us got into the car and drove back to our motel. We had hoped to head home that day, but it was already late in the afternoon, so we decided to stay the night and head home the next day. We stopped at a restaurant for dinner and then went back to our motel to settle in for the night. But the events of the day just kept running through my head, and I couldn't settle down or get to sleep.

"Well, that was an interesting day, wasn't it?" I asked Fr. Blair, trying to get his insight on it.

"*Interesting* is a good word for it," he answered me.

"Do you think Dr. Sharpton will come around?" I asked him.

"It's hard to say. I think she got a real shock. The best thing we can do is pray for her," he answered me. "Speaking of praying," he continued, "I was really impressed to hear you pray the rosary like that today."

"I think that's the hardest I have prayed in a long time," I answered him.

"Well, that's a good thing, right?" Fr. Blair asked me.

"Yes, I think it is," I answered him. "How about if we say another prayer, maybe a shorter one this time?" I asked him with a smile.

"Sure," he answered me, smiling.

We said a short prayer together, and I tried to keep all of the things that I had on my mind, especially Dr. Sharpton and Bob, in my heart and to pray that God would guide them and guide our mission here. I also prayed for a more peaceful night and for a peaceful sleep. After that, we went to sleep.

But once again, a peaceful sleep eluded me that night. Instead, my recurring nightmare occurred again, only this time it was even worse than before. I made it as far into my house as I had ever made it, and this time, I made it a little too far. This time, I couldn't hear the voices of my family calling out to me. Instead, this time I found their bodies, lying there lifeless. And I knew what had happened, and that it was too late to stop it, that I was too late. I started to scream, and the next thing I knew, I was waking up screaming *no* at the top of my lungs with Fr. Blair leaping out of his bed and racing over to see what was wrong with me.

"What's wrong, Tom?" he asked, still half asleep and almost tripping over the bed.

But I barely heard him as I woke up and shot out of bed in a cold sweat. I looked around the room and for less than a split-second thought that it was only a dream, but then remembered that it was all real again. I looked at Fr. Blair who was standing there on the side of my bed. Suddenly, I heard someone knocking at the door. Fr. Blair walked over to open it and a half asleep looking Bill came racing in, looking very confused. I glanced at the clock and saw that it was about two in the morning.

"What's going on?" Bill asked, sounding excited.

"Nothing, I just had a nightmare, that's all. Go back to bed," I answered him.

He looked at Fr. Blair, who didn't say anything, and then back at me. He looked like he was pretty tired, and I figured that was his motivation for simply leaving and going back to his room. I got up out of bed and walked around the room a little bit, trying to collect myself. I sat down on my bed, and a few tears started to roll down my eyes. Fr. Blair sat down next to me and put his arm around me.

"Do you want to tell me about your dream?" he asked me. "Was it the same dream as before?"

"Yes, it was, only this time…" my voice trailed off, I didn't know how to tell him. Fr. Blair and I had become very close in the time that we had known each other, and our relationship had reached a point where I felt like I could tell him just about anything. But I knew where this dream was going, and I also knew that I just couldn't face it, let alone tell anyone else about it. I didn't answer Fr. Blair's question, just fell back onto my bed, and tried to think. I was finally starting to make some progress, and maybe put my life back together a little bit why couldn't this just go away. And then I remembered what I had figured out before, that it wasn't going to just go away, and I was wasting energy trying to make that happen. So I tried to continue my statement: "Only this time, it…climaxed, I think that's a good word to describe it."

"What do you mean?" Father asked, sounding confused.

"I mean, tonight my dream turned into a true nightmare. Tonight, I saw a vision in my head that I haven't seen since my family died. Tonight in my dreams, I saw their bodies lying on the floor of my house, and it was not the first time."

Fr. Blair looked at me stunned for a second but then collected himself and tried to comfort me. "You have never told me about the day that your family died before," he said questioningly.

"No, I haven't," I replied to him. "It was a memory I vowed to never revisit."

"You were right about what you said during our first argument," I told him.

"What was that?" he asked me.

"That line you gave me about 'being Mr. hotshot detective' or something like that. Well, you were right about that. That's exactly what I was doing, and it cost my family their lives. I would give anything to go back and undo that. More than anything, it eats away at me to know that I spent all that time doing things I thought were right, but, in reality, I was blind to what was right in front of me. And now I've lost them forever. God, if I could just go back and do that over again, I would. I wouldn't be blinded by ambition, but, instead, I would look for love."

Fr. Blair's answer once again showed his humble wisdom: "You know, Christianity is all about forgiveness, forgiveness of others, that is. But I think that sometimes what gets missed is forgiving yourself. People do things to us that hurt us, and we have to learn to forgive them, but at the same time, sometimes people do things that hurt themselves, and when that happens, we have to learn to forgive ourselves. In your case, it's especially hard because you have to live with the fact that the things you blame yourselves for can't be undone. But I think that the best thing you can do is remember that each day is a new day, and that if you really make an effort at it, you can let yourself off the hook, and you can truly make life better for yourself."

I had to admit I was amazed at his answer. I couldn't begin to count the times I had kicked myself, thinking if I had only seen what was truly happening, if I had only gotten out of my tunnel vision. Maybe my family would be here with me right now, and maybe I would be happy. But in that moment, I began to see the flaw in my thinking. The past was the past; there was no way to change it. And I couldn't get back what I had lost. I realized that Fr. Blair was right: all I could do was live each day anew, learn the very harsh lessons of my past, and try to move forward.

And once again, I was amazed at the wisdom that this man had to offer me. This man whose friendship I had tried to reject, but who despite that, or perhaps because of it, hadn't given up on me. Instead, he had stuck by me and over a matter of months helped me to overcome some great issues and struggles. He even cared enough to be sitting here with me at two in the morning, helping me through this.

"So how is it that I learn to forgive myself and move forward?" I finally asked him.

"Well, I think you have to start by accepting the past and simply learning the lessons it teaches," he answered me.

"How do I accept the past when it's still so much in the present?" I asked him.

"Maybe you can start by letting yourself revisit those memories you don't want to talk about," he answered me.

I thought about his answer for a minute, and it occurred to me that there was something else I had to do on this trip, something I hadn't done in a long time.

"You want to take a ride with me, a little side trip before we head back home?" I asked him.

"Now?" he replied to me, sounding a little confused. "Where are we going?"

"To confront my past head-on?" I answered him. I also glanced at the clock again and realized it was still the middle of the night. "Maybe we should get some rest first," I continued.

I could tell Fr. Blair was confused, but, I guessed for my sake, he agreed. I turned off the light and crawled back into bed, but didn't get much sleep. As I tossed and turned, I could hear Fr. Blair quietly praying, praying for me. I was moved by his friendship toward me, and knowing that he was on my side once again helped bring me some peace. I lay in bed until about 5:00 a.m. but didn't get much sleep. I was too busy thinking about my dream and about what I was about to do.

As soon as I saw the first rays of sunlight and heard the birds start to chirp, I got up and got dressed. Fr. Blair heard me and started to get up too. He got dressed, and we headed out to the car. When we first walked outside, I was struck by how cold it felt. Fall really was in the air. My wife would have been thrilled. I went back into my room to get a jacket and then headed toward the car.

"What about Bill?" Fr. Blair asked me.

"He'll be okay," I answered him. "This is something I want to do with just you."

"Don't you think he will wonder where we are?" Father asked me.

"Don't worry, we'll be back before lunch," I answered.

"Okay, then," Fr. Blair answered me and got into the car.

"So where are we going?" he asked me.

"You'll see," I answered him.

After that, we drove along in relative silence for almost two hours. It wasn't that I didn't want to talk to Fr. Blair; I was just lost in my thoughts about what I was doing. As we got closer to our destination, I started to feel knots in my stomach, and once again, there was that temptation in me to just turn around and leave. But I resisted it. I turned down a little back road and hit a bump as I did. That woke up Fr Blair, who had fallen asleep on the ride. He looked around and asked again where we were.

"You'll see in just a minute," I answered him. I maneuvered the car around a curve and turned up the driveway into the cemetery. Fr. Blair looked around, confused at first, but then realized what we were doing.

"Are we going where I think we're going?" he asked me.

"Yes," I answered him, sounding sad, but knowing that I had to do this. "And I really need your help to do it."

Fr. Blair didn't say anything in response, just gave me a look of support, which told me all I needed to. I knew he was on my side. I drove around to where the graves were and then parked. I just sat there for a minute and watched as the sun began to fully come out.

"Whenever you're ready," Fr. Blair said, smiling a comforting smile at me.

"I'm as ready as I will ever be," I answered him and got out of the car.

Fr. Blair followed behind me, and we walked along a few rows of grave sites until we found the ones I had come here looking for. Four graves, one after the other. Each one bearing the name of someone I loved more than anyone in the world. Each one bearing the name of someone I would have given anything to have back, if only for five minutes. Jillian, Emma, Thomas, my children, Carly, my wife.

As I looked at the graves, I remembered the last time I had been there. I remembered watching as each of the caskets was lowered into the ground. I remembered looking over the fence of the cemetery at the road clogged with reporter's cars and news vans. Everybody. from the top news anchors to some online blogger with a camera, had wanted a piece of the story. Now it was five years later, and I turned and looked at that road and saw that there was no one there. No cars, no news vans, no reporters, nothing. The world had forgotten my family, had forgotten my story. But Fr. Blair was there with me.

He was there, looking very tired, expected from the sleepless night I had caused him. But he was there. And looking at him, I thought that really his presence was a symbol. A symbol that God was there too. That despite my complete renouncing of faith and rejection of him, he was still there. And I realized he had always been there. I turned back and looked at my wife's gravestone. And on it was a quote from a story I had not heard in a long time, but one I realized that day I had needed to hear all along: "In the times when there was only one set of footprints, that was when I carried you."

"That's quite a story, isn't it?" I asked Fr. Blair, who came up and stood next to me.

"What story?" he asked.

"That one," I answered him, pointing to the quote on the grave. "About how a man see's his whole life as footprints on a beach. For most of his life, there are two sets, one for him and one for God, but during the hard and dark times in his life, there is only one set. And the man asks God why God abandoned him during the hard times. And God tells the man that during those times, he didn't abandon the man. He carried him.

"Well, I don't know about that story, but in my world, God has always worked through people. And in my life, lately, he has been working through you. He has carried me, even if I couldn't see it. And he has done it with your help. Without you, I wouldn't be here. I would be back home, being angry all day, and crying myself to sleep all night. But thanks to your friendship, here I am."

"I don't know what to say," he answered me. "Other than to say I was doing my job as a priest and tending to one of the Lord's flock. Even if he wanted to run away from the ninety-nine others."

I hadn't thought about that parable in a long time, but now I could see how I fit into it. "You know, being here, remembering the last time I was here and thinking about all the memories of my family and of events surrounding their deaths, I have to face that there is one more memory that I haven't faced yet. One that I have never let myself face, or even think about, but that has always been there haunting me. I had hoped it would go away, but my dreams over the past few nights are proof that it won't."

"Do you want to tell me about it?" Fr. Blair asked, trying to comfort me through what he understood was about to be a very difficult moment for me.

I saw a bench near where the graves were, and I walked over to it and sat down. Fr. Blair followed behind me and sat down next to me.

"Last night, when I told you that you were right about what you said during our first argument, well, there was a reason for that. As you have pointed out to me, I've never told you about the day my family died," I said to him.

"Do you want to tell me?" he asked again in reply.

"Yes, I think it will make my nightmares a little clearer to you," I answered him.

"Okay, then," he answered me. "Tell me."

"The night my family died, I wasn't with them. Instead, I was out on a stakeout. As you saw in the newspaper headline the sheriff showed you that night, I was trying to capture John Fearhand, the man who called himself 'the most powerful criminal in the world.' He had beaten the rap so many times before. Everyone from the local DA's office to the US attorney had tried to prosecute him, and no one could ever get him. And that was if they even got that far. Usually, no one ever got past investigating him.

"But then, he finally slipped up. Well, technically, one of his lieutenants did. The lieutenant killed a man so that they could use his house as part of an underground drug tunnel they were running, but he accidentally left some of his hairs on the guy's shirt, and we had DNA to prove it. Guess, there really isn't any honor among thieves because when we finally caught the guy and informed him he was looking at life or worse, he agreed to flip on his boss and tell us everything. He had enough information to keep the guy on trial for the next ten years or more. And I was at the center of it all, simply because I caught the original murder case.

"We put out a warrant for Fearhand's arrest. It was a huge news story. And I was completely wrapped up in it all, and loving it. I thought for sure that this would put my career on the fast-track, and as a result, my family on easy street. But the truth I know now is I was just blinded doing what I thought was right, and it cost me the very thing I had worked so hard for."

"What happened?" Fr. Blair asked.

I stared out across the cemetery at all the tombstones and the falling leaves blowing around them and let out a breath. "Like I said, that night I was on a stakeout. You see, as soon as Fearhand heard about the warrant, and that I had stashed my witness somewhere he couldn't get him, he went on the run. But I was hot on his trail. The morning of my family's last day alive, I got a tip that that night he was going to be hiding in a drug house near the city limits. That he was going to be transported there very late. So I planned to stakeout the house until he arrived. Never mind that my wife and young children would be alone. They would be fine, I thought.

"Well, it turned out to be a trap. He was never going to be there at all. He had fed me the tip as a diversion, and I think you know why. Anyway, I waited in front of the house until almost 1:00 a.m., but he still hadn't arrived. I started to fall asleep when I woke up to the sound of my cell phone ringing." I stopped talking and looked at Father trying to draw the strength to tell him the next part, the most painful part. The part I had never even told myself, the part no one but me knew.

"Who was on the phone?" Father asked, somewhat confused.

"It was my neighbor. He had called to tell me that there was the sound of gunshots and yelling coming from my house. I started yelling at him to hang up and dial 911, but he said he had already done that. I wanted to tell him to go there, but he was an old man, and he probably would have only gotten himself hurt if he could even make it over there.

"I raced home as fast as I could, calling for help, again, as I did. But I was an hour away from home, and by the time I got there, it was all over. There were cops and paramedics everywhere. The detective you met yesterday was there, and they were putting up crime scene tape. I pushed past everyone and raced into my house, but I was too late. My entire family was there, dead. My wife was right by the front door. Apparently, she had tried to keep him out and was the first to go. Next came the girls, who had come to see what all the commotion was. Jillian was first, next Emma who was killed as she was trying to run away. Finally, my son, who had hidden in a closet. On the other side of the room from him was the home phone, with my phone number punched in but never dialed. It looked like he had hidden and tried to call me but was interrupted.

"After that, my life went from a famous news story to an infamous one. The reporters were in front of my house before dawn. As for me, I just sat out on the sidewalk in shock. A week later came the funeral, and the day I vowed to never enter a church or worship God again. That's why before a few nights ago, I wouldn't go inside the church. After the funeral, the cops tried to find him, but it was like he just disappeared. Personally, I threw myself into the search, looking high and low, searching day and night. We arrested every criminal we had ever so much thought about, but none of them knew where he was. Truth was there just wasn't any evidence anyway. There were no fingerprints, no DNA, no witnesses, nothing. The authorities interrogated everyone from his top lieutenants to the teenaged kids he paid to be lookouts for him, but no one had any idea he was going to do this or where he was.

"So, even though I knew he had done it—everyone did—there was never any actual evidence to convict him on it. He had spent his life playing the system, using our own rules against us, and it seemed like this was his parting act, his final goodbye. He had committed the ultimate crime against the justice system and now disappeared. It was a game for him. He always knew how to play people, and that included me. I guess he knew me better than I thought because after what happened, I just gave up. Seeing that no one could find him, a part of me wanted to search high and low, but it was outweighed by a part of me that just gave up that said 'no more, this is enough.' That part of me won out. So I just gave up. I put in my retirement papers, sold my house, and left the city to go and hide in Rocky Hills, where I hoped that no one would know who I was and where I hoped no one would find me. And no one did until the day you knocked on my door."

I finished talking and tried to catch my breath and control my tears and crying that had started. Fr. Blair didn't say anything to me, just looked at me. I thought maybe I had stunned him a little. He had known since that night he and the sheriff were in my house what had happened to me, but I had never shared the gruesome details with him, and I didn't think he was prepared for what I had told him. But, once again, he showed strength and wisdom I had never seen before.

"You know, I had a conversation just like this one once," he said to me. "Only I was in your position."

"What do you mean?" I asked him.

"I mean, after my fiancé and my mother were killed, I was just like you, distraught and lost, and just like you, I gave up on everything. And if it wasn't for the intervention of a wise old priest, I probably wouldn't be where I am today. And I certainly wouldn't be here to help you."

"What happened?" I asked him, not really sure how else to ask him about it.

"Well, like I said, after my fiancé and mother's deaths, I was at a loss. At the time. I was planning on going to school to be a therapist, but I couldn't go back to that. I just gave up on everything. One day, I was sitting in the church, back in Rocky Falls, just staring up at the cross and crying, asking God why he let this happen to me. While I was sitting there, the pastor at the time, Fr. James, came in and sat down beside me. He didn't say anything; just sat there with me and tried to comfort me.

"Over the next year or so, he counseled me, like I have tried to counsel you. He helped me to deal with my pain and anger and my trauma of what had happened. He also helped to show me that God had a plan and that there was a purpose for my suffering. And after some vocational coaching, we both came to see that that purpose was for me to follow in Fr. James's steps and enter the priesthood. After that year was up, and I had healed a lot, I applied to the seminary and was accepted. The day I left, Fr. James told me he was retiring, but to keep in touch and that he would always be there if I needed him.

"During my years in the seminary, we kept in touch by mail. The day I graduated, he came to see me and told me how proud he was of me for all that I had overcome. But he also told me that he had had gotten sick and that probably didn't have very long. We spent his last days together praying and talking about all that had transpired between us. He was the one who inspired me to do the missionary work I did overseas that you heard Dr. Sharpton mention the other day. The day he died, I went to see him in the hospital, and in one of the most powerful moments of both our lives, I heard his confession. I said goodbye to him and asked him what it was that had inspired him to be so loyal to me. And he gave what maybe the best wisdom I have ever heard."

"What was that?" I asked him.

"He told me 'One man's pain can be another man's redemption.'"

"One man's pain can be another man's redemption?" I said questioningly.

"I didn't completely understand it at the time either, and I didn't until sitting here with you today," he answered me. "But now I think I understand it completely."

"How?" I asked him.

"I don't know what motivated Fr. James to want to help me, but whatever it was, it really inspired him. You told me that if it wasn't for me, you would be back in Rocky Hills angry and crying and all that. Well, if it wasn't for Fr. James, I would probably be back there doing the same thing. But you're here because of me, and I'm here because of him. So, yes, now I understand what he meant by that. And I hope maybe I can help you to understand it too."

"I think I do, a little bit, at least," I answered him. "But what I don't understand is what you said last night about forgiveness."

"What don't you understand about it?" he asked me.

"It's not so much I don't understand as I just don't think I can do it," I answered him.

"Why not?" he asked in reply.

"How can I forgive myself for something that I believe may have made my life worse, and how do I even begin to forgive the man who murdered my entire family simply because of me?"

"I think the only way to do that is to figure out what obstacles there are inside of you, that prevent you from forgiving," he answered me.

"I'm not sure about that. But why don't we talk about it more on the ride back? I don't want Bill to get worried about us," I replied to him

He agreed, and we headed back to the car. On the way, I stopped and looked at the grave one more time: "Bye, honey, bye, kids, I love you, I hope to see you all again someday."

It was an extremely powerful moment for me, and it gave me hope that someday I would see my family again if, God willing, I found myself in heaven with them.

And at that, Fr. Blair and I left and headed back to our motel to pick up Bill. On the way, we talked more about forgiveness. He asked what I thought my obstacles to it might be. And I knew that the biggest one was my still-burning desire for revenge. I still wanted to find the *criminal* who did this and kill him. But more and more, in my heart, I didn't see what that would achieve. It wouldn't bring back my family, and it wouldn't take away one ounce of regret or hurt I felt. The two of us mulled that over for a while, and I tried to figure out how it was that I could learn to forgive both myself and him. But I knew that it would be a difficult task, and certainly not one that it was in my nature to take on.

CHAPTER 24

"Where have you two been?" asked a confused-looking Bill when we finally made it back to our motel. It was almost 11:00 a.m.

"We went on an adventure," I answered him sarcastically.

"Where?" he asked.

"Are you ready to head back?" I asked him, trying to dodge his question.

"Yes," he answered. "But I don't know how much longer I can stay."

"What do you mean?" I asked him.

"I mean I have been here for months now, and I have to get back to my life. I've been running a law practice out of a small-town motel in the middle of nowhere. It's not going to work forever. It doesn't look like your case is going to move forward anytime soon, so you don't really need me."

"If that's what you feel like you have to do," I replied to him.

"Look, I'm not running away. I'll still be around, and I'm still interested in helping you take down the sheriff. I'm just saying I need to start paying a little more attention to the rest of my life, that's all," he replied to me.

"Okay then, let's head back," I answered him.

We headed for home, driving most of the way in silence. It wasn't that we didn't want to talk, I figured; we all just had a lot on our minds. I figured Fr. Blair was thinking about his mentor he had told me about and his own family losses. And I was thinking about what Fr. Blair had said about forgiveness and about running into Bob and how I was starting to like this idea of confronting my past head-on instead of trying to hide from it.

My thoughts on this were suddenly interrupted by Fr. Blair and Bill telling me that I had almost missed our exit off the highway. I quickly maneuvered the car over to the exit lane and got off to the sounds of some unhappy driving honking their horns at me.

"Something on your mind?" Bill asked me. I guess he sensed some tension because he suddenly tried to ease it.

"George, do you think you could come back here and give me a confession and possibly last rites?" Bill asked Fr. Blair.

"Confession sure, but last rites are only if you're sick or dying," Fr. Blair answered him with a smile.

"Well, I'm sick of this guy's driving, and I'm dying to get away from him, does that count?" Bill asked.

"Think of it as your cross to bear," Fr. Blair answered him. "Just like I think of listening to you complain as mine."

At that, we all laughed, and for a minute, it was like we were just three friends out on a road trip together. And I imagined maybe someday, if all of this was ever over, we could be just that, three friends out on a road trip. And then, another powerful moment happened for me. I began to realize that the three of us really were beginning to form a powerful friendship bond, even if the circumstances that brought us together weren't ideal. But I was still bothered by the fact that I didn't know much about who Bill was or why he was here.

We drove along the rest of the way smiling, the three of us forgetting for a minute all that was happening. We arrived back in Rocky Hills late in the afternoon. Bill dropped Fr. Blair and me off at my house. I invited the two of them to stay, and the three of us ate dinner together. It was the first time I had had dinner at my home with anyone. And I had to admit it gave me a vision of a similar future.

"So are you going to go see your girlfriend?" Bill asked me teasingly.

"If your referring to Sarah, then, no, I don't have a reason to go see her," I answered him. But inside, I couldn't deny that I did have feelings for her and that I was actively trying to think up an excuse to go see her.

"So do you think next year when you guys get to seventh grade you, will be a little more mature?" Fr. Blair asked half-sarcastically, half-trying to say "let's act like adults." And again, the three of us laughed as if we were just three friends hanging out together. And again, I had a vision in my head of someday when we would be.

"So do they still have the fall festival around here?" Bill asked.

"Yes, I think they have something," I answered. "But I've never gone before."

"Maybe this year, we could go, and maybe your crush will be there," Bill replied with a smile.

"I think you have to be in seventh grade to go to the festival," I replied sarcastically, referencing Fr. Blair's remark.

"You know, that at least used to be a lot of fun," Fr. Blair said. "I don't know what it's like now, but it might be fun to check it out."

"Maybe it will be fun, why not try it, when is it? I asked.

"Usually, it's right before Thanksgiving, and then there at least used to be the Christmas fair, right before Christmas," Fr. Blair answered me.

"Yes, I think they still have that too," I replied to him.

After that, we cleaned up from dinner, and Bill left to go back to his motel and got ready to leave the next morning.

"So what do you think about what I told you today?" I asked Fr. Blair after Bill left.

"I think that the best answer I can give you is the one I gave you last night, that the only thing you can do, as hard as it is, is to try and learn from the past and move forward. And to try and forgive yourself," he answered me.

"I'm not sure I could ever learn to do that," I answered him. "And I definitely don't think I could ever forgive the man who killed my family."

"Maybe you can," Fr. Blair answered me, sounding hopeful.

"No, I could never forgive him for what he did to me," I replied to him.

"I know it can feel like he doesn't deserve it, that he deserves revenge, and he does, but really, that won't achieve anything. I know it feels like it will, but in the end, all you will do is hurt yourself. No, I believe that the only way to truly escape a situation like that is to try to learn to let go of your anger and your negative feelings. Let go off all of that and try to learn to love again. I think that is something we can work on together if you're willing to try."

I just looked at him for a second and was struck by the powerfulness of this moment. A few minutes earlier, we had been sitting there cleaning up the dinner dishes, and now, almost out of the blue, Fr. Blair had made this powerful statement. And I was moved by the power of his words and that he could just create a powerful moment like that, so moved that I decided to give it a try.

"All right," I answered him.

He didn't say anything, just smiled, and seeing him smile made me feel very encouraged. And in that moment, I felt something in my heart. I didn't know what it was, but it gave me a great feeling of hope. Like somehow I could see the light at the end of this dark tunnel I had believed was endless. That now maybe, just maybe, things could really get better. And that I could start to live again.

I smiled back at Fr. Blair, and then he said goodnight and left. I told him I would come to see him in the morning, and we would talk more. As I watched him walk back down toward the church, I thought about everything that had happened and how far I had come, and I felt something I hadn't felt in a very long time—optimism. I looked up at the beautiful night sky and thought about the great God up there somewhere who had helped me get to this moment. And I went to sleep with a smile on my face. I just couldn't help it.

CHAPTER 25

The gun was in my hand; he stood there before me back into a corner, down on the ground, helpless. I pointed the gun at him and just stood there. In the background, I could hear the sound of someone trying to get inside and the sound of someone yelling my name, but it was like those sounds didn't even register. Instead, it was just me and him. And I just stood there, pointing the gun at him, and I had no idea what to do.

I woke up and looked around my room, unsure of where I was or what was happening. I sat up and realized it had just been a dream. I sat there for a minute turning it over in my head, trying to remember all the details I could about it and trying to understand what it meant. As if my dreams from before weren't confusing enough, this one didn't make any sense at all. I looked at the clock and saw it was about 3:00 a.m. I got up and walked over and looked out the window. I stared up at the sky and down at the church. As I did, it occurred to me that, like my dreams of previous nights, maybe this one also had a purpose.

My dreams about finding my family had shown me that I needed to confront the memory of their deaths head-on and that I needed to share it with Fr. Blair. So I felt like I already knew something, that this dream was trying to show me something, but what? I wanted to think about that more, but instead, I just lay back down and fell asleep. I was just too tired from the long drive and short night, the day and night before to think about it anymore.

When I woke up in the morning, it was almost 11:00 a.m. I was surprised that I had slept that late. But I just figured it was because of how tired I was. I got up, got dressed, and went downstairs, not really sure what to do next. I still wanted to go and see Fr. Blair, but I also felt like maybe I needed a little break from all of that. Things had been pretty intense during our trip, and I wanted to rest a little. I thought about going over to Sarah's house, but I couldn't think up a good-enough excuse to go and see her.

After a little while, I decided I would just walk over to her house and think up an excuse later. I left the house and, as I walked, started to feel nervous. I felt like a kid in school walking up to their crush to ask them to the prom or something like that. That was definitely something I hadn't felt in a long time. And I had to admit, I was enjoying it.

As I approached the house, I saw that she and her son were out in front putting up some Thanksgiving decorations. I stood a few houses away and watched, not really sure what I should say to them. As I looked at her, I suddenly had this strange feeling. Like somehow she was different than everybody else, different in a good way. I didn't know much about her, but the one thing I did know was that I wanted to learn more. I wanted to know what she liked or didn't like. I wanted to know anything and everything there was to know about her. I wanted her to be able to share her sadness with me, and I wanted to be able to share mine with her.

Woah, this is big, I thought. It was definitely new for me to be feeling this way. I hadn't felt that way since I met my wife, and remembering that made me sad and made me long for those days. But at the same time, it was nice to feel love in my heart again. And it occurred to me that, while I could never replace my wife or the love we shared, maybe I could find something different, which was special in its own way. At that thought, I took a deep breath and walked up to the house.

"Hello," I called out to the two of them as I walked up.

They turned and looked at me. Jimmy looked happy to see me; his mom looked more surprised. But I was pretty sure I saw a suppressed smile.

"What are you doing here?" Jimmy asked me, walking out to meet me.

"Well…" my voice trailed off. Apparently thinking up an excuse later wasn't the best idea.

"Well, maybe you should work out what you're going to say before you say it," Sarah answered, coming up behind him.

"So you're back?" she asked me.

"Back?"

"Back from your trip?" she replied.

"Oh, right, my trip," I answered her, trying to snap back into reality. Apparently, something had me distracted, and I honestly thought it was Sarah. I could just hear Bill teasing me if he had been there.

"So what happened?" Jimmy asked, sounding very serious, a tone that reminded me of the seriousness of everything that was happening.

"Are you sure you want to know?" I asked, directing the question at Sarah.

"Yes," she answered me.

"Well, we found Dr. Sharpton, and we told her everything."

"Will she help?" she asked.

"Honestly, I'm not really sure. We gave her a pretty good shock. But I think with some time, she might come around, yes."

"What about the church?" she asked

"It's in the hands of the appellate court now?" I answered her.

"So what are you going to do in the meantime?" she asked me.

"I don't know. I still don't completely understand what all of this means," I answered her.

"Maybe that's a sign that we're doing the right thing," she replied to me.

"We?" I said questioningly.

"I'm a part of this too, aren't I?" she asked me.

"We're a part of this," Jimmy corrected her. "Whatever 'this' is."

"Yes, whatever 'this is'," I said, mimicking him.

"So do you want to help us decorate?" Jimmy asked.

No, I came all the way over here without an excuse because I didn't want to spend time with your mother, I thought sarcastically. And that thought brought home to me that I really was starting to have feelings for this woman. "Sure, if you want me to," I answered him.

"Why not?" Sarah declared.

So we spent the rest of the afternoon decorating the outside and inside of the house with Thanksgiving and fall-themed cutouts and carvings. And we cleaned up some leaves and things from the outside of the house. I also helped Sarah bring out some china plates for Thanksgiving dinner.

"It's just the two of us for dinner, but it's still nice to be a little fancy," she explained.

"Your brother-in-law doesn't come for dinner?" I asked her.

"No, he hosts a bunch of the town council members at his house. He only trots us out when he wants to brag about how great he is for looking after his dead brother's family," she answered me sarcastically.

"Why does he have the town council over to his house?" I asked her, a little confused.

"Well, I don't know what his official reason is, or if he even has one, but the real reason is because he owns them, so to speak, and I think he just likes the idea that they have to come and pay homage to him."

Her answer reminded me again how corrupt he really was.

"What exactly do you mean by 'owns them'?" I asked her.

"I mean he has dirt on them, and that's why they never oppose him and why he has managed to stay in power for so long," she answered me.

Her answer made me remember what Fr. Blair had told me that day about how power was the sheriff's motive. And it was apparently so strong, he was willing to kill for it.

"What's his problem? I mean what makes him so determined to be in control of everybody?" I asked her, trying to get some insight into the sheriff.

"I don't know. I always guessed he had some kind of inferiority complex with his brother, and pushing everybody else around is how he deals with it," she answered.

"Very insightful Dr. Freud," I answered her with a smile.

"Thank you very much," she answered me, lowering her voice to sound like a man's and pretending to stroke a beard.

And we both just laughed. I looked outside and saw it was almost dark. I was surprised and looked at my watched, realizing it was almost 7:00 p.m.

"Wow, looks like I have been here all afternoon," I said, trying to gauge how she felt about it.

"Looks like you have," she answered me.

"Where did Jimmy get off to?" I asked, realizing I hadn't seen him for a while.

"He went off with some of his friends. Guess he figured we had this covered," she answered me, still smiling at me.

"Well, then…" my voice trailed off. I didn't really know what to say. "I just wanted to stand there and stare at her, and to be with her, and spend time with her."

"So since I did spend all day in your house, how about if I buy you dinner?" I asked her.

"Well, since you spent the whole day helping me, how about if I buy you dinner?" she answered me.

"A modern independent woman, I love it," I teased her.

"Why, because we're so independent?" she asked.

"No, because I don't have to pay for dinner," I answered her playfully, and we both laughed.

"So where are you taking me?" I asked her.

"How about the diner? Ever eaten there?" she asked.

"No, I can't say that I have," I answered her after pausing for a second and remembering the day I overheard the judge and the sheriff talking there.

"Well, then, let's go," she said, grabbing her keys and heading out the door.

It was a pretty nice night for the midfall, and we decided to walk over. We ate dinner in a little booth. We sat and talked about everything: our spouses, our pasts, our careers, anything. We were having a good time, and I felt like I could tell her anything. Turned out we had a lot in common, and not just our tragic pasts. Before I knew it, the owner was coming over to tell us that we had to leave because he was about to close up for the night. We had been talking for almost four hours, and it was nearly 11:00 p.m.

We left the diner, and I walked her home, the two of us talking and laughing the whole way. It was the most fun I had had in a long time. We walked back to her house and then just stood there. A breeze came up and blew her hair around, and some of it into her face. I reached up and brushed some of it away, and we locked eyes and just looked at each other. I brushed my fingers along her hair and along her cheek. And then I kissed her. It wasn't like our first kiss—that was almost an accident. This time, it was intentional and passionate. This time, we both felt something for each other.

After a minute, we pulled back. I smiled at her, and she smiled back at me.

"So what did you have in mind for tomorrow?" I asked her sarcastically, and she just laughed.

"Why don't you come back tomorrow and find out?" she answered me a little playfully.

"Careful, or I might take you up on that," I replied to her.

"Well, then, I'll just throw caution to the wind," she replied playfully.

"So I'll see you tomorrow then?" I asked her.

"I hope so," she answered me.

I watched her go inside the house and then left and walked home. I could feel a little extra pep in my step as I walked. I really was feeling happy, happier than I had felt in quit a long time. But I was also scared and feeling a little guilty. Guilty like somehow I was doing something wrong, like I was cheating on my wife or something. I knew that wasn't true, but a part of me still felt that way. And I was scared because I didn't know how these new feelings fit into everything that was happening. And because there was a part of me that thought that if I really did fall in love with this woman, all I was doing was risking that I would lose her too.

But I tried not to focus on that and, instead, to focus on the positive: the happiness that I was feeling. Like my growing friendships with Bill and Fr. Blair, my relationship with Sarah that was causing me to have visions of a future. A future where we were together, where things were different, where they were better, where we were happy.

I got home and tried to go to sleep, but I was too excited. So I sat up reflecting on everything that had happened over the past months. How last spring I was so angry and hateful and vengeful. And how having met Fr. Blair and Bill, and now Sarah, and how each of them had helped to change my life for the better. I really was starting to feel better and happier with my life. But the anger and the desire for revenge still burned inside me.

And that made me think about what Fr. Blair had said to me the other night about forgiveness. And even though there was a part of me that knew he was right, I just couldn't let go of the anger I felt. It seemed unfair somehow. That the person who hurt me would just get away with it. That I was just somebody for him to treat however he liked, and I couldn't do anything to fight back. Feeling that way, like I was powerless and like no one cared, made me very angry. And I didn't know what I had to do to let go of that. But one progressive thing that was happening was that I did want to.

I must have fallen asleep on the couch because the next thing I knew, I was waking up from falling on the floor. I sat up and looked around confused as to why I was on the floor. As I woke up more, I started to remember my dream. It had been the same dream as the previous night, only this time it was more vivid. This time, I could feel a conflict, one that I didn't understand. Like I knew I shouldn't do it, but I felt like I had to, like I had no other choice. Again, I just stood there with no idea what to do; only this time, there were two conflicting forces inside of telling me what I should do.

I figured I had tossed and turned because of the dream, and that was why I fell on the floor. I pulled myself up and wandered upstairs, still half asleep, and just fell asleep on my bed. I was too tired to think right then, but I knew that these dreams were something that I needed to talk to Fr. Blair about. The rest of the night was peaceful, and I did manage to get some sleep. I woke up in the morning around eight and resolved to go and see Fr. Blair immediately.

I showered and got dressed thinking about how conflicted I felt. On the one hand, I was very happy after everything that had happened yesterday. I could once again feel love in my heart, and a part of me truly did feel like I was starting to put my life back together, and together the way I wanted it to be. But another part of me still felt lost and angry. It was a part of me that felt like things were never going to improve; they were just going to stay the same, or get worse. I didn't want to believe that, but my experience over the last five years told me otherwise.

I tried to keep a positive mind-set and keep looking to the future. I had so many visions of a friend-and-love filled happy future. I didn't want to give up on that. Instead, I wanted to carry on because something inside me was telling me to. Something inside me was telling me to keep going, to have faith, and to just keep trying. Yes, things had been hard, but they could, and would, get better if I just kept trying.

I ate some breakfast and then headed down to the church looking for Fr. Blair. I found him behind the church bringing out a rake and some shovels and bags.

"Burying a body where you think no one will ever find it?" I asked him sarcastically.

"Not yet, but the day is young," he answered me with a smile.

"So what are you doing?" I asked him.

"I thought maybe I would clean up some of the leaves and dead branches and things that have fallen all around here. I've been meaning to get to it since I got here last fall, but I just never got around to it. Want to help?" he asked, handing me a pair of gloves.

"Sure," I answered him. "But I was hoping we could talk."

"Can we do both?" he asked.

"Why not?" I answered him. Maybe some yardwork would be therapeutic.

We started out raking leaves that had built up about three or four feet high against the side of the church. Some of them looked like they had been there since last year.

"So is that when you got here last fall?" I asked him. I had been curious about his past ever since Dr. Sharpton had mentioned him being overseas.

"Yes," he answered me.

"Why did Dr. Sharpton say that you were overseas?" I asked him.

"Because I was. After I was ordained, they wanted to assign me to a parish, but I just didn't really feel like that was my place. My mentor Fr. James, he had been a missionary for most of his career, and I thought it would be good work. Plus, I needed a change of scenery."

"Where did you go?" I asked him.

"Africa, all over the continent," he answered me.

"What kind of work did you do?"

"Oh, all different kinds," he answered me.

We spent the rest of the morning and part of the afternoon cleaning up the churchyard and talking about Fr. Blair's time overseas. He told me all kinds of stories, everything from working on bringing food to impoverished areas to ministering to prisoners in a military camp. He had been all over the continent and had seen many things, some of them good, some bad. Some of his stories had happy endings; others not so much. Either way, it was clear that he had seen quite a lot and that he had truly poured his heart out and tried to help anyone he thought he could.

"Were you by yourself all that time?" I asked him.

He paused for a minute, as if a difficult memory had popped into his mind. "No, there were other priests, as well as nuns and monks and friars, many different people. And there were lay volunteers. And not just people from the Catholic Church. Many different denominations of Christianity were represented. I became friends with one woman in particular. Even though she wasn't Catholic, she had a strong devotion to her own faith beliefs that I couldn't help but admire."

"What happened to her?" I asked him.

"We were friends for about eight months or so. We met working on a clean water project for an impoverished area. There were a lot of children in the area, and it seemed especially close to both our hearts that they have clean water. During our time working together, we spent a lot of time talking about faith and God and things like that. I got the sense that she was trying to convert me to her church, and I would be lying if I said the same thing wasn't on my mind but it still bothered me. After our assignment there was complete, I got orders on where to go next from the local bishop.

The day I said goodbye to her, we had an argument. As we said goodbye, she talked about how our beliefs were not so different, and I guess that made me angry. We both said a lot of things. In hindsight, it wasn't fair of me to call out her faith or beliefs the way I did, but at the moment, I was angry and said what I was thinking. Eventually, she just stormed off, and I didn't care enough to stop her. Looking back on it, there were better ways to handle the situation than the way I did. I don't know whatever became of her, but I just tried to pray for her and pray that she would find her way. If I had it to do over again, I might do it differently. I truly don't know. But I guess that doesn't matter now."

He paused and sighed. I could tell that was one conflict he had not resolved, and he didn't seem sure that he ever would.

"What do you believe about members of other churches and denominations?" I asked him, looking for some wisdom.

"I think that people are all taught different things, and all believe different things. Personally, I believe that our church is the true church and that we have to continue to advance her missions. That said, I also think that while other churches may not have all their theology correct, the people who fill their pews are good people, who do good work, otherwise they wouldn't be there. And I think that if God allows those people to worship how they do, if that is his way of guiding them to do good work, like the work they did with me, then I am not the one who should judge that or put them down. The Lord works in mysterious ways, and I guess one is to bring good people to do his work in whatever ways he sees fit. I won't be the one to question that."

His answer truly impressed me. He had shown true humility. And I was inspired. It made me realize it was important to accept others with different beliefs. Even if you didn't accept their beliefs, it didn't mean you had to reject them. Once again, Fr. Blair had taught me a valuable lesson.

After that, the two of us continued to talk about his past and where he had been. Even though I had come there hoping to talk about the issue I was having, I was enjoying talking to Fr. Blair about his past and just having a nontherapeutic conversation. It was a little conflicting, but I figured if this was the direction our conversation was going in, that was okay, and we could always talk about my issue later. And once again, I was amazed at his devotion to the service of others, despite the sacrifices it had forced him to make.

"So why did you leave?" I asked him.

"The work I did there was good work, but after a while, I got the sense that God was calling me to make a change, to do something else. I heard, through the grapevine, so to speak, that St. Jude's here was about to become a lost cause itself. But I thought maybe I could rebuild it. I felt like this was the new call that God was giving me. That this church, like the people I served overseas, just needed a little love, even if everyone else had given up on it. And I thought maybe I could help the town a little too."

"Were you worried about what the sheriff would say when he found out you were back here?" I asked him.

"Some, at first, but then I remembered the story of Jesus and Pontius Pilate, how Jesus told Pilate that he would have no power over him unless it had first been given from above. I realized that the 'sheriff,' so to speak, I answered to was far greater than the one running this town."

His answer amazed me. As impressed as I was by his commitment to service to others, I was even more amazed by his faith. It was almost funny how in that moment, it occurred to me that maybe the whole reason for this reversion to faith I was starting to have was because Fr. Blair seemed to have so much faith in God that it was just contagious.

"So what happened when you first got here?" I asked him.

"The first day I arrived this place was a mess, to say the least. I could tell why, when I asked to be assigned to this parish, the bishop in charge had looked at me like I was crazy and told me that this place was a lost cause."

"And what did you tell him?" I asked.

"I said, 'Well, there's a patron saint for that. Maybe he will help me.' Guess I outwitted him because he didn't say anything else, just told me I had what I wanted, don't ask for a transfer if it doesn't work out.

"Anyway, like I said, day 1, I spent just trying to clean up the place. Day 2, I had to go out and buy some furniture for the rectory, and day 3, I was cold. That's how I remembered to turn on the heater. After that, I started trying to put together a group of parishioners again. Couldn't have a parish without them. It wasn't an easy task, but eventually, I got enough volunteers, and God was kind. Each of them was able to bring something: a skill, materials, money, whatever, and we were able to get going."

"So are you missing anything?" I asked him.

"Well, we could use a roofer," he answered me with a smile, but I knew that he actually meant it.

"Sounds like you have got yourself a real-life *Lilies of the Field* here," I replied to him, referencing the Sidney Poitier movie.

"I guess so," he answered me, laughing.

"So what happened to you yesterday? I thought you were going to come down here but you never did?" he asked me.

"Well…" I answered him with a smile before telling him about my day.

"Sounds like Bill was right," he replied with a smile.

I didn't say anything, just smiled and stared out into space, thinking hard about the future and what it might hold. And I also thought about the things that were holding me back—the hurt, the anger, the way things had been so different from how I always imagined they would be. And that brought me back to what I had come here to talk to Fr. Blair about in the first place.

"So about that forgiveness thing you mentioned the other day," I said, trying to change the direction of the conversation.

"What about it?" he asked in reply.

I just looked at him not really sure what to say. I had been through so much, and even though I had started to heal from the experience of it, I was still very angry that it had happened. And I didn't know how to even begin to let go of that anger or even resist the urge to feel it. I knew that I wanted to, but it seemed almost impossible. I just so often could not resist the urge to explode. It was like that was the only thing that had rewarded me at all, at least lately, was to be angry, so that was what I did. I walked over to a bench on the side of the church and sat down feeling confused.

"How do I learn it?" I finally asked after thinking about all of this for a minute.

"I'm not sure that it's something that can be learned," he answered me.

"Then how do I even begin to go about it?" I asked him, sad at his answer.

"Well, I think you have already taken one step forward. You have the wisdom to understand that forgiveness is important, and you have the willpower to want to try to do it," he answered me. "After that, I think that first thing to do, as in all things, is to pray to God for help and for the strength to learn how to forgive."

"I was kind of hoping to draw some inspiration from a source a little closer to home," I replied to him.

"Who?" he asked.

"You. You have been through so much, and yet you seem to have been able to learn how to forgive the people who hurt you. How did you do it?" I asked him in reply.

"I'm not sure that I really did anything. I think maybe I just had to learn a new way of thinking, that's all. Instead of thinking about how hurt and how upset I was, I thought about what could I do to help others facing the same tragedy. And with Fr. James's help, I thought about what it was that God might do to help carry me through this difficult time. In the end, I think I just learned to take all of the negative I felt and turn it into something positive. And it helped me to let go of what I was feeling, and that was a huge weight lifted from me."

"How can I possibly bring any good out of what happened to me?" I asked him.

"I think that you already are," he answered me.

"How?" I asked him.

"By what you're doing in trying to take on the sheriff and to help me fight to keep this church open. Maybe that's what God had in mind all along, maybe that's why he allowed what happened to you to happen so that he could bring a great good out of it. Good in the form of you helping to bring this church to fruition, and good in you helping Sarah to move on. It sounds like the two of you could really have something."

I smiled thinking about that, but there was one other thing weighing on me. Something I hadn't realized was there until that very moment.

"How do I forgive God?" I asked Fr. Blair

"Forgive God?" he asked in reply, sounding confused.

"How do I accept that he allowed this to happen to me. How do I get past my feelings that if he really loved me, he would have kept my family alive so that I would be with them and would be happy? How do I reconcile my visions of a loving God with one who apparently allows events rooted in anything but love to occur? It is so disillusioning to me to think that we are told we have this loving God, and yet, the picture I get is the picture of one who asks us to live a very hard way of life and to endure all of these sufferings. How do I possibly do that?"

A tear began to streak down my eye as I asked all of that, as I let all of the anger and hurt I felt at heaven and at God come out of me. It was clear to me that part of my struggle was with myself. Because deep down, I didn't want it to be this way. There was a part of me that had always felt that I was wrong for what I was doing. That said *no*, that I should be able to fight on, to stay on the path of living a faith-centered life. But I just couldn't do it. And like I had realized before, that it was my greatest loss, I felt as though, when it came to faith, I just couldn't do it anymore. I felt surprised the moment had changed so quickly from the two of us raking leaves to this powerful emotional moment I was having.

Fr. Blair looked at me confused at first but then very comforting. He came down and sat next to me and put his arm around me like he had done before. And once again, I felt the comfort of someone being on my side and being there for me.

"Do you remember what I told you that day at your house, the day that you first agreed to let me counsel you?" he asked me.

"Yes, I remember that," I answered him.

"You remember what I told you about God allowing you to walk this path so that he could bring something greater out of it?"

"Yes."

"I know it's difficult, but that is your answer. I know it's hard to understand, let alone accept, and that is something I have to work on myself every day. But in those times of doubt, I just try to look at the good that has come out of what happened. If what happened to my mother and fiancé hadn't happened, I would not have become a priest, I would not have been able to do the missionary work that I did, and I would not have been here to help you through this."

"And the good that can come out of what happened to me is what's happening here. With the sheriff, with the church, with helping you to fight this fight," I answered him.

Fr. Blair smiled at me. I could tell it made him happy to hear me say that. And in a way, it made me happy too. It helped me to understand God a little more and to stop being so angry at him. My heart healed a little, thanks to the wisdom I gained that day. But I was still very conflicted. Whatever I did or did not feel, that anger at the criminal who murdered my family was still there and still very strong. And that was something I didn't know how to deal with. I wanted to let it go, but the urge to feel it was too strong.

"What do I do about my anger?" I asked Fr.

"I think that the only way to really let it go is to focus on what makes you happy and maybe to replace your anger with something else. To not only let it go but to replace it with something positive. So my answer to your question is a question: what makes you happy?"

The first thing to pop into my mind was Sarah. I thought about our evening together the night before and how just spending time with her and talking with her made me feel like something inside me had come alive. I smiled thinking about her, and Fr. Blair caught it immediately and smiled back at me.

"So what are you thinking about?" he asked me.

"I was thinking about Sarah," I answered him, sounding like a kid with a crush.

Fr. Blair didn't say anything, just continued to smile at me, and I began to understand his answer. I began to understand that part of forgiveness was to take the anger you felt and replace it with something else. And what better thing to replace it with than love?

I dried my tears and tried to focus on the happy things that were starting to happen.

"Does that help?" Father asked me.

"Yes, it helps a lot," I answered him.

Fr. Blair invited me to stay for dinner, but I turned him down, telling him I had other plans. He smiled at me, and I left and headed back to my house to clean up from doing yardwork all day. I showered and changed and then left and headed over to Sarah's house. As I walked over, I thought about what we might do that night. I figured maybe we could go over to the diner for dinner again, but I was hoping we could do something different. Maybe a movie or just a nice walk around town. Or maybe she had something planned? It was exciting to think about all those possibilities.

I walked up to the front of her house, and I could see her through the kitchen window making something. I just stood there watching her, and as I did, I could feel something I couldn't quite put into words. It was something special that I had never felt before. It was like what I had felt for my wife but at the same time different. It was a different kind of connection, something entirely new and special in its own way. Something that I knew could help me heal from my losses and to find a new happiness.

She noticed me standing there and came outside to meet me. "What are you doing out here?" she asked me.

I just shrugged my shoulders and smiled at her. I didn't have an answer for her except to tell her how I felt. Since I still wasn't sure how to put it into words, I just smiled at her, and she smiled back at me.

"So what do you want to do?" I asked her.

"Well, since I took you out last night, I thought maybe tonight I would treat you to my own home cooking, and maybe afterward, a late-night movie," she answered me.

"Sounds good to me," I replied as she led me inside her house.

"So where's Jimmy?" I asked, wondering if he would be there too.

"What, afraid I'm going to kidnap you or something?" she answered me playfully. "He's off working on some school project with one of his friends."

"So what's for dinner?" I asked her.

"My famous secret chicken recipe," she answered me.

"Secret recipe?" I asked.

"Yes, it's been passed down in my family for generations," she answered.

"Guess it's pretty good then," I replied to her.

"It is," she answered. "Too bad I don't have anyone to pass it on to."

"What about Jimmy?" I asked her.

"Well, as much as he loves to eat, he's not much for cooking. Besides, I always thought I would have a daughter to pass it on to, like my mother did with me and her mother with her and on like that going back so far, no one even knows anymore. But, well…" her voice trailed off, and a very sad look came over her face. I imagined she was thinking about a larger family that might have been if her husband hadn't been killed. Maybe she would have had a daughter to pass her recipe down to. I walked over to the counter where she was standing, put my arm around her, and held her there in my arms. She wrapped her arms around me, and we stayed there like that, comforting each other. It wasn't a sad or dramatic moment; it was just a soft and tender moment, one where I was there for her. And I had to admit it felt good to be there for someone. It reminded me of what Fr. Blair had said about one man's pain being another man's or, in this case, woman's redemption.

"I think my chicken is getting cold," she said after a minute, smiling at me. We locked eyes for a second, and I could feel something powerful go through me. It was at that moment that I knew that I was starting to fall in love with her. I leaned in and kissed her, and we stood there embracing each other. It was a powerful romantic moment, and it felt like the most special moment I had experienced in a long time.

You don't deserve this. The thought came to me out of nowhere, a voice in my head so loud, it was almost like someone had said it out loud. Like someone was there just whispering it in my ear over and over again. I pulled away from Sarah and stood there staring at her. She looked at me, surprised and confused. As I stared at her, visions of my wife during our life together and of her lying on the floor of our home dead with our children kept going through my head.

"What's wrong?" she asked me.

"I don't deserve this," I said, retreating backward, tears starting to form in my eyes. "My family is dead because of me."

"What are you talking about?" she asked me, sounding confused and concerned.

"I killed my family. I don't deserve any of this," I said, continuing to back away from her and toward the door. I couldn't believe what I was doing, but I couldn't help it; this feeling was suddenly overwhelming me. I turned and walked out of the house and ran all the way home in a daze the entire way. I got home and went in the house and sat there confused and crying. I thought over what had just happened and tried to make sense of it.

It was like something inside of me refused to let what was happening go any further. I couldn't give up on my self-imposed isolation. I couldn't give in to actually being happy. I was supposed to fulfill the roles I was given in life, and I had failed to do that. And I deserved to be punished for it. I certainly didn't deserve to find happiness and love again, I deserved to be alone and be miserable. What happened to my family was my fault, and I had to be punished for it. I hated it, I resented it, I didn't want it to be that way, but it had to be that way. All those thoughts and feelings were racing through my mind, and I felt dizzy trying to make sense of them all.

I couldn't believe what I had just done, how I had just run away from Sarah like that, but I couldn't help it; it was like I couldn't let myself do it. I couldn't let myself fall in love with her and be happy again. I felt almost ambushed by my feelings. It was like they had just snuck up on me all of the sudden. Like I was having this great time and starting to put my life back together and feel happy, and suddenly here was sucker punch I never saw coming. In a weird way, it was like a breakthrough, like I had discovered these feelings that were motivating me without me having any idea.

I let out a deep breath and sat back. I felt myself calm down a little, but I was still pretty upset. I was about to get up and go down to the church to talk to Fr. Blair when I heard someone knock on the door. I thought it might be Sarah coming over to see why I ran out on her, but instead, it was Fr. Blair. I was happy to see him, but I wasn't sure why he had come over, not until I saw the look of concern on his face.

"What are you doing here?" I asked him.

"I heard you're pretty upset," he answered me.

"What gave it away?" I asked in reply, cheering up a little.

"To be honest, Sarah called me, she said you ran out crying and saying that you killed your family," he answered me, sounding confused and concerned.

"Maybe I did," I answered him, a tone of regret in my voice.

"What do you mean?" he asked me curiously.

"I mean, maybe all of this isn't God's doing or anyone's doing except mine. You told me earlier that God allowed this to happen. Well, what did he allow? He allowed me to be blinded by ambition so much that it cost me the most important thing I ever had in the world: my family. I failed at being their husband and their father. Maybe I deserve to be alone."

"Is that really how you feel?" he asked me.

"I don't know, maybe," I answered him.

"I think you're being too hard on yourself," he answered me. "I think that when we talked about forgiveness earlier, you left out someone you need to forgive."

"Who?" I asked him.

"You," he answered me.

"Me?" I asked in reply, feeling very confused.

"Yes," he answered.

"For what?" I asked.

"For being human," he answered me, speaking very softly. "For making a mistake, yes, perhaps a big one, but a mistake any person could have made. In the end, you were doing what you thought was right. I know that you feel like you were wrong and that you wish that you could have only seen that then. And I know that feeling as though you did everything right and the way you were supposed to, and the results being what they were can be disillusioning. And I know the way you feel seems hopeless now, but it can get better, You can make a new start. You are human, and you made a mistake. All you can do now is learn from it. You don't have to punish yourself like this."

"You know, it's really easy to tell myself that, but no matter how many times I do, I just don't believe it," I replied to him. "I never realized it before tonight, but no matter what I do, there is a part of me that will always be trying to punish myself for what happened."

"But what good will that do?" he asked me.

"I guess none," I answered him after turning his question over in my head.

"Then why do you do it?" he asked me.

"I can't explain it to you logically, it's just…" my voice trailed off. I just wasn't sure what to tell him.

"Guilt?" he said questioningly.

"Yes," I answered, almost surprised to hear myself say it.

"What do you feel guilty for?" he asked me.

"I guess for causing the deaths of my family," I answered him, still feeling very confused.

"But you didn't cause them," he replied to me. "And you have to stop telling yourself that, otherwise, you will keep punishing yourself for something you didn't do."

That statement was like an eye-opening revelation and, at the same time, a stinging wound to me. What had happened to my family wasn't my fault, but at the same time, it didn't feel right to think that way. It was like it had to be my fault, but the thought of letting that go felt good, and in a way felt right. It was very confusing, like there were two waring emotions jockeying for position inside of me.

And I knew if I could just work them out, I could have a much happier life.

"So what do I do, how do I forgive myself?" I asked him.

"I don't think you have to," he answered me.

"But what about what you said a minute ago about forgiving myself?" I asked him confused.

"When I said that, I meant that you had to allow yourself to let go of what you are feeling. Forgiveness implies that someone has done something wrong, but in your case, you didn't do anything wrong. You feel as though you made a mistake, and maybe you did in some sense of the word, but you never did anything wrong, and your intentions were always honorable. They say that the road to hell is paved with good intentions. Well, I say that doesn't make the intentions any less good. And that doesn't mean that good intentions have to lead to hell. In your case, they can lead to something much better if you let yourself let go of your desire to punish yourself. You didn't do anything to deserve punishment. So, in a way, yes, you have to forgive yourself, but simply by allowing yourself to be happy again."

"Happy again, I'm not so sure that's something I can ever achieve," I replied to him, even as I started to feel the weight on my heart lift.

"I think you can," Fr. Blair answered me with a comforting smile.

"That helps me a lot," I answered him, and I meant it. Once again knowing that someone believed in me and was walking this path with me helped me to believe I could reach the light at the end of this dark tunnel. And even though I was still plagued by my confusing dreams and by the feeling that what had happened was my fault, I couldn't shake the feeling that somehow things were finally starting to look up.

I laid my head back on the couch and started to fall asleep. I guessed my talk with Fr. Blair had worn me out. I heard Fr. Blair start to get up and leave, and I called out to him.

"Please don't leave, I don't want to be alone right now," I pleaded him.

Fr. Blair turned and just kind of looked at me.

"The chair reclines," I said with just a little bit of sarcasm that helped to lighten the moment.

Fr. Blair looked at me tired and like he just wanted to go back to the rectory and go to sleep, but I guessed his kind side won out because he went over and sat down in the chair.

"Thank you," I mumbled to him, half asleep. At that, I fell asleep, and I guessed Fr. Blair did too. Once again, that night, I dreamed of a fight situation, of facing down someone I had no idea who they were. I woke up midway through the night, turning the dream over in my mind trying to make sense of it. It occurred to me that the dream was metaphorical in a way. That the human villain I was facing in my dream was really the struggles I was having in life. And, like I didn't know the end of the dream, I didn't know what the end of this struggle would look like, but for the first time, it felt like I was in control and could write the ending. I looked over at Fr. Blair, asleep in the recliner, and I knew that without his help, none of it would have been possible. I fell back asleep confused but hopeful that I could write a happy ending to this story.

CHAPTER 26

I just sighed. I had walked over to Sarah's house to try and talk to her. It had been a few days since I ran out on her, but I didn't know what to say or what to tell her. I had realized Fr. Blair was right, that I didn't need to punish myself. It was very hard to do it, but I had to accept that; despite how it ended, I had always the most honorable intentions in the days leading up to my family's deaths, and that their deaths were not my fault. It still felt very conflicting for me to think that way, but in my heart of hearts, I was beginning to believe it. And I was also beginning to fall in love with Sarah, and I knew that she was a part of finding a new happiness. That was, if she would have me back after what had happened.

I stood out there in front of her house and watched leaves blow up and down the street in the mid-November wind. Thanksgiving was only a week away, and I figured she was starting to plan for her and Jimmy's dinner. She appeared in the same kitchen window I had watched her in a few days earlier, and somehow, she looked even more lovely than she had before. And, suddenly, I began to fear that if I didn't do something right, then I would lose her. And more so than ever, in that moment, I knew that a future with her in it was the key to a new happiness in my life.

She noticed me from the window and stopped what she was doing and stared at me. She looked very sad and very confused. I walked up toward the house, and she came out and met me outside. We stopped a few feet apart and just stared at each other. It reminded me of the day that I had met Fr. Blair at the church that same way. I hoped that Sarah would be as forgiving as Fr. Blair had been that day.

"Hi," I said, at a loss for what to tell her.

"Hi yourself," she answered me almost sarcastically.

"So I guess you want an explanation for what happened the other night," I said to her.

"Yes and no," she answered me.

"Yes and no?" I replied to her questioningly.

"Yes, I want to know why you ran out on me the other night. No, I don't want to hear you give me a list of reasons why you are not ready for this relationship. If that's really the way you feel, just tell me and let that be the end of it."

I was surprised by her answer; I hadn't known she felt that way. But, at the same time, I couldn't blame her what was she supposed to think. Her answer initially made me defensive, and I was tempted to fight with her. After all, what did she know about me? But in that moment, I realized that was an old me and that this was a perfect opportunity for a new me. I realized that the root of our conflict would be simply that she didn't understand me, and I didn't understand her. And I realized that the only way to really solve that would be for me to try and make her understand me, and for me to try and understand her.

"No, the problem wasn't that I wasn't ready for this relationship. The problem wasn't the present. The problem was that past still happening in the present."

"The past in the present?" she replied questioningly.

"Sarah, you and I relate in part because we share tragedies few other people can understand. You and I both live with what happened to our families and having to carry on without them, but for me, the struggle has always been feeling as though I was to blame for what happened to my family. And I hated feeling that way, and I hated myself for feeling that way, and all those conflicting emotions made me angry.

"So I came here to Rocky Hills to hide from all of it. But, more than that, I think, in a way, I came here to punish myself. I was imposing an isolation on myself. I had caused my family's deaths, and so I deserved to suffer for what I had done. And I certainly didn't deserve to be happy or to do things like fall in love with someone. I thought that I had roles to fill in life, and I deserved to be punished for having failed at them. But, now I know that I was wrong, and that I don't have to punish myself. I'm sorry for what happened the other night, but in a way, it had to happen. Because that last demon had to leave me. That final bit of anger and hatred and clinging to past had to go. And I know that now I can move forward. So the answer to your question is *yes*, I am ready for this relationship if you're still willing to give me a chance."

"You're falling in love with me?" she asked with an almost-blank look on her face.

I was a little stunned that after everything I had just told her, that was her response, but then I began to understand. I just smiled and answered her, "Yes, I am."

For a split-second, she looked at me like she wasn't sure what to do, but then, she walked over and kissed me. I kissed her back, and from that moment on, it was clear that I was hers and she was mine. I spent Thanksgiving with her and Jimmy and Fr. Blair, and it was the best Thanksgiving I had in a long time. Even Bill made an appearance. That year, for the first time in a long time, I had something to be thankful for. More than one something, in fact. I had Fr. Blair, I had Bill, and above all, I had Sarah. Our little group was starting to become very close and very important to me.

But there was still a lot weighing on my mind. I still didn't know what would happen with our appeal or the church, and I also wondered about Bob and whether or not he would be able to help at all. Because the truth was while I was beginning to truly feel happy again, I was also very nervous. If our appeal failed, and if we couldn't do anything to stop the sheriff, I didn't know what would happen.

CHAPTER 27

"And now, I officially light the town Christmas tree." That was the statement from John Walker, president of the Rocky Hills Town Council as he flipped the switch and turned on the lights on the town Christmas tree. It was the first Sunday in December, and the first snowfall of the year had greeted the town the day before. John stood up on a platform along with the other members of the council, four in total, along with the judge and, of course, the sheriff.

After John was done, the sheriff got up and talked for a while. I didn't pay much attention to what he said, just figured he was busy praising himself. I stood near the back of the crowd with Fr. Blair. I could see Sarah sitting closer to the platform with Jimmy. We had agreed to go separately in order to avoid the sheriff finding out about us. Neither of us could decide what he might do, so we decided to keep it a secret from him for the time. Although more and more I was inclined to just tell him. But I figured for now, it would be best to wait and see what happened over the next few months.

After the tree lighting, everyone spread out to view the setup and exhibits at the festival, while Christmas carols played out from the PA system. The town square was set up nicely, different businesses in town had booths, and there were sleigh rides, Santa Clause for the kids, and even a Nativity scene. I headed over to a booth where they were having a bake sale. Sarah was there; she made a cake for it. As I entered the tent, one of the town council members I had seen up on stage was looking around, along with a small child. It took me a minute, but I recognized him as the man I had a confrontation with that day at the grocery store. We stared at each other awkwardly for a minute.

"Long time, no see," I finally said, trying to ease the tension.

"Yes, the last time I saw you, we were shoving each other across the grocery store."

"I guess I owe you an apology for that," I said.

"Yes, well, I guess I owe you one too," he replied.

"Bygones then?" I asked, holding out my hand for him to shake.

"Bygones!" he replied, shaking my hand.

And I had to admit it felt good to make peace with someone. It was something I hadn't done in a long time, and wasn't very good at, even before my tragedy. But my good feeling quickly subsided when the gentleman pulled his hand away and quickly walked away from me. I couldn't figure out why he had done that until I looked around and saw that the sheriff had just walked into the booth. Guess he didn't want the sheriff to find out that he was talking to me. For what was hardly the first time, it was made clear to me just how much power and control the sheriff had.

I watched him walk in, and you could tell that there was an immediate increase in anxiety in just about everyone there. I was sure they all knew how much power he wielded. He walked over to the booth where Sarah was, and I just watched. I doubted he was any threat to her, at least in that moment, but I couldn't resist the instinct to protect her. I watched as he talked to her, bought the cake she had made, and then left. I thought about confronting him, but wasn't sure what to say.

As I watched him, I was struck by the fact that he wasn't wearing his uniform but regular civilian clothes. I wasn't sure why I was honing in on that, and then suddenly, I had an idea. I raced over to Sarah and pulled her away; I had to talk to her alone for a minute.

"Do you have any old pictures of your brother-in-law from before your husband's death? Old family photographs from holidays or something?" I asked her.

"Maybe, why?" she replied, looking puzzled.

"Because I've got an interesting idea," I answered her.

"What?" she asked me.

"Well, I was thinking, if you happen to recognize any of them as the same clothes that you saw that day at the sheriff's office, it might help to prove that he is responsible for his brother's death."

"That's an interesting idea," she replied. She looked sad, and I guessed that it was still hard for her to deal with her husband's death.

"Can we look?" I asked her.

"Guess it couldn't hurt to try," she answered me. "Why don't you come by tomorrow?"

"Sure, I'll see you then," I answered her.

After that she headed back to her booth, and I went back out into the festival and looked around some more. I was looking at the Nativity scene when Fr. Blair walked up and stood behind me.

"It's really amazing, isn't it?" I asked him.

"What?" he asked in reply.

"That a global religion, and all of the people and events and social movements that have come out of that religion, started with one baby, born with nothing, in a place where animals normally feed."

"Yes, it's pretty amazing," Fr. Blair answered me.

"Kind of reminds me of our little group here," I replied to him. "That is, if we can accomplish what we set out to do."

"Well, Rome wasn't built in a day, and neither was the Christian Church that calls the city home," he replied back. "But if we keep working at it and have faith in God, then we can achieve what we set out to do."

I didn't say anything, just continued to stare at the nativity scene, and thought about everything that had happened. I wasn't sure where things were going or what was going to happen, but I just knew that I had to keep pushing on because I just had a feeling that things were going to get better.

"How about a sleigh ride?" Fr. Blair asked me.

"Why not?" I answered him.

We got on board one of the carriages, and as it rode around the town, I looked around at the snow-covered buildings and streets that were just lightly and gently blanketed. I admired greatly the beauty of it, and it was an example to me of how beautiful the world could be and how that beauty could be so easily corrupted by man, or at least by some men. Because I knew that under the surface of that pretty snow-covered town was a town that had been rocked by two great tragedies that had altered it forever. And it seemed no one had yet been able to recover from it, but I thought that maybe I could help with that. It would be a new year in a few weeks, and I had the feeling that maybe it would be a good year. One where things would finally look up for me, for Fr. Blair, for his parish, and for this town.

After that, I headed home, feeling pretty peaceful and confident about the future. But once again, the peace I felt during the day did not translate into peace at night. Once again, I dreamed of a confrontation, one between myself and some unknown enemy. I didn't know who they were or what they wanted, or even why I was fighting them. And once again, the dream ended with them before me, defeated, and me with the opportunity to kill them and totally unsure of what to do. I woke up feeling very confused. I hadn't had the dream since before Thanksgiving, but now it was back, and in a way, it felt more real than before. I knew that in the morning, I would have to go and see Fr. Blair and hope maybe he could help me with it. I got out of bed and looked out the window at the snow that was falling again. I watched it for a little while and then went back to bed.

CHAPTER 28

In the morning, I headed over to Sarah's house. I still wanted to talk to Fr. Blair about my dreams, but right then, it felt more important to push forward with my case against the sheriff. But I was interrupted by the snow that had fallen overnight. Sarah, Jimmy, and I spent part of the morning shoveling her driveway. There was only an inch or two of snow, and it didn't take us long. After we had cleared the last bits of snow from the driveway, I looked at the piles of snow we had made on the grass and then looked at Sarah and smiled playfully.

"What?" she asked with a confused smile

I picked up some snow, made a little snowball out of it, and playfully tossed it at her, smiling the whole time. It hit her right in the center of her coat, and she looked up at me and smiled back. She didn't say a word, just fired one right back at me, and our snowball fight was on. We chased each other around the yard throwing snowballs back-and-forth and smiling and laughing. After a little while, our fight finally climaxed when we tripped on the snow. We landed on top of each other and playfully rolled around in the snow. I finally stopped with her on top of me and just lay there in the snow smiling at her.

"Guess, I won," she said to me.

"Why?" I asked her.

"Because I'm on top," she answered me playfully.

"Well, I can change that," I answered her, rolling around so that I was on top of her.

We rolled around some more and landed with her on top of me again.

"Nope, I definitely win," she said playfully.

"Guess you did," I answered her, smiling and leaning up to kiss her.

After that, we went inside the house and sat by the fire, trying to dry off and get warm. Sarah made us some hot chocolate, and we just sat there, drinking it and staring at the fire. It was such an amazing moment. My feelings for her were growing stronger by the minute, and just sitting there starting at her, she looked lovelier than ever. I hated to let reality back into our perfect moment, but I did.

"Sarah."

"Yes," she answered me, her voice dropping some. I think she knew what I was about to ask her.

"Do you have any old pictures that I asked about yesterday?" I asked her. Even though part of me was resistant, I knew that I had to do it—it was important.

"I know that this is something that we have to do, but please don't be upset with me for trying to resist doing this. It's not easy to deal with the loss of my husband, any more than it is for you to deal with losing your wife," she answered me.

"I know it isn't, but we have each other, and we can face these demons together," I answered her, surprised at how comforting my words sounded. I guessed Fr. Blair was starting to influence me.

"Together?" she said, like she was happily surprised to hear me say that.

"Yes, together," I answered her.

"Together," she said, wrapping her arms around me. I held her for a minute, and then she walked off and motioned for me to follow her. She led to a storage chest she kept in the living room. Inside were photo albums filled with photographs of her and her husband together, with Jimmy, and even a few from when they were first together. There was one of him being sworn in as sheriff. I could see Sarah standing in the background looking proud, and I could also see his brother, in his deputy uniform, with a bland, unhappy look on his face.

"Wow, there are a lot of old pictures here," I said.

"Yes, but I don't look at them much. It's just so hard," she replied. "Jimmy looks at them from time to time when he thinks I don't know about it." She chuckled a little when she said that.

"He really tries to take care of you, doesn't he?" I asked.

"Yes, he does. He's a good kid, that is, when he isn't spray-painting people's driveways," she answered.

I laughed at her answer. I hadn't even thought about that in a long time. "Boys will be boys," I replied to her with a smile.

We continued to look through the pictures, looking for old ones of the sheriff that maybe could help us. Eventually, we found several of him wearing the same types of clothes, and Sarah said that those were the ones she remembered seeing at the sheriff's office that day. Even though that was progress to me, I knew it would be hard to convince people that, despite the circumstances, she remembered all those years later. I sighed thinking that, and when Sarah asked what was wrong, I told her.

"Well, I think that there is one way we can assure them," she said, sounding hesitant about saying it.

"What's that?" I asked her, confused.

She took the album out of my hand and put it down. She reached all the way to the bottom of the chest and pulled out a manila envelope that was sealed shut. She broke the seal and opened the envelope to reveal pictures that hadn't seen the light of day in fifteen years. They were pictures of the bloody clothes she had seen that day, sitting in a box in a storage room at the sheriff's office. One of the pictures even showed the box addressed to the sheriff's office.

"Wow," I said, not sure how to respond.

This was exactly the kind of evidence that might actually convict the sheriff. That was, if we could get someone to listen to it. I thought maybe if we showed it to the town council at their next meeting, with everyone there watching, it might force their hand to vote no-confidence in the sheriff.

"I think you know what we have to do with these. We have to show them to the town council," she said, sounding determined and scared at the same time.

"Yes, we do," I answered her, but my voice trailed off as something occurred to me.

"What is it?" she asked me.

"Can we take a walk over to my house?" I asked her. "I want to show you something."

"Sure, what is it?" she asked.

"You'll see," I replied to her.

We walked over to my house, hand in hand, as the snow started to flurry again. It was strange to hold hands with someone again; it made me remember again my wife and the walks we used to take together. And then another emotion presented itself: happiness. Not just that I was with Sarah, but that it was her specifically that I was sharing this new love with. Like if I could have picked anyone in the world to share this with, I would have picked her.

We walked along in silence, me lost in thought about all of that and about what I was about to do. Finally, we arrived at my house and walked in the front door. As we did, I looked around at the house, or really at the lack of one. I remembered the day I moved in, I hadn't really cared at all about what the house looked like or what was in it. I didn't care if it had furniture or was painted a nice color or anything like that. I had brought some essential furniture, and that had been about it. I hadn't wanted to be there. I had wanted to be with my family, and my first few days in that house were haunted with the thought of the only way I could have made that possible.

But no matter how much it haunted me, or no matter how much I may have wanted to, I could never talk myself into ending my own life. And really, that was the first time I ever admitted to myself that I had actually felt that way or had wanted to do it. But, even if I wanted to, I just never could. And in that moment, I realized that it was God himself who had saved me from it. And now, I began to understand why. For all of this, for my love for Sarah, for my friendships with Bill and Fr. Blair, for my therapeutic relationship with Fr. Blair that had helped me so much. And for the role I was playing in helping to protect the church and the town from the sheriff.

I continued to think about all of this as I looked around at my nearly empty house. My empty house that, like my empty life, could be filled up again. But first, I had something I had to do.

"Why are we here?" Sarah asked me, obviously confused.

I didn't say anything, just walked upstairs to the room at the opposite end of the hallway from mine. I stared at the closed door, a blank look on my face. I knew what I wanted to do—I wanted to share with her the source of all my pain. Sarah walked up the stairs and stood there with me staring at the closed door.

"What's this?" she asked, sounding very confused.

I didn't say anything. I just pulled the key from on top of the molding over the door, turned it unlock, and opened the door. This time, I wasn't the first to go in, Sarah was. She walked into the room and looked around at everything in there. Kid toys, home movies, old pictures dusty inside their frames, all kinds of keepsakes and mementos.

"What is all this?" she asked.

"They're all of the things from my family that I kept. Toys my children played with, jewelry my wife wore, her engagement and wedding rings are in that box over there, old home movies, school projects my children worked on, cards and presents they made for me on Father's Day, all of the things that I have left from my past. It's all here, locked away in this room."

She didn't say anything, just continued to look around. "Why are you showing me this?" she finally asked me.

"Because I wanted to share with you the same things you shared with me: my memories. And because I don't know if I could have been able to face these memories at all if I didn't have you here supporting me. You being strong enough to face your demons set a great example for me, and now I want to do the same thing. So here it all is."

We spent the rest of the evening looking around at everything in the room. And I had to admit it wasn't as hard as I had thought it would be. In a way, it was almost cleansing. I was finally facing the past I had tried to run from for so long. Finally, we came to a shelf in the closet where I had hidden away my wedding album. I hadn't looked at it since before my family had died. I had looked through other photo albums, but that was one I just couldn't face.

I pulled it down off the shelf and looked at the cover. I sat down on the floor, up against the wall, and Sarah came and cuddled up next to me. And together, we opened the album. We looked through all of the pictures there together, her supporting me and helping me, and being a shoulder for me to cry on. We looked at every picture from my wife leaving her house for the wedding, to our altar pictures after the ceremony and every one in-between. Finally, we came to the last picture: it was the picture of my wife and I moving into our house. We had moved in a few weeks after we were married. I could still remember holding her in my arms as I carried her across the threshold. We had stopped to pose for a picture.

We looked at the picture for a while and then fell asleep, just sitting there on the floor, cuddled up together like that. And we stayed there like that together. It was comforting, like were both just there for each other. In the morning, I woke up and looked around, forgetting where I was for a second. And suddenly, I realized that for the first time in a long time, I had woken up not feeling lonely. I looked at Sarah, still in my arms, asleep. And in that moment, I knew in my heart that I loved her, and I knew that I wanted to spend the rest of my life with her.

She started to wake up and then got up and looked around the room and then back at me. And before either of us could say or do anything, I said something I hadn't said to anyone in a long time, and didn't think I would ever say again, but I knew that I felt it, so I said it: "I love you."

She turned around and just stared at me. She looked shocked but at the same time had a happy look on her face. It seemed like something had started to come alive in her as well.

"I love you too," she answered me. As she did, a look of surprise came over her face.

"Are you sure about that I asked her?" with a smile.

She stopped for a minute, and then a look of clarity came over her face. "Yes, I'm sure," she answered me, smiling.

I smiled back at her, and we embraced. After that, we went out and bought some Christmas decorations, and we spent the day decorating my house. We spent the rest of the holiday season spending time together and waiting on whether we could resume work on the church. Fr. Blair and I continued to work together. And Sarah and I made plans to spend Christmas together, and I even decided to host dinner. It was the first holiday I had hosted in a long time, but it was all a part of this new life I was building.

On Christmas day, I had everyone over at my house. We spent Christmas eve having a Christmas movie marathon. On Christmas morning, Fr. Blair said a small mass for us and few other people who wanted to attend. After that, the five of us exchanged gifts and then spent the afternoon preparing our Christmas dinner. We all pitched in, but Sarah did most of the actual cooking.

"No one would want to eat if you cooked, anyway," Bill, who had made an appearance, teased me.

"As long as I get to eat more than you," I shot back at him, and we all laughed.

We all had dinner together and then cleaned up. After that, we all said goodbye. Fr. Blair headed back to the rectory, and I walked Sarah home. I said goodbye to her and Jimmy, and as I watched her walk up the path to her house and go in, I couldn't help but smile. It was the nicest Christmas I had in a long time, and I was truly grateful for it. I could truly feel the tide of my life turning toward happiness once again.

I walked back to my house and looked around. Bill was still there; he was planning to spend a few days and was staying with me. He was already asleep on the couch, so I simply shut off the light and went upstairs and went to sleep. Before I went to sleep, I said a small prayer of thanks to God for blessing me with all of this. My heart was still troubled by all the things we had yet to figure out, like the church, the sheriff, and all of it, but I was still grateful and still happy.

CHAPTER 29

The next few weeks went by quickly. After new year, Bill returned to his office to wait for the court's decision. The rest of us continued to try and plan what we would do once they ruled. I thought a lot about Bob and about Dr. Sharpton and all the different people involved in this. Fr. Blair and I continued to work together, and he continued to help me face my past and the struggles that it still brought up for me. Sarah and I also spent time together, and as we did, I more and more could not help but envision a future for the two of us together. My relationship with both became stronger as the time went on.

And then one day near the end of the month, Bill came knocking on my door late in the afternoon. I had been home continuing to work on making my house more of a home and was surprised to see him.

"What is it?" I asked him as I opened the door.

He didn't say anything, just walked into the house, holding an envelope in his hand.

"What's that?" I asked him even though I thought I knew.

"It's the response from the appellate court to our appeal," he answered me.

"That was fast," I replied to him. "Have you opened it?" I asked.

"No, I started to, but I don't know. I guess I wanted you to be here when I did," he answered me.

I looked at it and started to open it, but then I decided that I couldn't do it alone either. I decided that Fr. Blair should be here for it. Bill and I headed down to the church and interrupted him just as he was sitting down to eat dinner. "What is it?" he asked.

I told what had happened and handed him the envelope. The three of us looked at each other, each of us knowing an important truth. If this attempt failed, our mission here could very well be over. And there would be no one left to stop the sheriff. Fr. Blair tore open the envelope and pulled out the paper holding the decision. He read it over and then looked up at the two of us.

"Well?" I said questioningly and feeling impatient.

"We won," he said with an almost shocked tone in his voice.

The three of us looked around at each other, and no one seemed to know what to say. I was the first to smile. "We won," I said with a tone of celebration in my voice.

"We won," Fr. Blair repeated after me, also smiling.

The three of us looked at each other in celebration. We were all smiling and all happy.

"Now what?" Bill asked.

"Now we finish the church," Fr. Blair answered him. If we work together and move quickly, we can have it finished in time for Easter. "We'll start first thing in the morning."

"Sounds good to me," I answered him.

After that, we made plans to get started early in the morning, and then we left. Bill spent the night. He agreed to stay for a day or two to help and then came back as much as possible. I went to bed feeling very excited but nervous. Even though I was happy that we could start working on the church again, I was nervous about what was going to happen. Mostly, I was worried about how the sheriff would react. Whatever the appellate court had ruled, they were far away, and the sheriff was here. There was no one who would stand up to him, and I didn't know what we would do if he tried to interfere. But I just had faith and fell asleep.

CHAPTER 30

We got started early in the morning. Fr. Blair had managed to get some of the other parishioners together, and we started working again. Some of the other parishioners were worried about the sheriff, but Fr. Blair assured them that the courts were one our side, and there was nothing the sheriff could do about it. Privately, I wasn't so sure. I couldn't shake the feeling that something had to happen. I had gotten to know the sheriff well, and I knew that he wasn't just going to give in without a fight. But I just kept working and tried to have faith. I remembered the Bible verse about how if God was with us, who could be against us. Either way, I knew something had to happen.

I didn't have to wait long to find out what. Near the end of the morning, I saw the sheriff's patrol car pulling into the lot in front of the church. Another car was following close behind him. The sheriff parked and exited from his car. As he did, everyone, including myself and Fr. Blair, stopped working and watched him walk up. The driver of the other car also stopped and got out, and I realized it was the judge.

"What's going on here?" the sheriff asked. "I thought I shut this place down?" he continued.

"This is a church, Sheriff. We are here to do God's work, not yours, and you are not going to stand in our way," Fr. Blair answered him.

"I don't care whose work you're here to do. Last time I checked, a court had ordered this to stop," the sheriff replied. "Isn't that right,

Judge?" he asked, turning to the judge who, until now, had been standing behind the sheriff.

"Yes, that's right," the judge answered him. "I ordered that this construction to stop. Now you had all better go home, or I will have you all in jail," he continued.

"Actually, your honor, we don't have to go home," I answered him.

"And why not?" he asked me.

"Because of this," Fr. Blair answered him, taking the order from the appellate court out and handing it to him.

The judge looked over the order from the appellate court and stood there, stunned. And then, in a repeat of what he had done that day in court, he looked at the sheriff and then back at me, like he had absolutely no idea what to do.

"Well, what the hell is this?" the sheriff finally yelled at him after a minute.

"It's an order from the appellate court rescinding my order and saying that we have to let them build their church," the judge answered the sheriff without even looking up at him. Instead, he just stood there looking so timid that finally, I couldn't take it anymore and had to say something. "Why do you let this guy push you around so much?" I asked, motioning to the sheriff.

"Why don't you mind your own business, son?" the sheriff replied.

"This is my business," I answered him.

"Since when do you care so much about this church?" he asked me sarcastically.

"I have always cared about it. I just lost my way for a while. But thanks to this man and these people, I have found my way again. And a bully like you has no place getting in the way of God's work," I answered him, feeling truly inspired.

"Well, last time I checked, I was in charge of this town. I'm the law, and what I say goes. And there's nobody around who can stop me."

"What do you say about that, Judge?" I asked the judge who was still refusing to make eye contact with the sheriff, instead just looking at the ground. He again looked at me and then back at the sheriff, like he still had absolutely no idea what to do. Finally, after a minute, he just turned around, got in his car, and left.

"I don't need him," the sheriff said. "I say what goes around here, and this church sure as hell isn't going to happen."

He started to move closer, as though he were going to interfere with the building of the church. Without hesitation, I stepped up and blocked his way, almost surprised by how passionate I felt about stopping him.

"What do you think you're doing?" he asked me. "Get out of my way," he demanded.

I didn't say anything, just stood there. There weren't more than a few feet between us, and the sheriff stood there, looking shocked. Fr. Blair, Bill, and the rest of the parishioners all just stood there watching this standoff between me and the sheriff. It was like the first standoff we had in my house that day, with the sheriff standing there staring at me, gripping his gun in his holster. It occurred to me that this time, I didn't have a gun, and that scared me a little. But then, it occurred to me that maybe I had something even more powerful on my side—God. Thinking about that gave me a lot of peace.

I looked up at the sky and realized that for February, the day was almost perfect. It was unseasonably warm, and there wasn't a cloud in sight. I stared at the rays of sun shining down, and off in the distance, I saw a butterfly. It was just like the one I had seen before, the one that I knew was my wife coming to visit me. And as I watched, it flew away toward what I realized was the only exception to the perfect day. One small cloud that was very close to us and moving toward where the sheriff and I were standing. As I stared at it, I thought about the story from the Old Testament, how the Israelites followed a cloud out of the desert. And I suddenly had this feeling that I was finally coming out of this desert I had been in for so long now. Seemed strange to be having a breakthrough like that in that moment, but I just went with it.

"What are you staring at?" the sheriff asked, bringing me back to the situation at hand. He continued, "Whatever. I don't care what you say, I'm taking this place down, and I'll shoot anyone who gets in my way," he said, pulling his gun from his holster and started to move forward again.

But I refused to back down and just continued to stand there.

"If you don't get out of my way, I'm going to shoot you," the sheriff threatened again. And the look in his eyes told me he was dead serious. But I felt so inspired, I just refused to be intimidated, and I continued to stand there. I guess I must have inspired Fr. Blair because he stepped forward next to me and stood his ground too. And Bill wasn't far behind. The three of us stood there, almost like a little minitrinity. Slowly, the rest of the parishioners began to step forward and gather together behind us. In that moment, we weren't all separate but one. One group of Christians united for their cause and refusing to back down. Bill, Fr. Blair, and I stood there at the front of them.

The sheriff looked at the scene unfolding in front of him and started to back away, with a look of confusion on his face. For a second, I thought he was going to leave, but then he started to move forward toward us.

"The hell with you people. This place is coming down," he said.

I braced myself for a showdown, some sort of fight, and I truthfully didn't know what was going to happen next. And then suddenly, as the sheriff stepped toward us, a bolt of lightning suddenly shot down from the cloud, as if out of nowhere. The sheriff backed away fast, but the rest of us just stood there. After a second, the sheriff collected himself and started to move forward again. I knew the saying about lightning never striking twice, but apparently, someone up there didn't get the message because a second bolt of lightning came down and hit the exact same spot.

All of us, the sheriff included, just stood there with look of shock on our faces. Even Fr. Blair was stunned and didn't react. After a minute, the sheriff backed up, got in his car, and just drove away. He never turned his back on us and had the same look of shock on his face the entire time.

After he drove away, the rest of us looked around at each other. It seemed like no one knew quit what to say, but somehow all of us understood the power of what we had just experienced. And as we all looked at each other, I felt like we had just grown stronger as a faith community. Even though we were all different, and all had our different ways of viewing or practicing our faith, we were united in our one faith in one God. It was almost as though that burst of lightning was the sign we all needed that what we were doing was right, and important. Even if it seemed like a small gesture or that, in the grand scheme of things, what difference did one church make? Well, clearly it did make a difference, a difference to God. That lightning bolt showed me he was with us, and if he was with us, then, like the Bible said, no one could be against us.

"Well, what do we do now?" Bill finally asked with a tone that said well someone has to speak up.

"We continue working on the church. Easter is coming fast," Fr. Blair answered him with a smile.

"What if the sheriff comes back?" someone asks.

"I don't think he will," I answered. "But if he does, well, let's just hope there's lightning in the forecast."

Fr. Blair smiled, and we all got back to work. As we did, I looked around and smiled and started to feel like I truly had a community and a family again.

CHAPTER 31

Apparently, Bill hadn't gotten tired of beating my door down early in the morning the first time he did it because the next morning, he was doing it again. I ran downstairs and opened the door, figuring, after last time, this must be important. He was standing there with a look of concern on his face, like he was worried about what he had to say would cause a problem.

"What's going on?" I asked him.

"Your friend Bob, the detective, called me early this morning," he said, letting out a sigh.

"What did he want?" I asked, immediately interested in what he had to say. "Did he find out something about the sheriff?"

Bill didn't say anything, just continued to look at me. The look on his face wasn't giving me a good feeling.

"What did he want?" I asked again, this time sounding frustrated and with more angst in my voice.

"He found something, but you might not like it. Why don't we sit down?" he replied to me.

"I don't want to sit down. Tell me what it is," I replied to him, sounding more anxious.

Bill let out a sigh: "He found a wanted criminal by the name of Harry Gaglini."

Hearing that name immediately started to bring back memories. Memories of my family, memories of what happened to them, memories of the criminals I could never catch, and his underlings, who had no idea where he was. His escape had always been brilliant.

He never told anyone what his plan was and never told anyone where he was going. He just put his plan together, sold of most of his assets, garnered all the cash he could, and left. And no one could find him.

A plethora of people and agencies tried. Every local and state police department from Maine to Mexico and the entire alphabet soup of federal agencies scoured the country and world for him. He was one of the most wanted men in the world and even cracked the FBI's top ten. Never mind that his picture was all over every television, computer screen, newspaper, and phone screen in the country. But no matter what anyone did, he couldn't be found anywhere. Most of his underlings were in the wind too; some of them were arrested; some of them were still on the loose.

Now Bob had found his second-in-command. I didn't know how to take the news. Part of me was angry, but part of me was also hopeful—hopeful that maybe he would talk.

"Where is he?" I finally asked, returning to reality.

"He's at the state police station where we your friend works," he answered me.

I stared at Bill, frustrated. Frustrated with myself for not knowing what was going to happen next, or how I was going to handle this sudden change of events.

"What do you want to do?" Bill asked me.

"I don't know," I answered him. "Have you told Fr. Blair about this yet?" I asked.

"No, do you think we should?" he answered.

"Yes, absolutely," I answered him. I was past the point to questioning him, and to the point where I knew I needed his help.

We walked down to the rectory and interrupted him, just as he was getting dressed for the day. He came and answered the door, still buttoning his collar, and looking very surprised to see us. "What's going on?" he asked.

I told him everything Bill had told me and asked him what he thought I should do.

"Why don't we sit down and have some breakfast?" he answered with a smile.

Seeing him smile and offer to sit with me felt very comforting, and we sat down and had breakfast together. We talked openly about all the things that hearing about Ganglini's again made me feel and how we could handle it. I didn't feel compelled to keep anything from him, and we had a very intimate conversation. We talked a lot about me moving forward with my life and about learning forgiveness. At the end of it, I felt peaceful, despite what was happening, enough to ask Fr. Blair for a favor. "Will you go with me to see him?" I asked him. "I know that we are still trying to get all the work done here, but we can leave one of the parishioners in charge and go."

"Do you think that's a good idea?"

I sighed. "I need to see him. I'm not sure how to explain it to you, I just need to see him."

"Okay," Fr. Blair agreed.

Within a few hours, Fr. Blair, Bill, and I were in route to the police station to see him. Sarah was also along for the ride because I asked her to come. I just felt like I needed her support. We drove along mostly in silence. I was lost in thought about what was going to happen, and I thought everyone else was too. Suddenly, I noticed that we were almost to our exit coming up. I got off and headed for the state police barracks. I didn't know what to expect, but I had the feeling that my long journey was somehow finally coming to an end.

As we approached the barracks, I began to feel a sense of anxiety. My chest started to tighten, and I just had this anxious feeling in my stomach. I parked the car, turned it off, and just sat there in the driver's seat. I looked over at Fr. Blair, sitting next to me in the front seat. He smiled the same comforting smile at me. "You don't have to do this, you know," he said.

"I know," I answered him, "but somehow I feel like I need to."

"Well, you know that we are all with you, no matter what you decide," he said, looking around the car.

I looked around the car at him and then at Bill and Sarah in the back seat. I knew that they were my friends, and really my new family, and in that moment, there was a feeling of connection and intimacy that I hadn't felt in a long time. And I realized that it was only with their support and help that I had come so far and that I could go further. I looked at all of them and then got out of the car, and the four of us headed into the barracks.

We were greeted by Bob who let us in and led us to his office. We sat down, and he shut the door behind us and sat down behind his desk.

"So what did you find?" I asked him.

"They didn't tell you?" he asked, sounding surprised.

"No, they did," I answered him. "I was just wondering if there is anything else."

"Not much, honestly. I wish I could say it was skill or effort, but I found him almost by accident."

"How?" I asked him.

"I was looking into the story you told me about the current sheriff killing his brother, and I couldn't find much. But I did find some strange things in his bank records around the time that your family was killed. I followed the money backward, lost it a few times, eventually found a loan shark, and he said that he had paid the money on behalf of Ganglini. And when I asked him where he was, he actually knew. There was still a warrant out for him from what happened to you, so I went and arrested him for it. We are still holding him here."

"I don't understand. How did the sheriff's money lead you to a loan shark? Did he borrow it from him?" I asked.

"No, it appears that it was payment to the sheriff, and from what I'm gathering, it looks like the loan shark was a buffer for the sheriff and Ganglini."

"He paid the sheriff through this loan shark?" I asked, confused and trying to make sense of what this information meant.

"Yes, but the payments are all about five years old. I can't figure out is why he made them, or if it has anything to do with you," he answered me.

"Where is he?" I asked.

Bob looked at me and didn't say anything. I was sure he knew I wanted to try and question the guy myself. Anyone who had known me as a cop, especially as well as he did, would have known that I was hands-on and never hesitated to dive right in and get something done. But he also knew that getting sucked back into that world could have some very negative consequences for me.

"He's here as you have probably guessed, but what good will it do you to see him?" Bob asked me, clearly trying to talk me out of what he knew I was thinking.

"Maybe I can get him to talk," I answered him.

"I've tried every which way I can think of to get him to talk. He's smarter than that. He knows how the system works," Bob answered me.

I sat there and stared at him. I couldn't understand how it was that this had just landed in my lap. But I was sure that it was a chance I just couldn't pass up. So, without saying anything, I got up walked out of the office and down the hall toward where the interrogation rooms were. Everyone else followed behind me, calling after me, asking me what I was doing, but I ignored them. I still wanted justice for my family, and I didn't think an opportunity like that would present itself again.

I made my way to the room where he was being held and stood on the other side of the mirror looking at him. The rest of the group followed me in, no one saying a word.

"You can't do this," Bob finally said.

"I don't know how to explain this to you, but I have to," I answered him. "Maybe, just maybe, this guy has some kind of heart somewhere inside of him, and I can make an emotional appeal to him."

I heard the sound of my own words and knew how crazy, and unlikely, they sounded. Everybody else just looked at me, like they were waiting for someone to say that I was crazy, but no one said a word.

"Please, just let me try," I pleaded with Bob.

"This is not a good idea, but all right," he answered me with a sigh. I guessed he figured so far, he hadn't been able to get any information out of the man, so why not try something out of the ordinary. I walked over to the door and stood there for a minute. It had been a long time since I had been in an interrogation room or questioned a suspect about anything. I let out a breath, opened the door, and walked in.

Ganglini was staring into the mirror.

"I told you I have nothing to…" he stopped talking abruptly when he turned and realized I had just walked in. I guessed he was expecting Bob. "Who are you?" he asked, looking confused.

"You don't recognize me?" I responded to him.

He stared at me for a minute, and then his eyes widened. "I thought you quit?" he asked me.

"I did, but I heard you didn't want to talk," I answered him almost sarcastically.

"Well, seeing you sure doesn't make me want to talk," he replied.

"Well, that's not new, you didn't want to talk to me years ago, why should now be any different? I mean, after all, you have your boss behind you, your second-in-command of a criminal empire, and the law has nothing on you, so you don't have to run," I answered him sarcastically.

He looked at me confused.

"Oh, that's right," I continued. "Your boss abandoned you, you have nothing, and you're on the run constantly."

"Wow, I haven't heard that sarcastic remark since your pal in there arrested me a few days ago," he answered me. "Your buddies have already tried every trick in the book to make me talk, and nothing is working, so you may as well go back to wherever you were hiding."

I stood there for a second, unsure of what to do but trying not to feel daunted. "Well, then, I guess we'll just have to charge you for all of your boss's crimes and let you take the fall," I told him.

"Do you guys rehearse all these lines together because you all say the same thing?" he answered me, still cocky and sarcastic. I could see that this was going to be harder than I had thought.

I tried to think of something original to say to him, but nothing was coming to mind. I thought about all the criminals I had interrogated over the course of my career, but now nothing was working. So I said a little silent prayer for help. I needed some divine inspiration to overcome this hurdle.

"Maybe there's some reward in it for you," I finally tried.

"What reward?" he questioned.

"There was a big reward out for your boss's capture. You help find him, maybe you get it," I said. I was probably more surprised to hear myself say it than he was.

"What reward?" he asked again.

"It doesn't matter. You have nothing to tell me," I answered him and started heading for the door.

He didn't say anything, just looked at me, smirked, and started to laugh. When I asked him what was so funny, he just kept laughing. "Do you people know why you never found him? You were looking all over the country and the world, and all the while he was fifty miles from here. But you couldn't get him."

"What are you talking about?"

"It was always the most brilliant part of his plan. No one was supposed to know, but I figured it out when the loan shark told me where he was sending the money."

"And where was that?" I asked. As I did, I started to have the feeling something big was coming, but I had no idea what.

"To some sheriff he was paying to hide him," he answered with a proud smile. "It was brilliant. He knew he would have to lay low for a long time, and he knew no one would ever suspect another cop of hiding him."

Bob walked into the room and looked at me and then back at him. We both knew what was coming, but even though I was stunned, I had to ask, "What was the name of this sheriff?"

"Sheriff Frank Marhave of Rocky Hills PA, a small mountain town where no one would look if the sheriff told them they didn't have to," he answered me.

I sat back on my chair, stunned. I looked over at Bob who looked equally stunned as well as appalled. Ganglini just sat there with a look on his face like "yep, just said that." I got up and walked out of the room. Outside, the faces of Fr. Blair, Sarah, and Bill were all stunned. Clearly, no one knew what to do next. I looked at them and then back at Bob. I was a cornucopia of emotions.

I closed my eyes for a minute and tried to ignore the world around me and become aware of my feelings. What I was experiencing, and how I could best address it. And in that flurry of emotions,

I realized I felt a ping of hope. Like, somehow, what this man had just told me about a fellow cop, albeit a corrupt and inefficient one, hiding the killer of my family was somehow good news.

"Maybe this is just the breakthrough we needed," I said out loud, not realizing I had done it.

Everyone just looked at me like I was crazy.

"How is this a breakthrough?" Bill asked, confused.

"Because maybe, we finally have something on the sheriff," I answered him.

"Yes, maybe you're right," Fr. Blair answered me, sounding hopeful.

"Even if that's true, what are we going to do, take him back to town with us and have him testify before the town council?" Bill asked. "The sheriff would never let us within miles of them with this guy in tow. He would just arrest him and send him back, and there would be nothing we could do to stop it."

"He would have to if the council told him to. Otherwise, it would look like he has something to hide," I answered.

"He has plenty to hide, we all know that, and they know it too," Bill replied to me. "But either way, they are all beholden to him, one way or another. They will do whatever he says."

"We would somehow have to convince them that something is more important or worth more," Sara added.

"What," Bill remarked, "I mean the only thing that might convince them is if you told them who you are and why they should remove the sheriff from power." Clearly, he meant that remark sarcastically, but it actually got me thinking. What if I did do that? Could I do that? I had never told my story to anyone before, except for Fr. Blair. To get up and tell it in front of the entire town council would be hard. I closed my eyes and tried to feel my own strength. I tried to feel whether or not I had enough strength to face this demon, enough to finally start to acknowledge to the world and others around me the feelings and experiences I had because of this tragedy. I had only recently begun to face them myself.

"Do you think you can do that?" Fr. Blair asked me, snapping me back to the situation at hand.

"Maybe," I answered him. "I can't do it alone, but with the help of everyone here, and above all with God's help, maybe I can."

"Well, then, we will pray for that strength," Fr. Blair answered. "And you know that all of us here are behind you."

"Yes, I know," I answered him. "And thank you."

"Wait, what did we just decide here?" Bill asked, sounding confused.

"I think we decided to take this guy and bring him back to testify before the Rocky Hills Town Council about the level of corruption of their sheriff," I answered him.

Bob suddenly got this confused look on his face. "What did he say the name of that town where you live is?' he asked.

"Rocky Hills," I answered him, not sure why he looked so confused.

"How did you wind up there?" he asked me.

"I don't know," I answered him. "At some point, I read about it," I answered him, but my voice started to trail off as I began to realize where he was going. I began to remember something I hadn't remembered in a long time.

"Wait," I finally said, "there was a report in the days after what happened, a report that Fearhand had been seen near there, but the sheriff had checked it out, and not found anything."

My voice became very serious as I finished saying that. I remembered reading the name of the town. Later, after the funerals, when I decided to leave, I went back and looked it up. It seemed like the perfect place to hide from my problems. So I went there, found my house for sale, bought it, and moved all my things there. And as I looked back on it, a part of me thought it seemed like a cruel coincidence, but another part of me also felt like it was a divine coincidence. Like if I hadn't wound up there, I wouldn't be able to take part in helping Fr. Blair and the church the way I was. I guessed my face gave away what I was thinking because Fr. Blair looked at me and simply said, "The Lord works in mysterious ways."

"Yes, he does," I answered him, understanding what he meant, but still struggling some to accept it.

"What about him?" Bill asked, pointing to Ganglini.

"There's one more thing I want from him," I answered.

"What?" Bill asked.

"The location of Fearhand," I answered him. "He knows, and I'm going to get it out of him."

The rest of them just looked at me; clearly, they didn't think it was a good idea. But in my heart, I felt like maybe this was my shot. This was my chance to get justice for my family. There was a difference between revenge and justice, I always knew that, and now I was going to look for justice. I turned around, opened the door, and walked back into the interrogation room, not sure what I was really walking into.

When I walked back in, he was still sitting there with that same "yep, just said that" look on his face. I stared at it for a minute, not sure how to feel. Part of me was angry at him for being so smug, but another part of me felt sorry for him. His life was a life of crime. He didn't have anything or anyone. He was always on the run, and now he was caught and would have to answer for his crimes. But above all else, I felt sorry for him because he lacked any faith in his life. And I knew that I wouldn't want to be him when my judgement day came.

"What do you want now?" he asked.

"You feel guilty," I said suddenly, almost involuntarily. It had just popped into my head, and I went with it. I figured it was divinely inspired.

"Guilty about what?" he asked, although his face said something different.

"Guilty that you played a role in what happened," I answered him. "As evil as you are, even you are above killing an innocent woman and children. You feel remorse for what your boss did and the role you played in it."

He didn't say a word, just looked at me, but the look on his face spoke volumes.

"I swear I didn't know what he was planning to do," he finally said. "I didn't figure it out until afterward. None of us did. We all knew our boss was ruthless, and we probably wouldn't have cared if he had killed you, but not your family. But there was no time for that. We all had to be on the run. The day the news broke, I didn't have time to grab anything. I just took some cash and jumped in my car. I knew that they were going to come for me and for all of us. And as for our boss, he was nowhere to be found.

"I think we all felt betrayed by him. I heard later that he had packed up all of his stuff and left. I knew he had been pushing hard for us to sell off everything, and he hadn't been paying us, either, but I never knew why. After the story broke, I figured out why he'd been acting that way, but by then, there was no time for anything. I had to be on the run. I almost got caught a few times but managed to elude them. Until your pal here came along."

"Do you know where your boss is now?" I asked him. I wasn't interested in him filling in the blanks of what happened.

"Last time I saw him was the afternoon of the day your family was killed. He had a meeting of his top bosses and collected all of the cash we had made. Usually, he let us keep our pay, but he told us to hand it all over. We had hardly any product left because he had told us to sell it all off."

"How much did you give him?" I asked.

"In total, he hoarded together a little over two million dollars. What I didn't know then was that was his getaway money. Like I said, by the time any of us figured it out, we were all on the run."

"Did your boss ever tell you what he was planning to do?" I asked, even though he had sworn no already.

"No, I told you that," he answered. "He just sold off everything he could, collected all his money, and left."

"Maybe he didn't tell you directly, but I will bet you know, even if you don't realize it," I pressed him.

"The only thing he ever said was that he was going to lay low in the small town for a while and then retreat farther into the mountains. Eventually, he would reemerge once the heat died down. He did ask me one final thing—to pay the loan shark the money. He gave me all of it, plus some for me to keep. But he never said where he was going or what he was going to do.

"The truth is you really got to him. Despite everyone who had ever come after him, you were the only one that really managed to get under his skin. You had him, and we all knew it. And as ruthless as he was, I'm sure he wanted to get back at you for causing him so much trouble. That, I always thought, was his true motivation: revenge. But I swear I didn't know what he was going to do until after he had done it."

I didn't say anything else, just looked at the criminal in front of me. He seemed different than he had earlier. He wasn't arrogant anymore; he just looked guilty and sad. I didn't say anything else to him; instead, I just left the room, needing to talk to Bob.

"We have to get him to help us. We have to bring him back to tell the town council what he saw. It will force them to fire the sheriff."

We tried to work out a plan. Bob agreed to talk to his supervisors and try to get him a deal to testify. Meantime, we had to go and see Dr. Sharpton too. I wanted her to come back with us too. I knew, between her and Ganglini, there would be enough evidence to force the council's hand. If we made it public, they would have no choice but to call for a vote of no-confidence in the sheriff, and then we could try and get him kicked out of office. And Bob also started the process to get a search party sent into the mountains to hunt for Fearhand, with Ganglini as a guide. When he told them what it involved, it didn't take long to get things in motion.

By the end of the day, a lot was happening, and I was starting to feel excited but also sad and scared. Sad at the memories of my past and scared at the prospect of facing them. The four of us decided to stay the night, and we went and checked it at a local motel. After we had checked in and had dinner, I went back to my room and was standing outside of my balcony for a while just looking out at the last remnants of the day's light as night began to fall. I thought about all that had transpired in my life since last Easter and how much different it would be this Easter. Was I really ready to move forward into a new life, a life free of this pain?

My thoughts were interrupted by Sarah coming out of her room and coming up next to me. "What's wrong?" she asked me.

"Just thinking about everything that's happened and what's going to happen," I answered here. "I'm scared," I admitted to her; the first time I had really admitted that to anyone.

She reached out and touched my hand and hugged me. "Don't worry," she answered me. "It will be okay. We are all here for you, and we are all in this together."

Feeling her embrace brought me comfort, and at that, I said goodnight and went to sleep, preparing myself for the events that lay ahead of me.

CHAPTER 32

"Don't do it," the voice called to me from somewhere. "You're better than this, you have come so far, don't give up now," another one shouted.

I knew the voices, but even though I did, I didn't know if I should listen. Instead, I just stared in front of me, a weapon in my hand. How I got here, I had no idea. I just stared at the face in front of me, totally frozen, not knowing what to do. There was a gun in my hand, and he was just staring at me helpless, and I was just staring back at him. The voices were urging me not to do it, but something inside me was screaming. This was my chance at revenge. I stood there, frozen, sweating with fear. I didn't know which path to take.

Suddenly, I woke up. I sat up and looked around forgetting for a second where I was. I rolled over and got out of bed. I turned over the dream in my head, trying to make sense of it. I didn't know who the face was, or who was yelling to me, or any of it. I walked out onto the balcony and looked up at the night sky. I looked at all the stars and thought about how I had always been fascinated by how many there were, even as a child. I smiled when I remembered I had wanted to be an astronaut when I was very little. And again, I thought about the passage in the Bible where God tells Abraham he will make his descendants more numerous than the stars in the sky.

Thinking about that gave me some peace. But I was still very troubled by my dream and what it meant. Again, I remembered the theme in the Bible of dream interpretation and how it occurs many times. Dreams had always been confusing to me. It seemed like they were always a bunch of things jumbled together that didn't make much sense. I said a quiet prayer for help in interpreting my dreams and then went back to bed. Much was going to happen, and I needed to rest.

In the morning, I talked about my dream over breakfast. The four of us discussed it, but weren't really sure what to make of it. In the end, we agreed on the path of praying for help in interpreting it. It seemed the be the best path. My dream was confusing, and as our day went on, I was constantly turning it over in the back of my mind. There wasn't much else to do. The four of us set out to find Dr. Sharpton. We made arrangements with Bob to contact him once we had found her and were headed back to town. He was going to lead a search party into the mountains not far from Rocky Hills to look for Fearhand.

It wasn't a far drive to the doctor's office, and we arrived there in the midafternoon. I parked the car and looked at the office, wondering if I was going to do this and what the ripple effect could be. After about a minute, I decided to just walk inside and see what happened, not waste time sitting there contemplating it. We walked inside, and she was sitting there waiting for us.

"I had a feeling you were coming," she said. "I had a hint when that police lieutenant called me."

"Does this mean you have decided to come back with us?" I asked her.

"I have spent my life trying to help others," she answered me. "I became a doctor in a time when many women were not doctors because I believed I could do good. And after all these years, one day someone comes along and tells me that, inadvertently, I helped a murderer get away with what he did. And now I have the chance to right that wrong. If I don't go with you and undo what I have done, I don't know that I could live with myself. So, yes, I am going with you."

The four of us just looked at her. Here was another victim of this tragedy that had brought us all together: the killing of a man by his own brother. In that moment, it became the five of us, as we added Dr. Sharpton to the list of people the sheriff had hurt. And the list of people now out to bring him to justice, the list of people strong enough and brave enough to stand up to him, despite his powerful position. Or, just maybe, because of it. Once again, I was reminded of the early church, and really Christians throughout the centuries who, time and again, had stood up to those vastly more powerful than them. And how the early church started out so small, just twelve apostles and other disciples, who stood up to the might of the Roman Empire and started a movement that became bigger than any of them could have ever imagined.

We headed to the car and set off for Rocky Hills. As we set off, no one said a word. We all had a look on our face like we were each lost in thought. We drove along for a while, and I was not sure why, but I was eager to break the silence.

"Did you say you had plans to go to school for psychology?" I finally asked Fr. Blair. I wasn't sure why I asked; it had just popped into my head.

"Yes, before I chose to go to the seminary," he answered me.

"What made you want to be a therapist?" I asked. As I did, I looked in the rearview mirror and saw Bill glancing at me with a sad look on his face.

"It was Bill's father, actually," Fr. Blair answered me after a minute.

"Bill's father?" I asked, confused.

"He was a psychologist," Bill answered me in a low, sad-sounding voice.

I knew from what Bill had told me before that his father was dead, but I had never really thought much about it before.

"He died a few months before the sheriff's brother did," Bill continued. "He used to have a practice in town. It was never much, but folks would come to him for help and advice with whatever problems they were having. He was a help to a lot people."

"What happened to him?" I asked.

"He went to sleep one night and didn't wake up. Natural causes. They called it stress," Bill answered me, sounding angry.

I got the sense that there was more to the story, and I couldn't resist asking about it. And for the first time, I realized that Bill was only about forty years old. It occurred to me that he must have been young when his father died.

"Is that all?" I asked, not sure how to express my curiosity.

"No," Bill answered me with a sigh. "When he died, I just graduated from law school and passed the bar. Like I told you the day that we met, I never liked it around town much, and as soon as I graduated high school, I left. We didn't see much of each other during those following years because of the distance. It's not that we were separated because of some fight, but there was a sense of disagreement between us. He accepted my choices and let me live my life, helped me in every way he could, but I always knew that there was this unspoken understanding that he wished I would move back home. Even talked once about clearing out space in his office for me to open one. But I never wanted to come back here.

"After he died, I had to go through all his things, settle all his business, sell his house, that sort of thing. I was still hanging around town when everything happened with Fr. Blair's fiancé and mother and then with the sheriff's brother. So there we were, two young men all alone in the world. And I left and never looked back. Guess I was afraid of turning into a pillar of salt," he concluded with a smirk.

"And you never came back?" I asked him.

"Not until the day I showed up in the courtroom out of nowhere," he answered me.

"How did that happen?" I asked, realizing that I had never really thought about that either.

"I read about the case online. It appeared in the Rocky Hills paper, and one of the bigger papers shared it on their website. The editor is like everyone else, scared of the sheriff. So, of course, the story read like he was the victim of a mob hit or something, but I knew better. And I knew who you were. Most people have heard of you at some point. So I saw a chance to stick it to the sheriff, and a chance to help someone else willing to stand up to him. So I told one of my associates to look after the office, packed up some clothes, and headed for Rocky Hills. I had no idea it would turn into all of this."

"What was your father's name?" I asked Pricley.

"Bob Pricley, Dr. Bob Pricley, licensed psychologist. Not that he ever used it to get out of that small town. I never understood that until his funeral. So many people who came were his former patients. They told how talking to him and working with him had helped them so much and all that. He helped with everything from marriage counseling to psychological trauma, and there were so many grateful people. And he helped me too, even if I couldn't see it at the time."

"Your father loved you, Bill, you know that. He was always proud of you for becoming a lawyer. He knew you would do good and help others."

"I know that," he answered. "I don't regret the choices I made. I just wish I had gone about it differently."

"Have faith, Bill, you're here now when you're greatly needed. Your father would be very proud of you for standing up to a bully like this," Fr. Blair answered him.

"Yeah, this group needs a good lawyer, but without one around, I guess we can settle for you," I said with a smirk. Bill smiled and so did everyone else, and it helped to lighten the mood some.

We drove the rest of the way back to Rocky Hills in silence, arriving just after dark. I looked at the clock and realized that just after dark was now pushing six-thirty in the evening. Slowly, the days were getting longer, and I remembered that Easter would be coming up soon and that we needed to have the church ready. I then headed toward the church to drop Fr. Blair off. As we parked, I looked at the church and thought about the days getting longer. I thought about how much had happened in my life over the past year and how I had slowly begun to feel better and to make peace with my past. Like the days growing longer, it felt like my dark winter was beginning to end. The three of us got out, and Bill and I helped Fr. Blair bring his things inside.

"Would you like to stay and have something to eat?" Fr. Blair invited us.

"What's for dinner?" Bill asked.

"What are you cooking?" Father replied with a smile.

"If I'm cooking, you better give everyone confession and last rites now, just in case," Bill answered him with a smile.

We all laughed.

"How about if I cook something? I'm not so bad at it?" Fr. Blair answered.

"Sounds good to me," Bill answered him, and we all agreed.

We all pitched in, and within about an hour had a good meal cooked up and ready to eat. We sat around the table eating and talking about all that had happened and what we thought would happen going forward. It was clear now that we were going after the sheriff. We talked about what to do and when. We talked about getting all of the evidence together and appearing before the town council. We agreed that we would do so at the next monthly meeting. Until then, we agreed that Dr. Sharpton could stay at the rectory with Fr. Blair, who had an extra room. And also that we had to be careful the sheriff did not see her; otherwise, he would send her packing.

"So this is it, we are really going to do this? After all this time of talking about it, it's actually going to happen?" Bill asked with a combination of excitement and nervousness in his voice. I think his feelings echoed how we all felt.

"Yes, we are really going to do this, and may God be with us," Fr. Blair answered him.

For what seemed like the thousandth time, I was amazed at the faith of this man and his ability to speak softly and make me, and I think all of us, feel safe. At that, I left the rectory, drove Sarah home, and then headed home myself. I went inside and sat down on my couch, going over everything that was happening in my head. And I wasn't sure what to do going forward, and I knew that I was nervous. But I decided to just keep moving along and keep having faith that even if I didn't know where this movement was going, we had to keep moving. At that, I went to bed, trying to put off today's evil as sufficient and put faith in tomorrow.

CHAPTER 33

I woke up in a cold sweat and breathing heavily. I looked at the clock; it was just past 3:00 a.m. I had the dream again, and this time, it was even more real. This time, I had raised my weapon and was pointing it. My hand was resting on the trigger, and I was millisecond away from pulling it. I rolled over and sat on the edge of my bed, once again trying to make sense of this dream. I still didn't know who I was pointing the gun at or why I wanted to shoot them. I got out of bed and went and looked out my window. I looked down at the rectory and was tempted to go down there right then. It occurred to me that Fr. Blair probably would talk to me if I went down there and woke him up; that's just how giving he was. But I didn't want to put him through that.

Suddenly, the phone started ringing. I ran over to get it, wondering why someone was calling me at 3:00 a.m. I had finally bothered to set up phone service in my house, and now my first call was someone at 3:00 a.m. Seemed a little humorous. I answered it and was pleasantly surprised to hear Sarah's voice on the other end.

"Everything okay?" I asked her, concerned.

"Yes, everything is fine," she answered. "I was just thinking about you, and I don't know, I had a feeling you needed someone to talk to."

"Well, you were right about that," I answered her, smiling. It gave me a warm feeling in my heart to know that she felt that way and was thinking about me. We talked for a while about my dream and about the two of us and what we thought would happen after we went up against the sheriff. It was true that neither of us knew what to expect, and I knew that I was scared but knowing that she was behind me gave me some hope.

After we hung up, I fell back asleep feeling a little more at peace, despite all the things rolling around in my head and in my heart. And before I fell asleep, I said a quiet prayer of thanks to God for bringing her into my life. I knew that she was the best thing that happened to me in a long time, and I knew that after all of this was over, I wanted the two of us to settle down together. And then, I realized the power of that thought: when all this is over. As if I could finally truly see a light at the end of this tunnel.

In the morning, I woke up early, got dressed, ate breakfast, and headed straight down to the church. I wanted to talk to Fr. Blair about what my dreams might mean, but more importantly, I wanted to get back to working the church. It still needed a lot of work, and Easter was drawing closer every day. As I arrived, Fr. Blair was already working on something. It was the same project I had seen him working on before, only now it was starting to take shape, and I could see that it was a cross. He was making it out of wood entirely by hand.

"I didn't know you knew how to woodwork?" I asked him.

"My grandfather taught me," he answered. "He was a furniture maker before he retired. After my father died, he went back to work for the man he had sold his business to, but he wasn't as young as he used to be," Fr. Blair paused when he said that. I remembered him telling me the story of how his grandfather had gone back to work to support him and his mother after his father died.

"Was he your father's father or your mother's father?" I asked him.

"He was my father's father," he answered me, "my paternal grandfather." He continued, "My mother's father died during the Second World War, and her mother raised her largely alone. She passed away while my mother was still pregnant with me. That was part of the connection that my parents had: both of their fathers had served in WWII, as had many people's fathers at that time."

"What was your grandmother's name?" I asked him. I wasn't sure why I asked.

"Both of them were named Mary," he answered me.

I was stunned by his answer. "Mine were too," I answered him.

"How about that?" he said with a smile. "The Lord really does work in mysterious ways."

"Tell me about it," I answered him with a smile.

"Are the two of you just going to sit there, and are you actually going to get some work done?" Bill asked, walking up, smirking.

"We were saving it all for you," I answered him with a smile.

And so the three of us began working. Fr. Blair was working on the floor of the church, seeing as he was a woodworker, and it was wooden floor. I was working on the roof, and Bill was busy trying to make a list of supplies we were still going to need and jobs that still needed to be done.

"I'm supervising," he joked.

As the morning went on, more and more parishioners arrived, and our work began to finish quicker. Sarah came too, and I taught her a little bit about roofing. As the day went on, we got a lot of work done, and then after it started to get dark, Fr. Blair sent everyone home.

Our days went on like that for the next few weeks. Each day, we would all work, except Sundays, of course, and slowly the church really began to come together. Fr. Blair finished the floor; I finished the roof, both with plenty of help from the other parishioners. Meanwhile, Bill pitched in wherever he was needed, but mostly, he spent his time going back-and-forth to pick up supplies from every place on the map.

"Guess, we needed a mule more than a lawyer," I teased him.

"I may be a mule, but I'm still better looking than you," he would shoot back, and we would laugh. We really were starting to become close friends.

We put in the windows, including a nice large one behind the altar, all of them stain-glassed. Even carved out a nice niche for that Mary statue that had been delivered that first day I ever helped work on the church. The windows were not the nicest windows in the world, but they did the job. And everyone donated and made a small sacrifice for it. That was what put real value into the windows and into the church. We all had to give up something, be it money or time or in most cases both, but by each of us sacrificing something small, we all as a community gained something large. And in a way, that seemed to me what Christianity was all about. We each give up something small, and together we all got something big.

After a few months, the church was almost done, and there was only one big job left to complete. We needed to hang up Fr. Blair's cross right over the altar. It really was a beautiful cross he had made, and I was impressed at his craftmanship. Bill, knowing that I was also interested in woodworking, joked that after the church was finished, we would have a competition to see who was better.

"Maybe we will build a whole new church again," Fr. Blair teased him.

"Yeah, we can turn it into a business. We each build a church for a parish that needs one, and whosesoever they like better gets the pay." And after that, Blair, Pricley, and Brado Church Builders Inc. was in business, jokingly of course.

It took a lot of effort most of the day, but we were able to get the cross hoisted into place. As we came down from the ladders, we all stood at the foot of the altar and looked up at it. And it looked beautiful. I looked around at the altar and at the pews in the church. They would still need some work, but really, I felt that by hoisting the cross into place, we had put the finishing touches on the church. I thought about my analogy of comparing myself to the church, and I knew that just like the church was almost complete, so was my journey.

After the church was complete and everyone else left, the five of us sat down to dinner in the rectory to talk about going before the town council. Their next meeting was that coming week, and we knew it was going to be our only shot to get them to act. We had to corner them at a public meeting where it would be harder for them to hide. The sheriff may have had them in his pocket, along with the judge, but that didn't mean he had everyone in town in his pocket. And if we could get enough of them to witness what we had to say and to make noise, then maybe we could get the council to stand up and act.

We talked until late into the night until we were all too tired to talk anymore, and on the verge of falling asleep. And I was reminded some of the story of the apostles falling asleep at the entrance to the garden of Gethsemane. And I thought about how that night was just the beginning of so much that was to happen. And I wondered if this night was the beginning of something very big too.

I headed home and went to sleep, thinking about all of that. But it was hard to focus on while I was tossing and turning, wondering if I was going to have my reoccurring dream again. I went on that way for over an hour, picturing it in my head and hoping I didn't have to struggle through it. Finally, I got out of bed, knelt down, and said a small prayer for a peaceful night's sleep. I looked up at the wall above my bed and realized that there was no cross there. I resolved to get one, finished my prayer, and crawled into bed and fell asleep.

The next thing I knew, it was morning, and once again, the phone was ringing. I was thinking about going back to not having a phone since it only ever seemed to ring in the middle of the night. I looked at the clock and saw it was just after six in the morning. I picked up the phone, still half asleep, and was greeted by the voice of Bob on the other end. At first, I couldn't comprehend what he was saying, but when I did, I shot up as fast as ever.

"We sighted him, and we're closing in. He got away, but we're right on his trail."

Bob's words activated a force in me I hadn't felt in a long time—the hunt for a criminal on the run. It was something I had experienced many times as a cop and detective. And I even caught a few of them too. But this time was different. Not only was this man the criminal who killed my family, but he was also the one man I could never catch. And now, I had the chance to undo that. The chance to right that wrong.

"I'm coming to help you search," I replied to Bob.

"No, you are not," he answered me firmly. "I didn't call you to invite you to help search. I called to warn you that he might be headed toward your town and that you could be in danger. I already called that priest friend of yours. He should be at your house any second."

It was like he was in the room with me because no sooner had he said that, then Fr. Blair was knocking on my door.

"Bob, you have to let me help you find him," I said, half-pleading, half-announcing my intention to do it, no matter what he said.

"No, if you get involved, it can taint everything. Don't worry, just trust me, we will get him. He won't escape justice this time."

I heard someone calling him in the background, but couldn't hear what they were saying.

"I have to go," Bob said and hung up the phone.

I turned his words over in my head and tried to figure out my next move. But it really wasn't any contest. I couldn't resist the urge to go after this man. I quickly got dressed. I unlocked a chest I kept in my room and took out a pistol and holster, along with a shotgun. I holstered the pistol and carried the shotgun in my hand. I headed to the door and opened it to find Fr. Blair still standing there, knocking.

"What are you doing?" he asked me as if he didn't know.

"I'm going to find him," I answered, a determination in my voice.

"And what are you going to do then?" Father asked me.

"I guess I'll figure that out when I find him," I answered him.

I started for the door, but he stood in my way. "Don't do this," he pleaded with me. "What about everything we talked about, about forgiveness, about moving on? What about Sarah and the church and all of it? Do you want to throw away what you have gained just to gain some brief euphoria of revenge?"

Somewhere inside of me, I marveled at the wisdom of his words, and I knew that he was right. But in the moment, all I could think about was revenge. Nothing else mattered. But he was still standing in my way, blocking me from leaving.

"I'm not going to let you do this," he said to me.

I didn't even bother replying, just grabbed him and pushed him out of my way. And before he could react, I was out the door. I headed off toward the woods that led to the outskirts of the town and the mountains surrounding it. I figured that's where he would be, and that if he was headed toward town, then maybe I could cut him off. As I set out, I wondered what Fr. Blair had done after I left.

It occurred to me that he might be coming after me, but I wasn't concerned about that. I just wanted to find him and hunt him down.

I spent most of the day wandering through the woods looking for any sign, but couldn't find anything. I spent a lot of my time avoiding the police and troopers looking because I knew they would just send me home. As it was starting to get dark, I didn't know what to do. I was all alone out there, and I was totally unsure of where to go next. It was kind of like my life: I was all alone in the woods, and no one was there to help me. And that included God. So I started yelling, yelling at the sky, yelling at the trees, yelling at God. Yelling about what was happening and how he couldn't give me a break or just let me have a little revenge—that was all I really wanted. Simple revenge.

I started to head out of the woods when I came across a small dirt road. And then I heard the sound of footsteps. I got down and hid in some bushes, weapon at the ready.

"Where is he?" I heard a voice ask.

"I don't know, but we have been out here all day, and if we don't head back soon, we're going to wind up stuck out here all night," another responded.

I recognized the voices as those of Fr. Blair and Bill. I lowered my weapon and stayed in the bush hoping that they wouldn't see me. Then I looked and realized that Bob was also with them.

"I hope he's happy," I heard Bob saying. "Instead of being out there leading my team looking for this guy, I'm stuck here looking for him," he said in reference to me.

I felt a little guilty when I heard him say that. For a minute, it occurred to me that I really was making life harder on him. He had put a lot of things on hold to help me, someone whom he hadn't seen in years. And because of his work, justice was now closer than ever. I let out a sigh and regretted it the second I did. I knew Bob, knew his training, and how good of a cop he really was. I knew he had heard it and was heading over toward me that very second.

And I was right. No quicker did I sigh and put my head back up than he was standing over me pistol at the ready. A look of recognition came over his face, and I knew that he had realized it was me but that still didn't seem to make him lower his gun.

"Are you going to put that thing down?" I asked him.

"Maybe," he replied, sounding angry, "or maybe I'll shoot you for all the trouble you have caused me."

"Shoot me in the face. I can't get any uglier anyway," I answered him.

"This isn't a joke," he answered me.

"You don't have to tell me that. Now why don't you lower your weapon and start looking for an actual criminal," I answered him, half-sarcastic, half-angry that he was still pointing a weapon at me.

He lowered his weapon, and I got up out of the bushes. The rain was still falling, and we all stood there staring at each other, wet and getting rained on.

"I'm glad we found you," Fr. Blair said. "Don't do this, come back with us, trust your friend. He will get justice for you. But this is not the answer."

For a second, I thought about taking his advice and giving up, but that feeling quickly subsided when I heard a branch break about one hundred feet behind us. I turned around just in time to see his face. It was the first time I had seen it up close in a five years, but I knew I could never forget it. We made eye contact, and the look on his face said that he was shocked to see me. He turned back around and ran. I grabbed my shotgun and aimed right for his head. I probably would have hit him too if Fr. Blair hadn't grabbed me and thrown off my aim. My shot hit a branch, and it fell to the ground with a loud thud. I instinctively hit the ground to avoid the branch, and each of us got thrown in a different direction.

I jumped back up without even grabbing my shotgun, which had gotten knocked away. I jumped over the branch and ran after him, pistol at my side. I ran as fast as I could sloshing through the muddy ground, a result of the rain. The rain began to increase until it was a total downpour, but that wasn't nearly as fast as my heartbeat, which was about to pound right out of my chest. I was breathing heavily and moving fast, keeping him in constant sight. As I ran the memories of doing this many times in my past, often with Bob, began to come back to me.

Our chase went on for about half a mile, and I expected to get tired, but something in me just kept me going, and I just kept running. And so did he. Suddenly, he turned and fired at me. It hadn't even occurred to me he might be armed when I ran after him. I ducked behind a tree, avoiding his shots and pulled my pistol and fired a few of my own. But it was raining and getting dark, and I couldn't see very well. I missed him, and he started running again, and so did I. Out of the corner of my eye, I saw a flash of lightning and heard a loud burst of thunder. It was as though heaven itself was holding its breath, waiting to see how this would play out.

I chased him to the entrance of an old abandoned cabin and watched him run in. He shut the door behind himself. I raised my weapon and kicked in the door, angrier than ever, and determined to get him, dead or alive. I searched through the house room by room, but couldn't find him. Suddenly, I saw him run behind me and toward the door. I turned and fired a shot, hitting him. He fell to the floor and crawled into the nearest room. I followed him in, and as I did, he turned and looked at me. He was down on his knees and barely holding himself up. It was obvious he was wounded badly.

As I stared at him, I had no idea what to do. I noticed he had this look of helplessness on his face. A look that said "please, don't kill me." The irony of the moment was overwhelming. Here was this man who had towered over so many people, and now here he was on his knees begging. And suddenly, I realized what this scene was. It was the scene I kept seeing in my dreams. And now I realized when I looked back that he was the one I had been seeing in front of me all along. I stared at him, holding the gun, totally unsure of what to do. Just like in my dreams. It was clear now that I was going to write the end of my dream, but I didn't know what that end would be. Part of me said to kill him, and if it had been a year earlier, I probably would have done just that and never given it a second thought. But now, something else was present: an urge to forgive.

"Well, what are you waiting for?" he yelled at me.

I stared at him, totally frozen, not knowing what to do. Part of me was screaming for revenge. But still that new part of me, the part that had come so far over the past year, didn't want to lose everything I had gained. And there, I stood on a crossroads, my old life versus my new one. Which one would I choose?

I heard the door to the cabin open, and I heard Bob calling out my name. He came down the hall and stood at the door to the room, weapon drawn.

"You don't want to do this," he said to me. "If you do, I'll only have to arrest you."

"He deserves it," I answered him.

"You're better than this. You have come a long way. Don't give up now," I heard another voice say.

I turned around expecting it to be Bob who had said it but, instead, saw Fr. Blair standing there in the doorway. I looked at him and then back at Fearhand. I listened to the sound of rain; it was pouring down harder than ever. And then, suddenly, the rain stopped. And even though it was late in the day, suddenly the sun came out. Its rays cast down right into the room where we were standing, as if a sign from heaven said "hold on, don't give up." I looked up at the rays of sun as they came in through the windows. And as the clouds parted, I could have sworn, for just a second, I saw my family. They were all there, the rays of the sun, smiling at me. And in that moment, I knew that this wasn't what they would have wanted for me.

I turned my eyes back to Fearhand and dropped my weapon. I couldn't do it. As soon as I had done that, Bob raced forward and arrested him and led him out of the room. I sat down in the corner against the wall and thought about what had just happened. There were tears in my eyes over the whole thing, but mostly, I was glad I hadn't done it. Fr. Blair came over and sat down next to me. As we sat there, I saw flashing lights and looked out the window to see some uniformed state troopers arriving, flashlights out as it was now getting dark. They stood there guarding Fearhand while Bob was standing there on the phone, I guessed calling off the search party.

I sat there for a few minutes with Fr. Blair, neither of us saying a word. And slowly, I began to feel peaceful again. "Let's get out of here," I said to him after a few minutes.

We walked outside, and I saw him still sitting there up against a tree, two state troopers guarding him. I walked toward him and just looked at him. He looked back up at me, and we stared into each other's eyes.

"Why didn't you just kill me?" he asked me.

That was the same question I had been asking myself since I let him go a few minutes earlier. And as I stared at him, I realized that the reason was complicated and yet simple: I just didn't have it in me anymore. The hatred, the anger, the desire for revenge. As I stared at this man whose life had been about those things, I thought, *There, but for the grace of God, would have gone me.* And I realized that instead of killing him, I had chosen to do something else.

"Because I forgive you," I said to him.

He looked at me like he had no idea what I was talking about. Fr. Blair looked at me stunned but proud. But the strongest feeling of all was the one in my heart. It was like the weight I had been carrying for so long was finally gone. I had finally let go of it all, and it felt right. It felt holy. It felt inspired.

"How can you say that when I haven't even said 'I'm sorry'?" he asked me.

I didn't really have an answer for him on that one.

"I don't know if you're sorry," I answered him. "I know that looking at you, I realize that could easily have been me sitting here if I had chosen to kill you instead. But I won't go down like that. Instead, I will encourage you to change your life. You're going to have to answer for all of your crimes now, but maybe, you can find peace and faith in your solitude in prison."

He didn't say anything, just looked at me. I guess it was the first time someone had ever shown him any kind of affection in his life. Kind of ironic. I had seen many criminals like him, and the one thing many of them were missing in their lives was love. They all thought they had it when really no one loved them; instead, they feared them, and they obeyed them because of that fear.

"Maybe there is a way you can redeem yourself," I said to him.

"What are you talking about?" he asked in response.

"You came here because you were looking for the sheriff, right? He hid you before, and you were hoping he would do the same again. When you heard from your loan shark friend that Lt. Simmons was looking for you, you decided to lay low and hoped that history would repeat itself. No one would look here if the sheriff told them not to, right?"

"What are you getting at?" he asked.

"I want you to come with us to Rocky Hills," I answered him. "I want you to tell the town council about how the sheriff hid you and the crimes he committed in the process. If you do that, then maybe you will win some points at your own criminal trial."

He looked up at me like a man who was defeated and tired. A man who had been on the run for a long time, and while he had managed to throw off the only person ever able to get close to him—me—it seemed clear that the weight of that crime seemed to be too much even for him to bear. Somewhere in his eyes was the desire to make up at least for that, if for nothing else.

Bob walked over, ready to take him away. I talked to Bob about him helping us, and Bob agreed to talk to the prosecutor and his lawyer about it. At that, the police led him away. As I watched him go, Fr. Blair walked up alongside of me and put his arm around me. "I'm very proud of you," he said. "You have come so far, and you have done very good work. You have learned one of the hardest lessons of faith: how to forgive. Just like Jesus sacrificed himself on the cross, you sacrificed your anger and desire for revenge, and in that sacrifice, you gained so much more. It is a lesson I had to learn myself many years ago, and it is a lesson I'm glad I had the chance to teach you."

Once again, I marveled at his wisdom, his faith, his ability to inspire me. This man who I had rejected, who earlier that day I had practically slammed to the floor. No matter what I did, he had forgiven me and given me new hope. I knew he was truly an example of Christian forgiveness. The same forgiveness God extends to all of us if we only ask and try to do better.

At that, we got up and headed home, the three of us, Fr. Blair, Bill, and me. When we got back to the rectory, Sarah ran up to me and hugged me. And then, she let go and hit me in the arm. "If you ever do that again, you are in so much trouble," she said.

I looked at her with a pleading I'm-sorry kind of look while the rest of the group laughed. And then, she embraced me again, and I just stood there and held her. I closed my eyes and felt the feeling of love that I had for her. And for the first time since I had known her, it wasn't counteracted by a feeling of hate or desire for revenge. Those feelings were gone. I looked around at our group and realized that I had completed something. That I had come through a great trial and had reached the other side. And now I had everything I had lost again. Like the story of Job in the Bible, I had everything I thought I would never have again.

And now, I knew I was strong enough to take on the sheriff. I had been planning it for a long time, but even with everyone else behind me, there had always been this little bit of doubt that I just wasn't strong enough. Strong enough, really, in faith to believe with my whole heart that God was on our side. But today, that little doubt was gone. Today, the Lord had shown himself, and now I knew that we could do it. I looked out at the group and, holding Sarah in my arms, knew that I was strong enough to walk with this small group of people toward opposing a great empire.

CHAPTER 34

The day had arrived. The day when we put everything on the line. The day that would make or break all of us, and possibly land all of us in jail if we failed to persuade the council. The usual monthly meeting was scheduled for 7:00 p.m. We had prepared all of our evidence, and Dr. Sharpton was set to tell the council what had happened on that night she bandaged the sheriff up. As for Fearhand, Bob said that the prosecutor and his lawyer were still going back-and-forth on what he would get if he talked. But Bob was trying to talk the prosecutor into giving him something in exchange. I could only hope, and pray, that something would be worked out in time.

That night, we all gathered at the rectory for dinner. In a comical sort of way, it reminded me some of the last supper. For better or worse, it was the beginning of something big. We all sat around the table quiet. No one seemed sure what to say. I didn't think we needed to reaffirm our commitment to what we were doing or how we felt about one another. Or our faith. And I knew that faith was strong enough to get us through. We all sat around quietly and ate dinner.

After dinner, we cleaned up, and I looked at the clock and saw that it was nearly six-thirty, and the meeting was very soon. Before leaving, we all went into the almost-completed church to pray. Fr. Blair led us in a prayer, and then we gathered ourselves and headed off to the town council meeting. I didn't know what to expect or what would happen next, but I was beginning to picture the outcomes in my head. As we entered the town council building, it brought back memories for me of going to meetings like this in the past. PTO meetings, town halls, and things like that. I smiled when I thought about how it had been my wife who had really made me go. She always felt it was important to be involved in what was going on.

Returning my mind to the scene at hand, we entered the meeting room and sat down. The room was clearly used for meetings of all different sorts. It consisted simply of a table at front with nametags for each member of the town council. There were only four. There was also a spot for the judge and the sheriff. The council members came in and took their seats. I recognized one of them as John Walker whom I had seen at the Christmas festival, as well as the other man whom I had fought with in the grocery store that day. There were also two women on the council I had never seen before except for the Christmas tree lighting.

John sat at the center of the table and called the meeting to order and then started talking about what items of business they would be discussing that night. The sheriff also came in and sat down and turned to look at our group.

And when he saw all of us sitting there together, along with Dr. Sharpton, for a second, he looked like he was about to faint, and his jaw almost hit the floor. He quickly covered it up and tried to look away, but I could tell for all his power something inside him was starting to get nervous. He turned his attention to what John was saying. He continued with what they were going to discuss that night and in what order. And then, he asked if anyone had any business they would like to be heard that wasn't on the docket for that night.

Everyone in our group turned and looked at each other and then, one by one, we all stood up. I spoke up first: "We have some business we would like for the council to hear," I answered, not sure what else to say.

"What is it?" he asked. The tone of his voice seemed to ask why he should hear from me at all.

The sheriff, for his part, just continued to sit there, as though he wasn't sure what to do. Even he knew that if he made too much of a scene in a public setting like this, it could start to turn the tide of things against him.

"I don't really think this is appropriate," the sheriff finally stood up and said. And when he did, he turned and looked at the council members. Clearly, he was trying to intimidate them. And for a minute, I thought it would work.

"The sheriff is right," John started to say, "we have other business to attend to, and there are people waiting who have already planned to be heard. I can't put them off for someone I have never even seen here before."

I stood there, not sure what to say. I knew that this was our moment, and if I didn't find a way to get us heard then and there, it was over. It occurred to me that maybe I needed a Hail Mary pass, but instead of a football throw, I simply said "a silent" plea for help. And it must have worked because at that moment, the door opened, and Bob walked in. Along with him was another man in a suit I didn't recognize. And then uniformed troopers walked in escorting Fearhand. Everyone at the meeting turned to look at them and began to murmur amongst themselves what was going on.

John banged his gavel, trying to call the meeting back to order. "Who are you, and what is going on here?" he asked.

"If you will excuse the interruption," Bob answered him. "My name is Lt. Bob Simmons, I'm an investigator with the state police, and I have a witness here that I think you should hear from."

I turned away from Bob and looked back at the sheriff. The sight of Fearhand had caused a bead of sweat to start forming down his face. He quickly wiped it away and tried to look powerful, but I could tell he was starting to get nervous.

"I don't care who you are," the sheriff spoke up. "This is a meeting concerning the people of this town, and the state police have no business here. I am the sheriff and the law around here, and you have no right to just burst in here and bring this prisoner into my town."

"Sheriff, there are some people even you can't push around," Bob answered him. One thing I remembered about Bob was that he was always levelheaded, but if he thought someone was challenging his power or disrespecting his authority, he wasn't afraid to tell them.

"What is all this about?" someone asked.

"Yeah, what's going on?" said another.

"What's going on is this man is trying to feed you lies to turn you against me?" the sheriff answered in reply. *Boy, he just never gave up his lies,* I thought.

"No, what's going on here," I spoke up, "is that the five of us are here along with the state police to present to you, the people of this town, along with your town council, elected by you to serve you, that your sheriff is corrupt. I don't think that fact comes as a surprise to a lot of you, and certainly not to the members of the council. But the truth is that you don't truly know the extent of his crimes. And once his crimes are revealed, I will ask the council to vote no-confidence in the sheriff."

"What are you talking about?" came a voice from the audience.

All the council members just sat there and stared at the president. He seemed to have no idea what to do.

"This is inappropriate, not to mention slander," the sheriff spoke up. "You are disrupting this meeting, and if you don't leave immediately, I'm going to arrest all of you for causing this disruption."

"I don't think that will hold up in court," came a voice that I turned and realized was the judge's. "In fact, I know it won't," he continued.

"What are you talking about?" the sheriff answered him, looking at him incredulous.

"What I'm talking about is that these folks are right," the judge answered him. "You are corrupt, you hold everybody here hostage and force them to do your bidding, and in doing so, you preserve your own power. You have been doing it for years. And it's time someone stood up to you. Yes, I know that you will expose me for what you have on me, but I don't care. Because effective at the end of this meeting, I resign my position as judge of this town."

Everyone at the meeting stood there quiet and stunned. I for one had no idea what to say. I had always sensed there was a part of the judge that wanted to uphold the law faithfully and stand up to the sheriff, and now he had actually done it.

"What do you mean you resign, Judge Smith?" John asked him.

"I mean that as soon as I tell you about how the sheriff has manipulated me into always siding with him and doing his bidding, he is going to tell you about some not-so honorable political moves I made when I was in law school. And once you know about them, you will pass it on to the authorities over me, and they will investigate me and revoke my law license, and my career will be over. So I'm beating them to the punch. But not before I issue this final order," he said, walking over to me and handing me a court order.

I opened it up and realized it was an order dismissing all the charges the sheriff had brought against me almost a year ago.

"He told me what really happened that night," the judge said to me. "Who can blame you, for how you reacted?"

"Judge, is there something you want to tell us?" John asked, trying to bring things to order.

"There is a lot that I could tell you, but right now, I think that we should hear from this man here," he said, pointing to me, "and anyone he wants us to hear from."

"I don't care what he says. We are not hearing from any of these people," the sheriff replied as if he was ordering the council what to do.

"Sheriff, I believe it is up to us who we hear from at this meeting, not you, and I second what the judge said to hear from these people," replied one of the members of the council.

The sheriff looked at him and then back at the president with the same look he had given the council member that day at the grocery store. The president looked at the sheriff and then back at me. "Inspired by the position of the judge and his actions, and based on the request of councilman Jones, the motion is granted, and this man will be heard."

The sheriff stood there incredulous. He had run out of arguments. He just sat down; he was outnumbered and outgunned for once.

"Then, without further ado, I present before the town council Mr. Ian Fearhand to testify to the crimes of the sheriff."

There was some mummering when his name was announced. Most people seemed to recognize it, but they didn't know from where.

"Wait, isn't he the guy who killed that cop's family?" someone finally asked.

And when they did, everyone suddenly turned and looked at me.

"Then, wait, that would make you—" someone said before stopping and finally realizing who I was.

"Yes, my name is Detective Tom Brado. I was a police detective before my family was killed by this man here. He killed them to get back at me for getting enough evidence on him to convict him of a crime and to throw me off his trail. And it worked. At least, until now," I answered them.

Everyone in the room sat there stunned. Even in a small town like this, everyone had heard the story at some point. And even after five years, a story like that still seemed to tear at people. I didn't like the idea of playing a sympathy card, but I had to get them to listen to me. And it was a key step for me too because it was part of not hiding from my past anymore.

"What is it you want for us to hear about?" another one of the council members finally asked.

I sighed. "I want you to hear about how the sheriff harbored this man after he committed his crime."

Again, no one in the room said a word. Finally, Fearhand spoke up and told the council everything. How he had been running, how he had hidden in the mountains around the town, how he had paid the sheriff to protect him. How the sheriff had harbored him, brought him clothes and food and kept other law enforcement from finding him. When he was finished, there was not a face in the room that didn't look stunned and angry.

"How could he do that?"

"Could that really be true?"

People were murmuring.

"This man is a liar," the sheriff finally spoke up. "He has every reason to lie to save his neck. And as for this guy here, he has lived in this town for years now and yet, before tonight, not a single person ever even knew his name or where he was from or anything. And now he shows up and expects you all to believe that I harbored a fugitive. Where is his proof?"

ONE MAN'S PAIN

I had to admit the sheriff was a good talker. And I saw some heads in the audience nodding. I spoke up: "This man has come here and admitted to you a series of very serious crimes. He doesn't have to admit to anything. He's an accused criminal, and he has every right to keep quiet. Why would he admit to all these things if he didn't do them? The answer is he wouldn't. No one would. But if you don't believe that, then maybe you will believe the evidence of the other crime your sheriff has committed."

When I said that, the sheriff suddenly got a look of pure panic on his face. You could see confusion in his eyes. It was as though a part of him knew what was coming next, but another part of him just could not believe it was possible that we could have any evidence of that.

"I think you all know Fr. Blair here. And I think many of you remember that several years ago now, his mother and fiancé were killed in a car accident with the current sheriff. The sheriff has made you believe that it was just an accident, that no one was really at fault. But that is not the truth. The truth is that night, the sheriff was drunk. That he caused the accident because he was drunk. And there's more. I'm sure you all remember the sheriff at the time, this man's brother. I'm sure you all remember how he was tragically killed by a robber one night and how his murder remains unsolved to this day, despite the supposed efforts of his brother to solve it. Well, the current sheriff hasn't made any efforts to solve the crime, and the reason for that is"—I took a breath, knowing that I could never take back the words once I had said them, and because I didn't know what they would start—"because the sheriff is the one who killed his brother in the first place."

As soon as the words were out of my mouth, I felt a sense of nervousness. I knew the weight and the seriousness of what I had just said. And I knew that I had now started down a path from which there was no return. But I said a silent prayer, no words necessary, and had faith. I thought about the sun coming out that day at the cabin and tried to imagine the sun shining again in this moment.

I looked around the room, and no one was saying a word. There was not a face in the crowd that didn't have a jaw almost hitting the floor. No one could believe what I had just said. The sheriff didn't say a word, just sat there looking stunned. In a way, it was almost like the roles had flipped from that day when he brought the newspaper printout to my house. Only now I had brought up his past that he wanted buried. But it wasn't out of revenge that I had said it, and I didn't enjoy that feeling at all.

"That's, that's, that's a very serious charge," the president of the council finally managed to get out. "Do you have any evidence at all to back it up?"

"Yes, as a matter of fact, I do," I answered him.

"What?" he asked me. The way he said was almost like he couldn't believe I had anything.

"I have the doctor that stitched up his wound that night, and I have a witness who saw the blood all over the sheriff's car and his bloody clothes hidden in his office, as well as pictures of the clothes and car and pictures of the sheriff wearing the same clothes previously," I answered them.

By now, the stunned looks and dropped jaws seemed to be a permanent fixture of both the town council and the crowd. But resisting the urge to be distracted by that, I turned and looked at the sheriff, and I could see that he looked nervous now, and he was beginning to sweat. For the first time, I looked at his face and did not see a look of evil confidence. And again, I was reminded of my years as a cop.

I knew the look on the sheriff's face well. It was the look criminals always got when they knew they were finally caught. Sometimes you saw it in an interrogation when they finally confessed. Other times, it took until the guilty verdict came at their trial. Now I could see it on the sheriff's face. I turned and looked at Bob, and he looked back at me. It was the same look we had given each other many times when we knew we had finally had someone dead to rights. And looking at each other like that brought back a feeling of familiarity for me. I was beginning to feel victory.

"Where are these witnesses?" the president finally asked.

"We're right here," Dr. Sharpton's voice called out from the crowd as she and Sarah stood up.

ONE MAN'S PAIN

The look on the sheriff's face the moment he saw them stand up could only be described as utter shock and panic. Clearly, he was beginning to feel the weight of the situation coming down on him.

"What is it you have to tell us?" the president asked them. It occurred to me that at this point he just couldn't resist hearing it.

Dr. Sharpton spoke first: "Fifteen years ago, I visited this town for the funeral of my friend. She had been killed in a car accident. It was a very sad occurrence. I had dedicated my life to saving other people's lives but wasn't there to save the life of a close friend. That is something I still struggle with. But I can't do anything about that. What I can do something about is the struggle I have over saving the life of this man here"—she gestured toward the sheriff—"I have never regretted saving the life of a patient, no matter who they are or what they did. But what I do regret is what I came to learn recently, and that is that I helped to cover up the murder of one man by saving another."

With that, she recounted the story of how the sheriff, the current one, had come to see her that night and how she had stitched him up, and how she had removed a bullet from his side and given it to him. She recounted every detail, leaving nothing out. When she had finished, Sarah stood up and did the same thing, recounting what she had seen that day at the sheriff's office. She showed them the pictures she had as proof. And by the time the two of them were done speaking, every single person in the room was staring directly at the sheriff. By now, we had heard how he blackmailed the judge, harbored a fugitive, and now was a cop killer.

"I think we should have that vote that was called for," came a voice from the crowd.

"Yeah, let's vote," came another voice. "All in favor."

One by one, every person in the crowd raised their hand calling on their council to vote no-confidence in the sheriff.

"Very well," said the president, looking out over the crowd, "I put it to the council for a vote. All in favor of voting no-confidence in the sheriff and holding a special election to elect a new one."

One by one, all the council members raised their hands. The sheriff stared at them stunned. In a matter of minutes, he had gone from having the whole town in the palm of his hand to staring down the possibility of being voted out of power, or even worse.

"It's unanimous then. The council votes no-confidence in Sheriff Blank's leadership, and a special election will be held to replace him," the president said.

"Fine, you can have your election," the sheriff spoke up. "But there is nothing that says you can stop me from running in it. And do you have any other people interested in the job?" he asked, beginning to sound confident.

Everyone on the council and in the crowd just looked at each other. They all had jobs and families and lives. It didn't seem that anyone was able to give all that up to run for sheriff. There was a moment of silence as everyone continued to look at each other.

"I nominate Tom Brado," came a sudden voice from behind me.

I turned to see Bill standing there and stared at him. He had just nominated me for sheriff. I wasn't sure how to feel about the idea of being a cop again.

"Will anyone second the nomination?" the president asked.

"I will," came a surprising answer from the judge. "And," he continued, "I ask that another election be held. An election for a new judge because, like I stated earlier, I resign the office effective at the end of this meeting."

"One thing at a time," the president replied.

"Do you accept the nomination for sheriff?" he asked me.

"Yes, I do," I answered him. Part of me was surprised to hear him say it, but a much-bigger part of me was happy. That part of me knew that I had found my way home again, that I had found my destiny. That I had rebuilt my life. I was always meant to be a cop and serve others, and it was what I always loved to do. Only now it was in a new place.

"Good then, I guess we will move on to nominations for the judgeship," the president said, almost as if he were just making it up as he went along at that point.

"Is anyone here even qualified to be judge?" someone asked.

"Is anyone interested in the position?" the president asked.

"I nominate Bill Pricley," I said, speaking up.

Everyone turned and looked at me and then back at Bill. Some of the older residents of the town had looks of recognition and surprise on their faces. They obviously remembered him. Bill just looked stunned.

"If he wants the job, that is," I added.

Bill just continued to look stunned, as though he had been made a surprise offer and didn't know how to respond in the moment. "Okay," he said, looking surprised to hear himself say it.

"Well, then, I guess we are having an election," the president said, again sounding like he was just making it up as he went along.

The sheriff just sat there and stared at me with a look of what I could only describe as hopeless hatred on his face. It was obvious that he hated me, hated me for standing up to him, for helping to expose him, and now for being a threat to his power. He knew what would happen if someone else took over. He turned from me and looked at the judge with the exact same look.

"Are we going to vote or not?" came a voice from the audience.

"We don't have the entire town here. We need to let everyone know that there will be an election," the president answered.

"An announcement will go out by phone and e-mail tonight and in the days to come. The election will be here one week from today," he continued.

At that, he adjourned the meeting and left along with the rest of the town council. I sat there with Fr. Blair and the rest of our group. The sheriff for his part had ducked out the door the second the meeting was adjourned. It occurred to me that he might try to influence the vote by going around and intimidating people. I started to follow him and was stopped by Bob.

"I'm way ahead of you," he said. "I've got someone watching him 24-7, and if he even tries to intimidate anyone, he will be arrested."

With that, we all said goodbye and headed home. After I got home, I tried to go to sleep but really couldn't. I had way too much on my mind. I was thinking about what was going to happen tomorrow and how I felt about it. I was surprised at how excited I was at the thought of being a police officer again. It was as though I really was getting back all the things I had lost.

And there was one other thing I wanted to do. One thing that would express how I felt once and for all. But I was even more scared at the thought of that than I was at my impending new career. At the same time, I was even more excited at the thought.

I finally fell asleep, finding some peace in the thought of an exciting and happy future I saw potentially on the horizon.

CHAPTER 35

I woke up early on the day of the election and quickly got myself ready. I headed down to the rectory and met Fr. Blair and everyone there. And together, we headed over to the meeting hall for the election. The members of the council were there along with the sheriff and the judge. There were voting booths set up across the room with a monitor at each one. It was only 8:00 a.m., but people were already lining up.

The president stepped up and announced that voting would officially begin. The five of us got into line, and we each went in and voted. As I wrote down Bill for judge, I smirked a little, thinking maybe he would vote against himself just to avoid getting the job. Then I came to my turn to vote for myself as sheriff. For a minute, I thought about running away. About leaving again, setting up shop somewhere else and hiding from all of this. But I knew that those days were over. That the sun had come up again, and it was time to embrace a new destiny God had set out for me, one I had not previously envisioned. But one I was beginning to like and wanted to embrace.

I exited the voting booth and went and sat with Fr. Blair and everyone else. The hours ticked by as people came and went to vote. The sheriff sat there too, trying to look confident but looking nervous. It was clear he was fearful of losing his grip on power. We all sat there for the entire day until finally in the evening, the president got up and announced that the voting had ended and that they were going to tally the results. Just about everyone in the town came in and sat and watched as he pulled the votes out and counted them one at a time.

All of us sat there, fingers crossed, praying. The sheriff was also watching closely. Finally, the president looked up, cleared his throat, and took the microphone to make an announcement.

"For the candidacy of judgeship, our winner is Bill Pricley, if he accepts," the president announced.

The judge sat there with a sad but satisfied look on his face. It was clear he wished things could be different, but he knew he had done the right thing in resigning. He walked over to Bill, shook his hand, and wished him good luck. "Do this job better than I did it," he said. And at that, he left the room.

"And now, the results for the election of sheriff," the president announced.

The entire room became quiet, and everyone held their breaths. I closed my eyes, took a deep breath, and in my heart said I was ready, if this was the Lord's will.

"The winner of the election and the sheriff for the town is Thomas Brado," he announced.

No one in the room said a word. Instead, everyone stared at the sheriff waiting to see his response. He was just sitting there with a stunned look on his face. In a matter of a few months, he had gone from ruling the entire town to being kicked out of power in one full swoop.

"Sheriff, at this time, I will have to ask you to surrender your badge and weapons to the council," the president said.

The sheriff sat there for a minute, not saying anything, and then a look of total anger and smugness came over his face. "I don't care what you people say. I'm not giving up power. I don't care who stands up to me. I rule around here, and you had better get used to it."

"Sheriff, you have been voted out in a fair and legal election, and you need to turn over power immediately," the president answered him.

"No," he answered.

I finally stepped forward. "I believe this man asked you to turn over your badge and weapons, and you need to comply."

He stood there, staring at me with a smirk on his face. "You don't have the guts to stand up to me," he said.

Some of the citizens in the meeting began to form up behind me.

"If he doesn't, we will," one of them said, and one by one, they all began to fall in behind me.

The sheriff stared out over them and knew that he had lost. He was defeated. He would rule no longer. I approached him, grabbed his hand, and twisted his arm around his back to arrest him. I removed his handcuffs from his toolbelt and placed them on his hands.

"What are you doing?" he asked me.

"My first official act as new sheriff of this town," I answered him. "I'm arresting you for the murder of Sheriff Merhave. As well as for the murder of Mrs. Mary Blair and Ms. Susan Moore. You killed each of them, and now you will face justice for it."

The entire room began to clap. As they watched, I removed the now former sheriff's weapons as well as his badge and handed them to the president.

"I think these belong to you," he said, handing them back to me.

I took them back from him and stared at the badge in my hand. It was the first time I had held a badge in my hand since I had turned in my police badge five years earlier. I had sworn I would never wear a badge or serve the law again; it had betrayed me. But I felt the pain of the memory and then let it go. I put the badge onto my belt and turned to look back at the now former sheriff.

"*Mr.* Merhave," I said, emphasizing *Mr.* to make clear that his title was no longer sheriff, "You are under arrest for murder."

I led him out of the hall and down to the courthouse. There I locked him up in a holding cell in the jail and sat down at his desk. I looked out over the office, and a part of me thought, *Well, what do I do now?* The now former sheriff wasn't saying anything; he was just sitting in his cell. He looked tired and defeated. He had lost, and he knew it, and like Fearhand before him, it was clear now that he felt the weight of the things he had done to keep himself in power and that, ultimately, his craving for power had destroyed him.

The door opened, and Fr. Blair, Bill, and Sarah came in.

"We just came to introduce the new judge to the new sheriff," Fr. Blair said.

"Your honor," I greeted Bill, reaching out my hand.

"Sheriff," he responded, shaking my hand and smiling.

"Everyone went home, but the council members said they expect you at the next meeting and every meeting after that," Bill said with a smirk.

"I will be there," I answered.

"Where's Bob?" I asked.

"He went back. He had to get Fearhand back to jail," Fr. Blair answered me.

I looked out over our group and felt a sense of satisfaction and of victory. I felt as though today, I had contributed, in a small way, to the great mission that was our faith.

"Don't you have a church to go finish?" I said to Fr. Blair.

"Yes, I do," he answered, leaving along with Bill.

That left Sarah and I alone in the courthouse together. "You want to take a walk?" I asked her.

"What about him?" she asked.

"I don't think he's going anywhere," I answered her.

At that, we left and walked out back toward a small trail in the woods. It was getting close to spring, and the leaves were blossoming on the trees. As we walked, I thought about how to say what I wanted to say to her. To tell her how I felt, how I was sorry about how I had acted before, how I wanted her to be a part of my life forever and always.

"You know, it looks like my future is set, but not how I ever pictured it," I said to her.

"There's just one thing missing," I continued.

"What?" she asked.

"You," I answered her.

And with that, I got down on one knee and proposed to her. She accepted, and from then on, we were engaged to be married.

In the weeks that followed until Easter, we all finished up work on the church. It came together beautifully. I settled into being the sheriff of the town, and Bill settled into being the judge. Sarah and I made plans to get married just as soon as the church was finished. Fr. Blair worked with us on wedding preparations and pre-Cana classes, a requirement to get married in the church.

As for Fearhand, he pled guilty to all his crimes and received a sentence of life in prison. It was in some ways a sad day because he had ruined his life, but he needed to face his crimes. And, as for the sheriff, the decision was made to try him outside of the town for it to be fair.

Nevertheless, he was found guilty and received a life sentence for his crimes. As they led him away from the courthouse that day, he turned and looked at me as if he had something final to say, but instead, he didn't say a word. I guess he couldn't decide what to say and wasn't sure how to feel about his fall from grace. Clearly, he would need more time to decide how he felt about his actions and to make peace with any regrets he may have.

With all of that finished, the only thing left to do was work on the church. We put the finished touches in on Good Friday, in preparation for its first mass on Easter Sunday. As we finished up that night, I pulled Fr. Blair aside and asked him a special favor. I just couldn't wait any longer. He looked at me surprised but then smiled and agreed.

CHAPTER 36

The day had arrived. On a beautiful Saturday morning, I greeted Fr. Blair at the church. Not for mass but for something else special—a wedding. I couldn't wait any longer; I wanted to be married to Sarah and spend the rest of my life with her. And so, with Bill and Dr. Sharpton there as witnesses, as well as Jimmy to give his mother away, the two of us were married. It was a small ceremony but beautiful, nonetheless. We each took our vows, and then Fr. Blair declared us husband and wife. It was simple and yet so powerful. I looked at Sarah, and I knew that I loved her and that there was nothing that made me happier than spending the rest of my life with her.

We didn't have much of a reception, just a small celebration with our small group of friends. But, in a way, that was even better. We may not have had a big friend group, but we had a special, close one. And that was what counted. We moved all of Sarah and Jimmy's things into my house that day, and Sarah made plans to sell hers. We even talked about having a family of our own.

"Maybe I will have a daughter to pass that recipe down to after all," Sarah said.

When she said that, I smiled. The idea of having children again was a nervous one, but even more so, a happy one. And in that moment, I knew that I had regained everything I had lost—love, a family, and, above all, faith. I smiled at Sarah, and she smiled back at me. I looked out the window of our house, and this time, I saw two butterflies take off. I pointed it to Sarah, and she smiled. And I think we both knew that our spouses had come to see us off into this new life. We looked at each other and smiled.

CHAPTER 37

Easter Sunday morning greeted all of us as the most beautiful morning I had seen in a long time, maybe ever. I thought about how just a year earlier, my life had been so different and how it had come so far. I had not foreseen many of the things that had happened, and if you had come to me and told me they were going to happen, I would have looked at you like you were crazy. But now, I had everything that I had ever wanted, and the future looked bright. The Lord had been patient with me and called me back at a time when he knew I was finally ready.

Sarah and I headed to church along with Jimmy to celebrate Easter. As we entered, I saw the two choirs sitting on either side of the altar. Clearly, there was still one more thing to be worked out.

"What are you going to do about them?" I asked Fr. Blair.

"I don't know. I guess they will have to work it out for themselves," he answered me.

"Maybe God has a trick up his sleeve for this," I replied, smiling.

We all took our seats, and Fr. Blair moved to the back of the church to proceed in. The canter walked to the microphone and asked us all to join her in singing "How Great Thou Art." I opened my hymn book to the page and listened as the music started to play on the organ and watched as Fr. Blair began to process in. The first choir began singing the verse with the second one not far behind. Gradually, and then quickly, their voices became louder and louder as they tried to outsing each other. Finally, they got to the last line:

how great thou art. Each choir sang as loud as they could, but instead of a negative moment, it was a positive moment.

As they sang out the very last line, their voices connected, and the sun shined directly over the church, as though it was a sign from God himself. They stopped singing, and Fr. Blair stood up to talk. "I think the Lord has given a sign that our two choirs are equally good and should begin working together. Who's with me?" he asked.

Most people in the church raised their hands, and one by one, the members on one side approached the members on the other. They moved their chairs around, and they all sat together forming one new church choir. Fr. Blair smiled at them and then continued to speak. "I'm so happy to finally be able to say mass in this church. As many of you know, I grew up in this church, and it holds a special place in my heart. I was very sad to see it decay the way it did, and I am thrilled to see it rebuilt again. In a way, this church is like someone's life. At times, they may find themselves down and out. Feeling defeated. But with hard work and with faith in God, and with his help, they can build themselves back up again and become someone even greater than they were before.

"And I am even happier to say that the first sacrament celebrated in this church was a marriage. Two people pledging their lifelong love to one another. And that is ultimately what will save us all, love. It was God's love that saved us all from sin, and it is love for each other that can save each one of us. The example set by the former sheriff is perfect for what can happen to someone who stops looking out for others and instead starts looking out for themselves only. They may be powerful for a while, but eventually, it will destroy them.

"Instead, we all need to love on another. A perfect example of how division is bad for both sides is our choir. Separately, they may have been good choirs, but they were each limited by the energy, they were losing fighting with each other. But united, they are a much more powerful force. The same is true of faith. There are many different Christian faiths, and while we all may not agree on doctrine or practice, we all claim the same Jesus as our savior, and we all worship the same God. I learned a long time ago what can happen when two people part ways simply because they can't agree on matters of faith.

What could be a powerful force for good, instead, becomes a powerful force for nothing. We need not fight with one another but instead love one another, even if we are all different.

As we conclude this journey of building we have been on, I look out to the future with optimism. I know that moving forward, we will all face obstacles, and there will be times where our inner churches look destroyed, and it seems as if there is no hope at all. But, like I said, we can all rebuild. And if we have faith in God, then we all will. My message here is not one of ending but one of beginning. At least one man here today has found his way back to faith, and with that, back to love and to a life of happiness and fulfillment. But he found it through a path he never thought he would walk, and he walked that path with divine guidance.

And so, as we celebrate this opening mass and this Easter Sunday mass, I want all of you to forget the past and, instead, look to the future. Let the evil of yesterday go, and focus on the good of tomorrow. Love each other, love your fellow Christians, love God. If we hate, we will be destroyed. If we love, we will be lifted up. It is so easy to stay angry, but all that does is hurt yourself and others around you, even if you don't realize it. Instead, love and let others love. If someone loves a person you hate, let them do it, and try to follow their example. The past is gone, and really the future is right now. The choices you make today are what will guide tomorrow and the rest of your life. And so, after this long speech, I will make my lesson short"—Fr. Blair smiled—"choose love!"

With that, he began the celebration of the mass. I sat in the pew with Sarah and Jimmy and looked up at the altar and the cross. I looked behind the cross to the sun shining outside the window. And I smiled. I knew that the sun was shining again, and that it was shining because, with the help of friends, I had chosen love. And I vowed to spend the rest of my life heeding Father's words. I vowed to choose love.

ABOUT THE AUTHOR

Dominic Branca is twenty-five years old and lives outside of Philadelphia, Pennsylvania. He works part-time in support services for developmentally disabled adults and attends graduate school at night, studying clinical psychology. In his free time, Dominic enjoys reading, cheering on Philadelphia sports teams, and spending time with his friends. *One Man's Pain* is Dominic's first novel.

CPSIA information can be obtained
at www.ICGtesting.com
Printed in the USA
LVHW031058311220
675393LV00004B/496